PATHWAY
to
PERDITION

Sam Ayun

Dedication

Thank you to my biggest fans Johanna Turnbull and Cristy Overturf for supporting me through this huge endeavor.

A special thank you to my very talented editor Annie Jenkinson. You have made my work shine brighter than I ever could.

Into the Void

Matt's Story

Lightly tapping on the door, I slowly enter the white single-wide trailer home. I close the door behind me, giggling playfully, using my shoulder because of the two large plastic bags in my hands. *Oh, this stupid goddamn door!* It wants to swing shut before I'm even in the place, making the entrance with bags of any kind almost a wrestling match. It's as if the door doesn't want me to come in. The smell of stale cigarette butts, mold, and musky laundry saturates the air when I enter. It's depressing but I know the mood will lift soon—because I have a plan to do just that.

"Honey, I'm home! Well, I see you haven't cleaned up yet. Geez, this place is a shit hole. It's okay, I'll take care of it later. Don't you worry about it. I'll soon have it all nice for us."

Placing the bags gently on the kitchen table, I grab a can of beer from the refrigerator.
Then I plop myself down on the seat in front of my new 'roommate'. *Shit, this beer tastes foul. Jesus!* I swallow, then reach into one of the bags to remove one of the items it contains.

"Aww yeah. Hey, what do you think about pliers? I couldn't find those needle-nose ones I wanted so I had to settle on the regular ones. Oh well, I'm sure they'll do. We'll get it done."

Next, I remove a disposable rain jacket and shake it a few times to flatten it out, then place it flat on the table, rubbing my hands across it to remove the wrinkles. Reaching back in, I remove a roll of duct tape, a face shield, a tube of extra strong super glue, zip ties, lawn shears, and a propane torch.

"This is going to be great, Bo! Are you as excited as I am? I hear you rolling around in there, so I know you're excited. By the way, the good news is, I got a face shield so I can take the tape off. The bad news is I can't have you screaming, so I also got some glue.
"Feel free to use your imagination."

Muffled moans and pounding echo throughout the small trailer. Its pathetically thin walls threaten to break apart with each impact. I quietly focus on the oven clock, listening to Bo's frantic efforts to escape.

Bang... Bang... Bang...

"You having fun in there, Bo?"

I imagine the thumping in perfect cadence with every second.

"Hey. It's nine-fifty-four! We can start in exactly six minutes if that suits you. I like to start on the hour if you're ok with that. I know you like to be in control all the time, but this is kind of my thing right now, so I hope that's alright. I mean, say if it's not, Bo."

With the banging dying down, he begins faintly sobbing, but my eyes never leave the clock as I await the moment I can start. It gets my blood racing around my body, my heart pumping, the adrenaline flowing. I feel it; every vein in me is warm from anticipation. The instant the clock shifts to ten, I jump up excitedly and walk to the closet in the bedroom. Bo begins to thrash wildly, howling through his nostrils when I slowly open the door.

"Here's Johnny! Nah, just kidding. Hey, settle down, man. You don't want to get yourself all worked up before we start. Otherwise, you won't experience the full excitement, Bo. Start calm, let the moment take you... But I can tell you're ready, same as I am."

Lying on the floor below me is a terrified sixty-year-old man wearing nothing but blue jeans. I've taped his feet together around the ankles, deep welts and rub marks now showing in his leathery skin where he's tried to wriggle free. His hands are still strapped behind his back, and copious tape covers his mouth. He looks sore all over, around the mouth especially, as though the tape is pulling, all the skin from his dry lips, tugging layers away, making his lips bleed and pare back, showing his yellowy teeth slightly like a rabid wolf threatening to bite.

He isn't threatening to bite, of course. His cracked lips are stuck to his teeth. But, that's no surprise, is it? That's Bo's own fault. It's from how he's chosen to live his life. His choice. His face is worn from all the years of heavy drinking and drug use, and his hair is disheveled, greasy, and dirty brown with streaks of grey.

I can't begin to describe the smell. Putrid, maybe? A stench that thickens the air. *He's shit himself.* He must have to get a stink like this. But it could also be that he hasn't been near a tub lately.

"So, it's time to pay for your life of evil now. Did you think this was ever going to happen? I mean, probably not. You made it this fucking far in life and never had to pay for the pain you caused everyone. Let me tell you, you're about to understand what you did. Today's the day that you get what you deserve, Bo."

As I'm reaching down and grasping his strapped feet, he immediately pulls them back and thrusts them into my abdomen, knocking me down. *You fucking shit,* I think. But I stay calm. *Breathe now, breathe. The best is coming soon.* I slowly pick myself up, put my hands on my hips, and let out a short sigh.

"Well, I guess you still have some pep left in ya, old man. Tell ya what. I'll just add that to your tab. Kick to the stomach. Check! Okay, now let's try this again. Try to behave better or I'll add more, Bo."

Bo begins flailing crazily as I re-enter the closet.

"Seriously, man? The sooner you accept it, the sooner we'll get it over with. You're only dragging it out."

He attempts to kick me again, but I am prepared, easily pushing his feet aside before climbing onto his chest. He freezes and locks his wide-eyed gaze on mine. Gradually, I slide my weight to his stomach and lean in closer.

"You remember this, right? That night thirty years ago, when I was sitting on your chest choking you? I really should have killed you then. Do you think this is fortuitous, Bo? After all, I am who I am because of you. It's me reaping what you sowed. You did this all to yourself."

I knock him out cold with one full-force swing and then remove the tape from his face, tugging it hard, seeing the skin peel away shiny and yellow, as if he's smoked himself. Hell, he doesn't even bleed. The skin has given up. Bo's body can't be bothered to save his soul.

Retrieving the bottle of glue from my back pocket with my right hand, I grab his chin and squeeze as hard as I can with my left. With the lid of the glue bottle in my mouth, I bite, twist, then spit it onto the floor next to him. Slowly running the tip of the bottle left and right, I build a substantial mound of glue across his lips, then blow on it lightly to help it set.
Blow, blow…
Patience is what it takes. I have time.

"There we go. Now I can see your whole face. Not being able to see your expressions was eating at me. Now, let's get you somewhere more comfortable. Smells like piss and shit in here."

Bo feels light as I effortlessly drag his unconscious body through the bedroom and into the kitchen. Wrapping my arms around his torso from behind, I try to lift him, but can't get leverage. I can't get a hold of him. Maybe he'll be easier to move when he's dead if I let the rigor mortis take him. Then, I can position his arms out and wait for the stiffness. Put him into a position that'll be easier to shift. Why does no one think of that? Just lay the body right out and wait for it to harden. Anyway, it's not time yet. He's still alive. I'm not ready to finish him off for good.

"We have to do something about your arms, man. They're making this way too difficult, and don't even suggest I remove the straps. I've seen that movie before. They always get away."

Straddling his motionless body, I scan the room for options, noticing a foldable metal chair against the wall next to the fridge. Positioning Bo on his side, I force the unfolded chair behind him with the seatback between his arms and torso, then use an entire roll of duct tape to secure him. In a deadlift position, it only takes one short heave to bring the chair upright. Bo's chin now rests on his chest, and he begins loudly snoring. In and out, the sound is grating on my ears, each instance causing me to clench my teeth. Pouring a jug of ice water slowly over his head ends his peaceful yet annoying rest, his eyes instantly widening as he realizes his predicament.

"Did you have a good nap? Don't worry, I didn't start without you. Now, let's get those pants off. You like taking people's pants off, don't you? Well, let me return the favor."

The lawn shears purchased hours earlier easily slice through his denim jeans. He lets out a high-pitched nasally whimper after each cut. Making my way up his pant leg, I begin humming random cheery tunes, bobbing my head to the beat. Once I reach his thigh, he begins rocking his body in a panic, causing me to jab the tip of the scissors into his stomach. The pain triggers a long-muffled scream and even more hectic rocking.

"Are you fucking kidding me? Be careful, man. You did that to yourself. I wasn't going to cut you. You know what? Fuck it! Let's get started since you're in such a hurry."

Donning the rain jacket slowly, I set off humming again. My eyes fix on his, wondering what's going through his mind. The face shield headband is fully extended now. To drag out the tension more, I tighten it a single click at a time, long pauses in between. Each click causes him to squint, tears dripping out with every blink. I stand statuesque for one last menacing pose, then take the pliers from the table.

"Here we go! What is it you told me before? Oh yeah, take it like a man!"

I kick him in his chest with every muscle in my body, and the chair falls back.

"Ouch. Well, that was supposed to be in your stomach. Sorry, man."

Lying on his back still strapped to the chair, I raise my foot and crash it into his stomach. Only a quick, barely audible scream comes out as he struggles to catch his breath. Rolling the chair onto its side triggers him to panic, and he repeatedly slams his head into the floor.

"Here, let's get you back up before you take another nap."

He's sweating and shaking profusely when I use the pliers to grab his right pinky. Applying sideways pressure causes him to stiffen his body, head to toe. I hold the stance for a few seconds, then put my face next to his.

"You know I wrote a book? You're in it. The shit you did to me is in it. The whole world knows now. It's called Born into Darkness, and I tell everyone about you. Maybe one day, I'll write a book about what I did to you today as well. Would you like the world to know about all this too? I would! That'd be fun, wouldn't it?"

Crack!

His muted screams echo off the kitchen walls when I force his pinky fully to the side. Immediately, I grab hold of his ring finger between the teeth of the pliers. His remaining fingers desperately clench tight to his palms.

"One… Two… Three!"

Crack!

Again, the room fills with his speechless wails. One by one, the snapping and popping of each finger produces a howl-like response that only excites me more. Dragging over a chair in front of him, I take a seat and lean in.

"How are you feeling so far? I know that shit had to hurt. I'll tell ya what. Do you want me to keep going? Blink once for yes and twice for no."

Through tear-soaked eyes, he slowly blinks twice.

"Wow! Double yes? You really are a madman, you know that? All right then, I'm gonna finish getting those pants off and if you move, I'll stick these shears in your fucking leg. Got it?"

My eyes lock with his as I make my way up his right pant leg. His terror feels like a cool, calming breeze, sending a tingling sensation down my spine. Cutting the jeans across his groin, he thrusts his hips violently, knocking the shears out from my hands.

"Dammit! Are you fucking kidding me? You asked for it! I told you what was going to happen if you moved. This is on you. You should have tried keeping still."

One forceful swing leaves the shears deeply embedded in his left thigh. Again, he lets out a long howl, followed by a few whimpers. I silently analyze his response to the pain, waiting for his distress to wane. I don't want to waste a chance for him to focus on every bit of anguish I've planned for him.

"Know why I didn't buy gloves? Because I wanted to feel your skin while I was slicing into it. Didn't really think it out though because this next part's gonna be kinda gross. I don't blame you though. I was the one in charge of shopping, so it's all on me. I can't blame you for that."

Abruptly pulling out the shears causes bright red droplets to spray my face shield. An anticipated wail fills the room.

"Well, it's a good thing I had this face shield on. If this shit gets on my face, I swear, I'll lose it. Probably a moot point from where you're sitting though, huh?"

With the tattered remains of his jeans, I gently wipe at the bright red beads. Crimson drops streak across the plastic, creating a thin red film that makes it impossible to see through. I remove the face shield angrily, slap it across Bo's head, then drop it to the floor.

"Well, that didn't quite work out how I planned. Wanna hear something funny? Half of this shit has gone off-script. I had a pretty specific idea of how this was gonna happen and you're fucking it up, Bo. Still, I think it's going pretty well. Don't you? Oh, and there's some good news. It seems you didn't shit yourself after all."

There's no shit. Not yet anyway. He just stinks something rotten. Hardly surprising. I press my knee firmly on his right thigh and with my left hand, reach deep into his crotch. With his testicles tightly grasped within my fist, he goes into an incessant panic that elevates the closer I get with the shears. His eyes snap wide, his body freezing at the cold, sharp steel in the vicinity of his gonads. They seem to shrink away as if they know what's coming to them. As if his testicles have a will of their own.

"Don't need these anymore, right? You've gotten more use out of 'em than you deserve."

The more pressure I apply, the faster his breathing becomes.

Snip!

There is no discernible resistance when I close the blades. Taking the remains of his balls in my hand, I display them to him before dropping them onto his lap and wiping my hand on his shirt.

"Fucking disgusting, dude. If you don't mind—and even if you do—I'm gonna wash my hands before we continue. We're almost done. Only a few more things left."

Washing my hands a few feet away, his childlike whimpers draw a large smile on my face. I carefully sit back down in front of him and begin to explain more.

"You did this. I want you to realize that. I've never been able to be a normal person because of you. I don't care about anyone. I don't love. I only hate. Guess what? I hate you the most. I know I don't seem angry, but you know as well as I do that when you embrace the anger, it's sort of just action with no emotion. Before I started this, I was going to pray for you, then I realized God sent me to you. Did you know that my name, Matthias, is a form of the name Matthew? It means 'Gift of God'. Well, God doesn't give a shit about you, I'm sorry to tell you." *No, I'm not sorry at all, you bastard.*

With a long groan, rising to my feet, I slowly walk, then stand behind him.

"I can tell you'd still do it all over again, wouldn't you? You aren't even sorry about any of it. I want you to see what you have to look forward to. The fires of hell."

I retrieve the knife from my pocket, and the sound of it locking open triggers squirming. Reaching over his head, I take a firm grip of his eyelid and slice it off in one deft motion. Going for his second eyelid, his screams grow clearer; the glue is starting to separate. One, two, three strikes to his face and he's out again. *This guy has no pain tolerance.* But then again, maybe I'm misjudging. He's taking a lot of beatings.

"I have to admit one thing. You are a tough old bastard even if you do keep passing out. I gotta finish this up because I have to be back in Tucson in the morning. Sorry to have to rush it."

Now that he's unconscious, I easily remove his other eyelid and reapply glue to his lips. It takes him five minutes to come to, and when he does, he meets with me holding a portable propane torch. He looks surprised even though he has no eyelids, permanently wide-eyed.

"Remember what I said about seeing the fires of hell?"

As I inch the flame to his face, he shakes his head forcefully. I follow his face back and forth, scorching flesh and hair with each pass. It smells like a pig roast I attended many years ago. I remember it being delicious. The thrashing sharply stops, and I realize he's only passed out from the pain. He's still breathing. Holding his chin straight, I finish the job, flames melting his eyeballs like wax now, followed by crackling and popping, creamy white fluids oozing down his cheeks. It feels like a job well done as I stare at the skin falling off his face and holes where his eyes used to be.

It takes three trips to the woodpile out front for enough to build a bonfire around him. He stirs awake as soon as I begin pouring gasoline over his blood-soaked body. But he still doesn't move. He seems defeated. Limp. Almost as if he welcomes the idea of ending the pain through death. The thought causes me to look back at my own life of suffering.

"Bo, you know I tried to kill myself a few times? If I'd succeeded, I wouldn't be here, and we wouldn't have managed to meet up today. Crazy to think it, right? I was in so much pain that I would rather have been dead. Is that what you're feeling right now? Then I'm sorry for you."

Not so much as a moan comes out when he lightly nods.

"Well, I failed at killing myself, but I promise you, your pain is about to end. You are going to have to suffer a little bit more first though. Believe me when I say this, I do pity you."

With a lit rolled newspaper in hand, I take in the scene one last time. Bo sits motionless, awaiting the inevitable. There is no fight left in him. He's already moved on, his soul gone someplace, or he's desperately wishing that it would. I think about how much harder it was to break him than I expected, wondering if I could take even half of what he's just taken, everything to which I've subjected him.

When presented with pain and death, most people would fight, wouldn't they? It's a natural instinct to flinch, kick, writhe, lash out. Self-preservation is a strong instinct. It's just remarkable coming from a sixty-year-old man who looks and smells as if his body actually gave up a decade back due to the drink and abuse he's meted out to it.

Tossing the makeshift torch into his lap, the fire instantly envelops him, his squeals turning to screams as he forcefully rips his lips apart. He doesn't even attempt to rock in his chair before the shrieks of agony stop abruptly. The complete event from ignition to silence takes less than a minute.

I quickly turn on all the gas stove burners, toss my rain jacket into the fire, then rush to the door and into the yard. Fearing that the tiny mobile home will be engulfed in minutes, bringing the fire department, I waste no time getting into my rental car and tearing out of the dirt driveway.

Driving down the maze of backroads, I start to analyze what's just happened. Or rather, what I made happen. *Yes, I did it. I finally did it.* From start to finish, I replay every step of torture. With each image, I become more elated and aroused. I've never done anything like this before, though I've dreamed of it for as long as I can remember. But doing it… Well, that's created a whole new emotion. It feels strange, a heady mixture of arousal, excitement, and a feeling of power all rolled up into one.

I thought finally killing Bo would bring me peace and closure but instead, it seems to have created something even worse than emotional anguish. It has shown me a new unexplainable feeling. A new side of myself. Luckily, it's a feeling that seems to fade the farther I get from his still burning body. Even in death, that bastard continues to influence my emotions.

"Hope you're happy in hell, you piece of shit. I'll be seeing you again soon. Very soon."

The Long Road Home

Matt's Story

I don't remember the last forty minutes that got me here. Fifty miles have vanished in a single blink, imprisoned in a deep daze. Bright city lights streak across the windshield as I pass by the Reunion Tower in downtown Dallas. Staring at the enormous microphone-like structure, I wonder how it would have been if I'd never moved to Tucson twenty years ago. The brilliant colorful strobes drag me deeper and deeper into a daydream of what-ifs until suddenly, a constant loud blast of a horn pulls me out.

Swerving back into my lane, I look out through the right window to see an outraged man flipping me off, shouting and swerving his car repeatedly. I can't understand him, so roll the window down. Staring at him blankly, I wonder if he would have given that gesture knowing what I'd done not an hour earlier. The smell of blood and scorched flesh still coats my nostrils. Recalling the scene, it immediately transforms into images of strapping him to a chair and twisting his vulgar finger off.

"Learn how to drive, you fucking idiot!"

Noticing my still expressionless face, he goes from angry to visibly nervous. He speeds ahead. My eyes are back on the road now, but my brain's imagining the day's events with him instead of Bo and can feel the excitement returning. The scene is the same, but my acts are not. I'm toying with him. I start with a light scratch on his arm, then a deep cut to his cheek, then embed the knife into his thigh. Adding more progressively intense cruelty to the fantasy, I force myself to stop.

"What the hell is wrong with me? This is crazy. Am I...crazy?"

This whole thing has always been about Bo, not anyone else. Why would I now take pleasure from envisaging doing this shit to someone else? Even if he did flip me off and shout obscenities. I just wanted Bo to pay for his life of malevolence, that's all, for what he happily did to me over thirty years ago. Once he was gone, I thought I'd be able to move on and find happiness, but instead of happiness, I feel...different.

This is not the contentment I've been hoping for, even though it's what I have been dreaming of for so long. But don't get me wrong; it's not as if I feel sad for him. After all, he deserves what he's got and more. I feel sad for me though—kind of low. My sight begins to tunnel as my mind wanders.

***

At eleven years old, I'm home alone in a house located deep in the woods. My room looks over our front yard, but I never hear the truck pull in because I have a box fan blowing in my face as usual. I always sleep better when I have a noisy fan blowing on me. But this night, sleep eludes me.

At around two in the morning, the piercing noise of a woman screaming rattles me awake, followed by shattering glass and a man shouting, yelling his head off. I jump out of bed and grab a baseball bat before running to the front of the house, still in my underwear. With no idea of what I'll find, the adrenaline running through my body makes my heart race almost to the point of exploding. Out the front door, Bo is right there, standing over a half-dressed woman, his foot on her throat. She is choking and blue in the face, grasping, clawing at her neck, the sounds horrific.

Before this night, I had never met Uncle Bo. Let me tell you, it's nothing like the sweet introduction any kid would hope for. He's not the magnanimous uncle who comes in bearing gifts and ruffling my hair, saying how it's great to meet me at last. No, this is an uncle who lives to hurt people, who has no love in him at all, only a narcissistic desire to get his own pleasure at any price. I recognize him from the one family picture that hangs in the living room.

"Stop! What are you doing? You're hurting her!"

I'm saying the obvious. No other words will come. That's because I don't know any other words for what I see him doing. He's killing her, in fact. I dare not speak it. It's way too horrible. My words are effective. He leaves her now, easing his heavy booted foot off of her throat.

Slowly looking up, he starts walking toward me. In a panic, I pick the bat up and wield it above my head intending to swing, but there's no point. He's already grabbed it from my hands. Using the tip of the bat, he jabs at my right temple over and over, then the same at my back as I fall. He wears a grin. Oh, he's loving this. I lie on the ground cursing him as he walks away. Attempting to check on the woman, I crawl toward her, but he's suddenly there again. Now, Bo steps between us, standing there, towering over me.

"You little shit!"

He's kicking at me repeatedly with the tip of his cowboy boot. After a few blows to my face and head, everything goes black.

Hours later, I awaken to the dogs licking my bloody face covered by a few cuts, but otherwise unscathed. My head is littered with knots and each heartbeat is a pounding hammer in my brain. A slight burning sensation comes from my backside, but it isn't unbearable. Not yet anyway.

Slowly turning and putting my hands down to lift myself, however, causes an extremely sharp and stabbing pain to radiate from my rear, all the way up my spine, and down my arms. Only then do I notice that my underwear is down to my knees, and Bo has left me with my own bat partially inserted into my backside. With my right hand uncontrollably shaking, I reach back and remove the bat slowly, wanting to scream with every millimeter that it comes out of my body, then I somehow manage to pull my pants up.

I lay the weapon down on the carpet, hoping it doesn't stick and make a mess. Then, I'll only be in more trouble, no doubt. The bat wears blood smears, top to bottom. The smell of it is atrocious—the odor of feces and fresh blood that covers the wooden bat till about four or five inches up. It's slimy, revolting. Makes me heave my guts up. Or I would if it didn't hurt so much. I can't even hope to reach the bathroom as quickly as I would need to if I'm going to throw up. So, I heave again, swallowing. It's all I can do.

After a long period of crying, I clean myself up and I never say a word to anyone. That is the birth of it—the birth of that godforsaken will for revenge, for retribution, for hurting so-called 'Uncle Bo' the same way he's just hurt me. I plan to get my revenge another day, even if it takes me the rest of my life. And for every twinge of hurt he's brought to me, I vow to hurt him a hundred times more.

***

Red and blue strobing lights stir me back into the present, and I instantly fear they are here for me. They've come for me! My body tenses in the seat, my mind saying repeatedly, *oh God, oh shit*... Watching anxiously in the rear-view mirror, I slowly veer into the right lane. One by one, five patrol cars race by, and my heart rate calms with each successive pass. Now, all the cars have gone by and I'm in the clear again. *So far, so good.* I need to stay under the radar. Being pulled over would place me in Texas, and on the list of suspects.

A combination of this day's events and lack of sleep are taxing, each mile marker seeming further away than the last, my eyes growing heavier with each pass. High-pitched horn blasts echoing from every direction whip me out of microsleep, so I grudgingly accept that continuing is dangerous, pulling into a rest stop outside of Fort Worth.

***

Nothing but darkness surrounds me, thick and vile to the point it's almost tangible. Waves of black ripple and reflect light with no visible source. I can feel evil within it.

"Hey Matt, can you come in here?"

The voice sounds familiar and haunting. I don't want to go in there.

"Get in here right now! Don't make me beat your ass!"

My feet anchor in place, my pallid skinny legs trembling violently at hearing that voice again. The shimmering obscure reflections focus on a single point, partially illuminating a figure. It sluggishly draws closer, gliding in the dim light. It's a man. I can tell by his silhouette. The details of his face gradually become sharper, and I realize, it's Bo. The trembling in my legs now radiates throughout my body and I begin to urinate, the warm liquid coating my inner thighs as it flows to the ground beneath.

"Remember how it works. It's gonna happen whether you want it or not. Take it like a man."

Slowly, he reaches out and places his hand on my shoulder. The mere contact sends a jolt through my whole body, freeing me from my cage of terror. There's a deluge of power as I grab his hand, breaking his wrist back, sending a thunderous crack echoing through the darkness as his unnatural, almost robotic wails feed my resolve. My knuckles crash into his face repeatedly.

One, two... Three!

His skin and bones adapt to the impacts and begin distorting like wet clay. Releasing a massive surge of anger in one last blow, his body bursts into ash, drifting slowly and gracefully to the ground. But this is not good. This is not what I have craved or yearned for.

Loneliness creeps in with the realization that I am the only one left in the darkness, surrounded here by endless still and quiet. The silence itself becomes painful to my ears, and I find myself wanting Bo back so I can at least have a purpose, even if only hate and revenge.
Bo has always been the face of anger for me and now that he's gone, I'm left with the emotion but no one to focus it on.

A tap on the car window transports me from the dark chamber. I jolt awake, pain assaulting my eyes and brain with the shaft of light streaming in. I find myself curled up in the front seat of my rental car. Through hazy eyes, a woman in her mid-thirties comes into view, her blonde hair disheveled and hastily tied up with a scrunchy. It blows across her face.

The flower pattern button-up blouse she wears is dotted with wrinkles and her tan cotton skirt barely reaches all the way to her slim thighs. She looks an absolute mess, not what I want to see in the state I'm in. She's almost skeletal, emaciated, rough as hell. *The look of a druggie,* I tell myself, sighing with annoyance. *Why do they always come to me?*

"I'm sorry to wake you, but… do you have a few bucks I can have for gas? I'm traveling with my baby to California to get away from my abusive husband. And my baby needs to eat and I don't have any money for formula."

Rubbing my eyes, I inhale deeply and exhale with an annoyed moan. I've seen this trick before, scammers pulling at the heartstrings of decent people by using the ploy of a child in need. Invariably, the poor kid doesn't even exist, either hasn't been born or created yet or—more likely—has been taken away to give to a home that can care for it better.

"Sure, just show me your baby and I'll give you twenty bucks right now. Show me two kids to make it thirty bucks."

Opening the door, she starts to protest, looking annoyed.

"He's sleeping. I don't want to wake him. And no, there's only the one."

Yeah, sure there is, lady.

"That's fine. I'll just look through the window. No need to open the door."

Looking around, I notice only one other car in the lot and walk toward it. She attempts to grab my arm in stride but stops short of contact. Sure enough, the only thing in that goddamn car is a pile of clothes in a laundry basket in the back.

"Can't afford a child seat either? Or maybe you have the baby under the clothes, huh?"

"My baby is with my abusive husband."

"You know that people with a baby don't refer to them as their baby, right? They call them by name or gender. You're just another scammer. Besides, you'd only get laid for money."

Before I can make a complete turn away, she grabs my arm and pulls me to face her.

"Okay, I was lying. I really am trying to get to California though. And my ex was abusive, but that ended a year ago. Is there anything else I can do for the money, sweetie?"

Oh, sweetie, huh? Let's see how far she'll go for the twenty.

She notices my gaze fall from her face, down to her body. Glancing back up, I can tell she is weighing her options. With a defeated sigh, she begins unfastening her blouse.

"Okay, but I'm not doing this for twenty bucks. One hundred. You good with that?"

"Sure, let me grab my wallet."

Handing her the one-hundred-dollar bill, it's obvious she's done this before as I watch her open the glove box, pull out a roll of condoms, and rip one off with her teeth.

"You'll have to wear this. Well, unless you want to pay extra."

"Nah, I'm okay with wearing it. How about kissing?"

"Are you fucking kidding me? What do I look like? Your girlfriend?"

"Okay fine. Just sex. Got it!"

Waving her blouse back from the sides, I have a clear view of her breasts cradled within a black lacy bra. I become aroused at the sight, but not wholly, having to concentrate for even the slightest bit of stimulation. The belief that physical contact will increase my sexual excitement gives me the motivation to continue. Once laid down in the back seat of her car, she pulls up her skirt. Now, she displays herself to me like a subserviently married woman on her wedding night.

Confidently, I maneuver into position and caress her breasts through her bra. Her soft skin against my palm stimulates my mind, but my body refuses to respond. Embarrassment grows to irritation, then to anger, and within seconds, I am cursing Bo. *You did this to me, you piece of shit!*

Images of Bo's transgressions against me flood my mind. I push through each of them to find the memory of the day I almost killed him at thirteen years old, my hands firmly clasped around his throat, feeling his heartbeat against my fingers. The sounds of cracking and popping produce a thrilling sensation that surges, then cascades into a massive discharge of tingly energy.

"What the fuck is wrong with you, you fucking psycho!"

I look down to see the woman prying my hands from her throat. She gasps for air as I gradually release my hold.

"I'm so sorry. I didn't mean to—"

"Shut the fuck up and get out before I call the cops!"

In horror, I look down at my hands, then flee, sluggishly walking to my car. Her scream of "fucking psycho" repeats over and over in my head, and the worst thing is, I agree with her. Closing the door, I immediately slam my palms against the steering wheel. She's right though. I must be a fucking psycho to do what I just did.

"What the fuck did I just do? I…really am crazy."

Knowing that she's probably called the cops on me anyway, I rapidly start the car and drive away, seeing a plume of exhaust smoke in the rearview as I speed away. So, they've got me now. If they don't arrest me for Bo, they'll arrest me for trying to strangle the girl. *Well done, Matt. You really fucked up.* I leave the car lights off so she can't read my license plate if she hasn't noted it already.

A lot of whores do memorize them before they even agree to anything, worst luck. She came up to the car before we even started talking. *She'll have the plate. She's planned all that. Fuck.*

Less than a mile away, I realize I still have the condom on. With one hand on the wheel and the other inside the front of my pants, I pull it off. Concern rapidly follows; the condom has semen in it.

"How the hell? I didn't even have sex with her. How could I have finished?"

The conclusion, although obvious, takes me far too long to establish. Uneasiness overcomes me when reality finally hits.

"Bo. *Fucking* Bo… he's even responsible for this. The thought of killing Bo's made me so excited that I…What

those legs walking brisk till you reach your door, the correct key clutched at the ready. Straight in, slam that door. Done.

"Damn, hot one today isn't it, Matt?"

And there it is.

"Yep, it's hot, Hans."

That's it then, my social obligation completed, our obligatory weather chat over and done. My pace increases toward the entrance to indicate something pressing to take care of and no time to talk, giving Hans just the slightest wave as I flit by, almost in a jog. Sometimes, I press my cell phone to my ear to make a point, indicating to it. 'I'm on the phone, otherwise I'd love to talk, Hans…'

On this occasion, I don't even have my phone with me. But I don't need to go that far today because Hans is down on his knees, busy, and I can easily pass by. Breaking the door seal causes a slight pop to ring through the sparsely furnished living room. A blue suede love seat, a two-foot-wide stained-glass table, and a sixty-inch television make up the minimalist décor, just as I like it. Neat and clean, no clutter, everything where it ought to be.

The open floor plan allows for a clear view of the kitchen from the front door. On the counter sits a solitary coffee pot, and on the stove sits the pan I like to cook with. Jasmine-scented Glade plug-ins are in almost every outlet of the home, saturating the air with an aroma reminiscent of the fields I used to walk through as a child. A better aroma than the alternative, though it will always manage to break through, of course, depending on which room I enter.

Down the dark hallway to the left are two bedrooms that share a bathroom. Across the hall and around the corner from them is my room at the end.

After guzzling down two large cups of ice water, I make my way to the bedroom to rest before work in six hours'. Even though every inch of me is filthy, I'm too exhausted to shower, just collapsing my grimy and sweat-soaked body onto the bed. Blindly snatching my cellphone from the nightstand, my eyes check for any missed calls.

"Yep, usual. Don't know what I expected. Who the hell woulda called me anyway?"

I had put it on the nightstand before I left for Texas, in case it could be used to track my travels. The possibility of anyone calling while I was gone was improbable. I have no family, friends, or obligations that would necessitate communication, much less over the weekend. As for my three kids from a marriage that ended over a decade ago, I haven't so much as spoken to them in years. My own emotional bankruptcy has ruined any chance of being in their lives.

Lightly tossing the phone back onto the table, I begin wrapping myself into a cover cocoon. The soft blanket feels like gentle kisses on my bare skin, rocking me to sleep, and it only takes a few minutes to feel my body fading out into the blackness. The closer I get to it though, the more those random flashes burst in to stop me. Like a carousel projector, each light darts in and out of frame so quickly I can't make out the images, streaks of random colors shooting by faster and faster. As the speed increases, it begins to overlap and create a moving picture.

***

From the forest, I watch Bo leave in his late-model blue Ford pickup. His taillights fading into the distance signal the all-clear and I approach the dilapidated single-wide trailer. Not knowing if anyone else is inside, I lightly knock on the door.

"Hello! I'm looking for Bo! Is he home?"

My heart races, listening for the slightest response. I fear what I may have to do if someone else is in there. My lungs are frozen, my eyes locked wide as I gradually open the door.

"Hello! I just want to talk to Bo. I'm his nephew, Matthias. Is anyone here?"

The air is warm and sour with a powerful stench of stale cigarette butts. Piles of clothes lie haphazardly strewn about the floor and couch. The laminated floors in the kitchen are riddled with huge gaps, exposing the cheap and rotting plywood beneath. The counter and sink are overflowing with filthy dishes and half the cabinet doors are missing. Rat and roach droppings scatter across almost every surface.

"Good Lord, there's nothing like home, huh? You fucking dirty bastard. Maybe I should just leave you here as punishment."

It takes less than a minute to make certain the place is empty and position myself next to the doorway. With bat in hand, I lightly tap my fingers against it as if playing the bass guitar. I have had this bat for over thirty years. Bo once used it on me when I was a child. It seems fitting that I would return the favor. Time feels as if it's moving at half speed as I patiently sit thinking about it.

The memories attack any doubts around what I'll do, like a fly swatter slapping my conscience mid-air. The oven clock reads 7:26 p.m. when lights pull into the driveway. My heart starts pounding faster as if trying to escape my ribcage but I am overtly aware that it's not because I'm nervous. The enormous smile on my face tells me that I'm excited like a kid about to get on a roller coaster. Listening to his footsteps getting closer and louder, I slowly raise the bat above my head, the palpitations making me dizzy.

When the door opens, a case of Miller Highlife beer comes across the threshold, shoved in from the other side. The top of Bo's head instantly follows. *There's the target,* I think. The light reflects off his shiny bald spot. Couldn't fail to know him by that. He's had that shiny pate ever since I can remember. The sign of an abuser. Don't they always seem to have one? Kind of funny but gross at the same time. Swinging the bat full force down into his skull, his body goes limp and flops to the floor.

"And that's how it was supposed to go, man. You know, I thought it was gonna take a few hits to knock ya out. Never got to use this bat but I'm really gonna miss her. Jesus… thirty years. She's been with me for a long time, but now she's finally about to serve her purpose."

A piercing snap rings in my ears as I break the handle of the bat over my leg. Determined, I force Bo's gangly, rigid body into the fetal position and pull his jeans down to his knees, then thrust the bat grip and shaft deep as I can into his anus.

"Payback's a bitch, ain't it? Guess this makes us bat brothers, huh? Now, let's get your pants back on. By the way man, you really should wear fucking underwear."

After securing his jeans in place, I quickly wrap duct tape around his mouth and feet and use thick zip ties to secure his arms behind his back, then wait patiently. I don't want to force this. I want it to flow organically. The calm before the storm allows me to take in all of the scene. Bo lies there helpless and unable to fight back. I feel powerful and in control.

"Is this how you felt your whole life? Did you feel powerful when you were beating and raping people weaker than you? Did you, Bo? Did you, you fucking pussy?"

Cradling my fingers around his chin and moving closer to his face, I examine every crevice and pore.

"You never did have any real power, Bo. You see, you've always been a weak and spineless worm of a man, preying on the innocent. You know… I see the evil within you, and it will all be cleansed tonight. Because I'm gonna rid the world of your wickedness."

His eyes flash open without warning, scanning aimlessly around the room. I imagine he's trying to figure out where he is, why he's bound, and who this man is kneeling next to him. He hasn't seen me since I was a boy. A lot has changed in my appearance over the decades and he's having a hard time placing me in his memories. The moment the light comes on though, he shows a change in demeanor. It's instant, that flash of recognition, the expression on his face that says, *shit. I'm in trouble.*

"There ya go. I knew you could do it! You remember me now? So…yeah. Okay, this is what's going to happen. You're going to suffer everything you put me through and then some. Then, I'm going to kill you, Bo… 'Uncle' Bo, I should say. You understand the plan?"

He starts kicking and squirming violently as I take a seat on the couch next to him to watch the show.

"Do you feel that pain in your ass? It's not nice, is it?"

He stops as if to ponder.

"Yeah… That's right. This is the same bat you shoved up my ass all those years ago. Does that knowledge turn you on, Bo, does it? Well… actually, it's just the bottom five inches of it, so if you struggle too much, you might tear out your insides. Be careful."

His erratic behavior subsides, and he concentrates on me.

"As I was saying, you're gonna suffer everything that you put me through. You remember that, right? I kept the bat as a reminder all these years. Cleaned it, of course. One thing is bothering me though. I didn't have shoes or a shirt on that night. We should do this properly."

As I grip his shoes with both hands, he pulls away frantically, but they easily slide off. I throw them into the corner one by one. Catching sight of the folding knife I pull from my pocket, he rolls onto his belly and attempts to worm away like the slithering snake that he is.

"Oh! Is your plan to wiggle your way out of here? Like the fucking worm that you are?"

With the heel of my foot, I push firmly into his backside, driving the bat handle deeper. A tiny droplet of blood is beginning to ooze by the place where the bat enters his anus. *Oh, what a shame. I must have torn your guts. Sorry, Bo.* Stifled screams instantly follow as he smashes his head repeatedly into the floor. Once again, I wait patiently. After more than a dozen impacts, he abruptly stops and lets out a long moan.

"Okay then. Now can I get that shirt off? I'm in a bit of a time crunch and still have my shopping to do. Come on, Bo, let's get this done."

My mind is already running through the shopping list of things to buy. He better not make this difficult. Pulling his shirt with my fingertips, I slice the thin cotton fabric a little at a time. Halfway through, he attempts to struggle, but pushing my blade to his cheek in response advises him of the implicit consequences if he doesn't stop. He gives no more resistance, remaining still while I finish.

"There we go, buddy. Are you comfortable? Now, let's get you into the closet. I gotta run to the store before it closes."

He doesn't fight back when I grab his feet and begin dragging him down the hallway. The carpet must be rough on his skin. *Friction burns, just what he likes,* I think. He loves a bit of that…

"There, that turning you on is it, Bo? I know you like it because you always told me you did."

I think the idea of me leaving for the store is also exciting him, giving him hope that he can escape while I'm gone. Settled into the closet, he stares at me in the doorway.

"I know you're thinking you can escape when I'm gone and I'm on board with you trying. If you do happen to get out of those huge ass zip ties, I'll even let you live. Just know that I expect you to get it all out of your system now because when I get back, I won't put up with it, right?"

I hear just a stifled *mmmf* from his taped mouth. The duct tape is doing its job, holding firm. Before the door fully closes, he's already kicking at the walls and twisting his body back and forth. Unconcerned, I walk away. No way on this earth is he going to get out of that.

"Get it out of your system now! Won't be too long, Bo. Not long enough for you to miss me."

***

The alarm rattles me awake. Bleary-eyed, I turn off its unrelenting siren and let out a powerful yawn, then drop my head back onto the pillow.

"Today's a new day, Matt. All that shit's well behind you now. You ready to move on?"

With my arms extended and breath held, I stretch my whole body, then bounce out of bed with a purpose. This is a feeling I haven't had since I can remember. There's nothing bad in my world anymore. That pervert has finally reaped what was coming to him. And even better, I am the one who's given it to him. It feels good, and freeing.

"Yep, today's a new day! Let's do this!"

Cutting the Surface

The hangar doors are fully open when I arrive, which means we're about to receive a new aircraft for maintenance. The airlines usually send the ones that are due for inspection straight to our hangar after their last flight of the day; now, they'll be getting their yearly two-week-long checkup and repair. As anticipated, the supervisor's already handing out maintenance assignments to the crew when I enter.

"Jack, I need you to grab Tim and do the prechecks on 781 then pull her into bay 2. Goron, get your stuff together for the nav upgrade. I wanna get it done before we cut power. Matt and Doug, you guys are on panels. Leave the stabs for last. We need to do backlash checks first."

On the first night of a newly arrived aircraft, I'm always assigned panels. I don't know why he even bothers telling me anymore. He hands me the twenty-page list of panels and then turns back toward the assignment board.

"All right Doug, usual? I'll take the right side and you take the left?"

"Sure, I still have your speed handle, by the way. Can I use it till tomorrow? I'm grabbing a new one on the way home in the morning."

"Dude, keep it. I told you, I still have two more."

"I know, man. I just don't like taking handouts."

Doug is in his early twenties, and this is his first job as an aircraft mechanic. He's quiet and shy with most people, but for some reason, easily talks with me. His awkward demeanor is probably the reason why none of the other mechanics like working with him and why they always assign him to me. They like a good chat and banter while they work, but I don't. He's too quiet for their liking. But he's too irritating for me too.

Our conversations are grating on my nerves; I only endure them because I know what it's like to be odd, and I pity him. I suppose he pities me too. He attempts to make conversation, struggling to remove one of the screws.

"Did you do anything exciting this weekend?"

Stopping mid-screw turn, I stare at the panel. His question triggers a barrage of images, each assaulting my mind and slowly dragging me deeper.
"Hey, I said did you do anything fun?"

Snapping out of the trance, I look slightly in his direction, but not directly at him.

"Oh, you know me. Not really. I just…watched tv. My life's pretty boring, man."

"Yeah, me either. What did you watch?"

Well, screw you, Doug. Just stop with the questions.

"This and that. You know how it is. Channel flicking."

"Yeah."

Minutes turn to hours as I remove panel after panel, enduring Doug's relentless talking. This job's terrible enough without having to deal with his nonstop chatter about nothing, and I can feel my limit approaching. I'll have to stop him before my impending eruption. I feel it welling up in me, something I can't control. An explosion of anger is on its way.

"Hey, can we just work in the quiet for a few minutes? I drank a lot last night and my head is killing me."

"Sure, man. I know what that's like. I once had a hangover so bad that I couldn't open my eyes because the light hurt so bad. I was drinking Everclear with orange juice all day and—"

"Dude… just a few minutes, man. Please. I just can't keep talking."

"Oh yeah, sorry."

I can tell he's embarrassed and a little sad, but the alternative would have been worse. There's been a change in me. I'm not the same person he remembers. My ability to block out frustrations and act how society wants me to now hangs by a thread. I can feel it, the burning fire inside that awaits its release. Pulsating and expanding to the surface, it takes every bit of focus to quell it.

"Look man, I'm just not feeling well right now. Promise I'll let you finish your story later. Just give me some time, okay?"

"Of course! We can talk later."

The first minute of silence in six hours brings a much-needed moment of relief and my frustration begins to wane. The relief is replaced by anxiety though, considering what would have happened had I allowed him to continue. He's just a lonely kid looking for friendship. He doesn't deserve my anger, or worse, what my anger could evolve into… physically. *What would I have done to him?* Still staring at the same panel I've been working on for an hour, overwhelming visions of what I could have done attack my conscience.

***

Plunging my scribe pick deep into his eye, he screams and flails violently.

"How's it feel, Doug? Is that answer enough for you, man? Still wanna know what I did this weekend? Huh? This…This is what I did this weekend! I made someone pay for being an evil piece of shit by killing him. Is this what you wanted to know?"

He collapses to the ground crying, and I position myself on top of him.

"You still wanna talk about it, Doug? Come on, let's talk!"

I wrap my hands around his throat, squeezing with so much pressure that his tongue rolls from his mouth.

"This is who I am. You wanna know me? Here I am! Look at me, Doug!"

His bulging bloodshot eye reminds me of one of those rubber stress balls with a face on it. Alternating pressure causes it to pop in and out from the socket. The other eye still impaled by the pick doesn't move. Releasing my right hand, I reach down and—

***

"Hey, it's quitting time."

Slowly turning my head, I see Doug drumming on my shoulder. My hardened gaze cuts through him like a knife and he senses the tension.

"You okay? It's six, man. Time to go home."

"Yeah, I'm fine. Just tired."

My stomach spasms and churns watching him walk away. Thinking about where my imagination has just taken me, I bury my face in my palms. *Something is wrong with me. I can't live like this. Why do I keep having these thoughts?* All my life, I've had thoughts of killing only one person… Bo. He was the one who ruined my life. My pursuit of vengeance is what's always consumed me. Now that I don't have that purpose, what's left? Hate? An addiction to torture? The longing to inflict pain is still there, maybe stronger now. But there's no face to put to it.

My guts twist and writhe, torment overtaking me, that kind of knotted stomach that makes you either want to thump or stab or burn someone, hearing them scream. Or it makes you want to kill the sensation with opiates or Valium, to get rid of it. Nothing works. The feeling won't go. The feeling has become a part of me, only I never knew it until now. The only time I ever felt anything other than hatred was while fulfilling my revenge. The scary thing is, I want that feeling back. It was stupid to imagine that a feeling that's been with me all my life since being eleven years old was going to go just by getting back at Bo. It's as much a part of me as breathing or drinking water or taking a piss. I need to get help. Still carrying the nervous cramps in my gut, I approach my supervisor.

"Hey, Mike. I'm gonna need to take a few days off. I'm not feeling well."

"What's going on?"

"I don't know. My stomach's cramping bad, and I can't focus. I mean, ask Doug. I've been out of sorts all day. I'm kind of scared I'll mess up if I keep on the job and it's not like we work in a mailroom, is it? I can't afford to fuck up this job; I got too much riding on it, Mike."

"Yeah, I was wondering why you didn't get finished with the panels. That's not normal for you. Hey, go take what time you need to figure this out. Doug can finish up tomorrow."

The sun is barely peeking over the horizon from the east when I leave the hangar. The thirty-minute drive home is filled with ideas of how I can get some help for whatever this is I'm going through.

Suicide hotline? Hmm, but I'm not suicidal, am I?
Banner University Hospital has one of those psych wards. Yeah, but it's for the real crazy people.
Not people like me. Psychiatrist? Psychologist?

It's hard to know who the right specialist might be. What's the difference between one and the next? Years ago, during my divorce, I began seeing a therapist through the Veterans' Affairs Clinic down the road in Green Valley. The sessions did help me through severe depression back then. Maybe they could help me through this. But I don't think I'm depressed either. What I am is vengeful, even after taking the revenge I've been thinking I needed. Turns out it wasn't enough. *But yeah—I'll go talk to someone.* Coming up with a practical solution relieves my cramping and puts me at ease.

"I'll call 'em in a few hours when I get up."

Lying down in my bed, I gaze at the ceiling, pondering. My windows are blacked out and only a small hint of light sprinkles through, the dark abyss offering a blank canvas for me to paint upon. Although I fight the urge to see, the illustrations gradually overpower me and squinting only brings the visions more into focus.

"Just one more time, then I'm done with this madness. All right, Bo. Here comes retribution."

The thrill of recalling the suffering I have caused to Bo grows, and the more I concentrate, the clearer it becomes.

***

In the front yard of my childhood home, I stand petrified at the door.

"This isn't what I wanted! What is this?"

Storm clouds roll and roar violently behind me with constant strikes of blinding light. Scanning around the moonlit yard, debris sails by, carried on the powerful continuous gusts. The wooden door swells and contracts as if breathing and sighing. Deeper and heavier, it creaks and grumbles. Suddenly, it stops, and the door begins fracturing. Brilliant white light sears through the cracks of the expanding web until it explodes into a million fragments. I feel the shards grazing my face as they pass. In the wake of the explosion stands a figure.

"Grandma?"

The shadowy figure remains still and doesn't respond.

"I'm sorry! I swear! I won't do it again…!"

I'm interrupted by its dark hand grasping my neck and lifting me off the ground.

"This isn't what's supposed to…"

Tossed onto the ground like a rag doll, I proceed to beg for forgiveness.

"Please! I swear! It won't happen again! Grandma!"

***

Lurching from the bed, I clench my chest, gasping for air. My sheets, saturated with sweat, cause me to shiver from the cold.

"Holy…What the fuck was that shit?"

Rejected memories of my grandmother beating me with anything she could get her hands on rush into my mind. Recollections of how close I was to death. How readily she was willing to distribute corporal, even deadly, punishment. I'm certain she would easily have killed me, then blamed me for being too weak.

"If only you were still alive. You would be next on my list, you old hag!"

I lie in bed for ten minutes, unwillingly reliving the abuse my grandmother put me through as a child before pushing the memories back down where they came from.

"Nothing I can do about it now."

Even without 'talking therapy', I am quite sane enough to know that when the perpetrator is long since dead, dwelling on the 'what might have been' can only serve to drive you more insane. *Let it go, Matt,* my inner voice says to me. In fact, my inner voice is begging me not to let these thoughts take over everything. Life is going to spiral rapidly downhill if I don't get a grip—and right now.

Thumbing through the contact list on my cellphone, I stop at the number for the Green Valley Veterans' Affairs Clinic, then stall for a few minutes, contemplating what to say. I mean, what *can* I say? Angry thoughts? That's relatively serious, but not enough to make people think I'm nuts. So, I'll just say I've been angrier recently. But then again, what if there's a waiting list? What if being 'angrier' isn't enough to put me at the top of the list? Isn't everyone angry these days? I just don't know. So, I vow to play it by ear, to take my time and see what they ask me. Each time the phone rings, my stomach knots a little tighter. I want to throw up. Six rings pierce my ear before someone answers.

"Green Valley VA Clinic, how can I help you?"

"Hello, my name's Matthias Ellis. I was wondering if I could book in to see a therapist soon?"

"Sure. I just have to ask you a few questions before we get you scheduled. Mr. Ellis, do you have thoughts of hurting yourself or others?"

The question of hurting others throws me off for a second.

"Uh…no."

"When did you notice a change?"

"I don't know. Around a month ago, I guess."

"What changes have you noticed, and would you say it's gotten worse, better, or about the same?"

"About a month ago, I noticed I was more irritable. I get angry more easily. I don't think it's gotten worse or anything, but it's definitely not getting better."

The clicking in my ear is so fast I can't imagine how she knows what keys she's hitting.

"Okay, a few more questions. Have you noticed any unexpected weight gain or other health issues?"

"No ma'am."

She continues her lightning-fast clicking. Listening patiently, I unexpectedly hear three strange beeps. Confused, I look at the phone. 'Crystal Cousin' illuminates the screen. My heart begins pounding through my chest. I haven't spoken to Crystal in years. There's only one reason she would be calling me out of the blue: to tell me about Bo.

"All right, you're in luck, Mr. Ellis. We've had a cancellation for an appointment with Doctor Ruiz, today at one if you are available."

"One o'clock is perfect!"

"Great! I have you down to see Doctor Ruiz at Green Valley, at one o'clock today."

"Awesome, thank you so much."

As soon as I hang up, the phone starts to ring loudly but all the panic coursing through me won't allow me to answer. The ringing stops and is immediately followed by a string of texts.

Call me back ASAP Matt! Some crazy shit happened yesterday! Call me!!!

My hands tremble uncontrollably when I press call.

"Oh, my God, Matt! Bo is dead! Someone killed him!"

"Holy shit, are you serious?"

"Yeah, they found his mangled body all burned up in his trailer. Well, what's left of it. I guess it's all burned to the ground. I don't know any more than that, only that he's gone."

"Damn! Well, that bastard deserved it. But are they sure it's him?"

"Yep. They're questioning everyone. They asked me about family, if I knew of any enemies and stuff. I don't know about enemies, but I told them what family we had left. Oh, and that you lived in Arizona."

My panic is now at crisis level, hearing how my name's been brought into conversation with the police. But it'd be odd if she didn't mention me, wouldn't it?

"They think it was drug-related. They found a shed behind his trailer that looked like it was used to store weed in it, but it was empty, and all torn up."

"Knowing Bo, it was drug-related, Crystal."

"Yeah, He was a piece of shit. I wish I was the one that killed him."

"Don't say that. Trust me, it wouldn't bring you peace."

"True. Oh well, I'll let you get back to it."

"All right. Have a good day. I'm sure we'll talk later."

Putting the phone down feels like dropping a hot stone. The cops will be contacting me soon to see what I know, and I need to prepare for what they're going to ask. Going down the list of possible questions, the best defense I have is that I haven't seen him in thirty years. No one, even a seasoned investigator, could think any person could hold onto a grudge for that long. If they were going to act in retribution, they'd do it sooner, wouldn't they? I'm hoping that's what they'll think. The more I rehearse my response, the easier it gets to say it aloud.

"Holy shit! Haven't seen him since I was fifteen. I just assumed he was already dead from all the drugs."

Satisfied that my reaction is perfect to steer suspicion away, I finally relax and get ready for my approaching appointment. Clean and dressed, I take one last look into the mirror. Alternating tucking and untucking my shirt, frustration is mounting again. I could rip this fucking shirt off my own body and set light to it. It's not even a big deal, yet it somehow feels as if it should be. In or out, for Christ's sake? Relaxed or professional?

Hmm, should I wear slacks instead? If I go in these jeans, will the therapist think—
Holy shit, man! What are you doing? You aren't going to a job interview.
You could go in fucking swim trunks. Who gives a shit? Stop thinking so much!
He's not going to judge you based on your fucking clothes.

Settling on a casual look, I drape my polo shirt over the waistline of my jeans and step back.

"Yeah, looks good. You're gonna be fine. Let's go fix this, Matthias!"

Picking at Scabs

Matt's Story

This waiting room reminds me of a wake. It's tiny, a fifteen-feet by ten-feet space filled with elderly military retirees, all quietly staring into their laps and picking at their yellowing ridged fingernails. Every few minutes, a patient who's completed treatment walks out and a receptionist calls out a name to promptly replace them. One out, then one in, like an assembly line. It's almost entertaining watching them get herded through the process.

Checking my watch, it's forty-five minutes past my scheduled appointment. My left leg swings over my right one. I pick invisible fluff from my pants. The frustration is building in me again, anxiety and agitation causing a well of stress. Now, I have just joined the ranks of the finger-picking crowd as if the clinic has just inaugurated me into a secret society. Going in to see the doctor while actively outraged would not end well, so I breathe deeply, trying to concentrate on calming thoughts.

***

The clinic tries its best to put us at ease. The only thing they're not doing to de-stress the visitors is handing out pills at the door, worst luck. But a nice cool breeze on my face carries a light scent of jasmine flowers. The scent of them seems to pursue me everywhere, yet I like it. Chimes delicately clank from a gentle wind. Water slowly flows over rocks in a creek. The sound of a fire is crackling and popping, and an image appears on a wall-mounted screen, flames dancing and flickering. Watching the blades of fire feather back and forth, I am entranced. Constrained by its power and beauty, I can't move on, its bright red glow attracting and pulling at me like a magnet. It suddenly rips me from serenity, the blaze surrounding me.

My flesh blisters and melts in the inferno. Frantically spinning in circles, looking for an escape, there is only fire. Spinning more rapidly, the flame becomes thin bright streaks. Faster and faster, the light molds into a solid wall of red, then…smack! As if hitting a brick wall, I abruptly stop and find myself staring into a mirror. Within it, there's the truth.

***

"Mr. Ellis? Uh, Matth…eye?"

"Matthias. Yeah, that's me."

"Sorry about that. I'm really bad at names. Doctor Ruiz is ready to see you."

The room is a typical medical evaluation room, not what most people imagine when they think of mental health treatment. No nice, soft, comfortable couch. Instead, the bland room has been kitted out with a PC, the doctor's own rolling chair, a stationary chair, and an examination table with the usual pointless white curtain. I mean, what's the point of going behind a curtain only for the doctor to enter the space with you? I hope he won't have me stripping off...*Yeah, what's even the point of a curtain when it's a psychiatrist*? I shudder. *God knows.*

"Mr. Ellis."

"Yep, that's me."

"Ah, okay. Mr. Ellis, please have a seat."

The spindly static chair is where I'm directed to sit. Opposite me is a woman, not a man. For some reason, I envisaged a man. Not that I care either way right now; I am not interested in her sexuality. She motions again toward the chair. My inner agitation draws me toward the other one, however, the one with wheels, the one to which she does not send me; at least I could keep some element of movement if I claimed it.

There is not one limb that wants to keep still, to keep from juddering, rocking, jittering. Being still for too long right now feels like I'm about to be caught, captured, arrested, then interrogated and found out. But the wheeled chair sits on the wrong side of the therapist's desk. I can hardly go and claim it. Then the clinic would really know that I was mad. If I did that—or anything akin to that—they would make me leave.

There are signs all over the walls, almost as if they know what has brought me here, as if they read inside my mind. *Abuse of our staff, whether verbal or physical, will not be tolerated and the police will be called in all cases. If you cannot control your outbursts, please leave the room.*

"You can just call me Matt," I hear myself say in a pleasant enough tone. I take the chair, the static one that looks way too uncomfortable for a whole hour-long therapy session. A very attractive blonde with deep blue eyes now sits on the rolling chair in front of me. It's hard to determine her age. I can tell she's mature by her gestures and the tell-tale furrows, but her magnificent form and perfectly symmetrical face complicate the normally easy assessment.

"Please, start in your own time. Tell me whatever you wish. Everything stays in this room unless I believe someone may be at risk of physical harm. That means you, or anyone else."

So, she really did read my mind, I think. Now, I don't know what to say, how much I dare to reveal. This is more than awkward. She has just applied conditions and limitations to what I can talk about. *Fuck this.*

"Well, Doctor Ruiz, I—"

"Please, call me Cristy."

"All right, Doctor Cristy."

As soon as the words leave my mouth, I realize how ridiculous they sound, and she laughs almost immediately before I can correct myself.

"Just Cristy is fine, Matt."

Her smile at my faux pas projects understanding and openness; it relaxes me.

"Right. Uh, I've been feeling emotionally unstable lately. Angry, really."

"Unusually angry? Would you say you've been thinking about hurting others or yourself?"

The wheels are turning in her head as she studies my reaction. She's not listening to my words as much as watching for my mannerisms. She eyes my fidgety hands, the fingers that won't keep still, the swinging leg, just as though I must have caught some disease of agitation from the old men in the waiting room. *Keep still, for God's sake,* my mind tells my extremities. They collectively refuse to obey. I have no control over myself. My right foot keeps jittering upward, my legs crossed again. Nothing on my body will listen to my instructions. And the more I think about it, the worse the tics become. My right eye twitches now too.

"Yeah, I'm not an angry person, but I *have* had emotional issues in the past, and you might already have seen that I came here to see someone about them. But I don't want to hurt anyone if that's what you mean. I wouldn't do anything. But I get so angry I want to escape them. Oh, and I don't feel suicidal or anything, no."

She writes a few lines on the clipboard in her hand and then stares above her glasses at me.

"What I mean is, are you actively *thinking about* hurting anyone when you get angry? Whether you would do it or not—are your thoughts taking you in that direction?"

Her stare is intense when she pauses for my reaction. I feel her piercing blue eyes probing for observable changes in my behavior. Her eyes flick between my face and these restless hands that I want to pin down.

"No, not really."

"Not really? Okay, we'll come back to that. I'm interested in something you said previously. You said that you had emotional issues in the past?"

"Yeah, I had some pretty severe depression. Like I said, I saw a therapist for it here. It's not in my notes?" She doesn't seem to know about what I went through the last time.

"No, Matt, we don't keep notes as such. Once a couple of years have passed, we write out to you to ask if we can destroy our records, If we don't hear back, we go ahead. It's not ethical to hang onto—"

"Oh, right. I suppose that's good, then."

They must have destroyed all records of me. When I last came to this place, I'd been moving around a lot. I wouldn't have received any follow-up letters.

"Yes, it is good," she says and smiles. She appears to have all the patience in the world yet at the same time, she's taking everything in. Every small word, every movement.

"Did it help to talk to someone about it last time? I suppose so if you've come back!"

"I'm not depressed anymore, so I would say, yeah. I also wrote a book to help me through it. I think it was something the therapist said would help me, actually, and it did."

She stops in the middle of jotting on her notepad and slides her frames down slightly.

"A book? That's an amazing accomplishment. Would you like to tell me more about that?"

"It's called Born into Darkness, about how I grew up abused and managed to find a way to be happy. Not that I'm especially happy now, but… at the time, it helped."

She returns to writing on her notepad. She has a big smile and is nodding as she writes.

"That's so good to hear, Matt. Look, I'm sorry we started so late and must cut this session short, but I want to go back to your answer earlier. You said that you 'don't really' think about hurting people when you get angry. What did you mean by that? What does it feel like?"

"I don't know. I mean, sure. Doesn't everyone wish they could punch assholes?"

She smiles as if thinking about an instance when she wished she could punch someone.

"Yes, I'd say that's pretty common. It certainly doesn't mark you out as unusual or in need of any treatment! Well, we didn't get near enough time today and there's so much more I'd like us to explore. Would you mind coming back Mondays and Wednesdays for a few weeks? We'll talk more about your emotions and explore your childhood if you're comfortable with it."

The thought of discussing my childhood causes anxiety, but my urge to be normal overshadows it.

"I can come Wednesday, but can't plan after that until I check my schedule."

There is no schedule. I just hate making multiple commitments. I always did hate committing to things.

"Great! I'll see you then. And hey, if you start to feel angry, try this. Close your eyes and imagine what it is that's making you angry. Don't open your eyes to see it. Keep it in your mind, then change the event to something else that makes you happy. You think you can try that?"

"Sounds simple enough. Thanks."

"Terrific! I'll see you on Wednesday."

The fifteen-minute interaction does little to encourage me that I can get better. All I'm left with is the strategy to think happy thoughts when I feel rage. She has discovered nothing about me, and a fifteen-minute session has done so little that I feel rage right now, in fact. Rage and an overwhelming sadness. My guts roil. *That was seriously a waste of my time.*

Nothing planned for the day, I sit in my car thumbing through movie listings to see if there are any upcoming showtimes. The only movie showing within the next hour is Candyman, a horror movie about a ghost or something who kills people after they say his name five times into a mirror. I have always loved horror movies, but looking back, wonder if it's contributed to my current problem. *That's ridiculous. If horror movies caused people to become crazy, there'd be no sane people left in the world. They'd all be dead.*

I start the car. The notion was absurd and not worth a second of my time. The theater is only a quarter filled when I take my favorite seat in the middle row, immediately bombarded by sharp crinkling and crunching sounds all around me. Barely audible whispers fill any voids between the awful chaotic noises. I feel it coming. At first, a slight itch with no way to scratch it. It spreads and builds to more of a burning sensation.

"Stop it! Stop it! Stop it! Shut the fuck up!"

Who are these people going to the movies at two-thirty in the afternoon? Don't they have jobs?

No one notices as my manic self-whispers are consumed by the surrounding murmurs and fade into obscurity. Clasping my hands together, I close my eyes.

"Happy thoughts, Matt. Where's a peaceful place we've been?"

Crunching transposes into the sounds of the ocean crashing into a rockface. The crinkling becomes the patter of crabs skittering along. The various whispers mold into the cawing of seagulls in the distance. I feel myself being rocked side to side by the warm salty breeze, synchronized with the swaying of the palm trees. *This feels nice. Maybe Dr. Ruiz's advice wasn't so dumb.* The ability to control my emotions seems possible until I am interrupted by someone's obnoxious voice.

"Ahh, this shit's 'bout to pop off!"

Peering through partially open eyes, I see an obscenely large man taking a seat in front of me, joined by a woman only half his size. Unlike everyone else in the theater, they speak not only at full volume but almost as if trying to talk to the people in the next auditorium. Most of the whispers are now comments about this couple.

The slight burning returns as a searing fury. I clench my eyes tight in response. It's strange, even to me. It seemed so easy to pull myself away from the many annoyances, but now with just one, I can't focus away from it, irritation building with every word from the big guy's mouth. *I wish I had glue right now.* My vision begins to wobble and color fades to grey.

"I didn't mean it. Please, don't…"

***

The room starts to vibrate and hum, steadily increasing in intensity. Higher and higher, the pitch becomes painful to my ears. The instant I cup them with my hands, everything goes quiet, and the already scarcely lit room slowly dims. I give it no resistance. The theater is empty now, except for the man who was seated in front of me. He is still there and facing the screen, throwing random concession snacks, waving his arms. He makes no sound, although his lips are moving. The closer I get, the more stoic he becomes.

Now within inches of him, he still doesn't move as if he's a rock. He doesn't even breathe. Gently pushing my finger onto his cheek causes no reaction. His skin feels firm yet soft and slippery. Pulling my finger back causes blood to stream out and I step back from its crimson path. Still, he gives no response. I bring my hand up to examine my finger, only to discover a small knife within my grip. *What? A knife? But how?*

"Is that? Oh my God!"

It's the knife I used on Bo one of the last times I saw him as a child. I stare at it for a moment to make certain it's the same blade, then look back at the man in the

~ 67 ~

theater. He's no longer bleeding. He's not even human anymore. He is only a statue, except the statue is pointing toward the screen. Terror fills me at the thought of turning to see what it's pointing at. My gaze locks on the statue's arm. Slowly following the guided path causes chills and tremors throughout my body, and almost as if on cue, as soon as I get sight of the white background, rolling pictures and sound begin playing.

There I am, lying in bed late into the night, unable to sleep. I can tell a storm is coming because the wind has been gusting for the last hour. The windowsills are uneven with small gaps, which causes a whistling sound with each blow. I know what these nights bring, and I'm done with them. My hands fiddle with a small box knife while I wait for the storm to arrive. *Click...Click...Click.*

I stop the clicking, noticing the first faint creak of the thin wooden floors. Concentrating, I listen for another warning. Nothing. My heart starts to calm, then another squeak speeds it back up. Concentrating even longer, the sounds seem to be all in my head. An eternity passes. Then Bo is standing in the doorway.

"Remember how it works. It's gonna happen whether you want to or not. Take it like a man."

He moves through the moonlight toward me and onto the bed. It sinks from his weight when he rolls into the middle. I haven't said a word. Normally, I've protested by now. It makes him suspicious.

"You okay? You seem quiet. Are you finally done fighting?"

I stare at him purposefully helpless.

"Yeah, I'm all right, finally taking it like a man. It took long enough."

When he touches my arm, current jolts through me. I begin stabbing blindly in his direction.

"What the fuck? Goddammit! You little fucker!"

Every thrust of the knife carries hot red droplets that splatter onto my face. Each drop causes me to be more excited and to stab more vigorously. Bo jumps up and runs out of the room with me in tow, swinging the tiny knife at him.

"Crazy motherfucker! I'll fucking kill you!"

Slipping his bloody hands in and out of the door handle, he finally climbs into his truck. The roar of it starting up feels like my cage exploding into a million pieces. I stand free, my bloody arms outstretched in the beam of his headlights, the chill in his eyes unmistakable even beyond the dirt-covered windshield. He nervously revs the motor and places his hand on the gear lever. Defiant and unafraid, I slowly swing my arm around to point the dripping red knife at him.

***

"Aww, shit! They playin' this shit backward, yo!"

Opening my eyes, I'm stunned to see that the movie is still in the intro scene. Even more incredible is that the man in front is still talking so loudly during the actual movie. Feeling I could easily plunge a knife into his fat neck and flabby jowls right now, I need to get away from the situation and rush to the aisle to leave.

"Hey, where ya going, man? This shit's about to get crazy!"

I look back at him with contempt. If only he realized how *crazy* it already is. If he understood how his actions really affect the people around him, and how close he is to being assaulted… *If you knew how crazy it almost was…you would have shut the fuck up.*

Shattered Chains

Matt's Story

Pushing through the door and out into the courtyard, the rage isn't subsiding. The short brick wall surrounding a small flower garden beckons me to sit, and I rub my hands together forcefully.

"Stop it, you crazy bastard. Do you want to be normal or not? Just stop!"

The friction from rubbing my palms so intensely creates a heat that could ignite at any moment. Harder and faster, I watch for embers to appear, softly cursing myself.

"Hey, are you okay?"

Looking up, there's a couple holding hands, overdressed for a typical trip to the movies, so they must be on a date.

"Me? Yeah, I'm okay. It's just been a bad day. You know how things get sometimes."

"We've all been there. Hang in there, man. It'll get better."

As they walk away toward the theater, I contemplate why he would bother comforting a stranger. That makes a change, someone trying to help a man they don't even know. But it doesn't take long to figure out his motives; I hear the woman speak as they walk on.

"That was so sweet of you."

"Looked like he needed some encouragement, poor bastard. Like a stray dog."

"Aww!"

So, his attempt to be sympathetic was just for show. Like everyone else I have ever met, he is a total fake. Acting, to portray himself in a way that will get him what he wants. Not that I've given him anything, of course. Well, maybe a small smile, though it was hard to do. My current suffering has presented the perfect opportunity to be a pawn in his elaborate game of wooing a gullible woman. The thought of someone using me like that enrages me for a moment until I am hit by a profound understanding.

"I'm fake too."

I fill my days constantly trying to hide who I am so that people won't feel uncomfortable around me. The pretend grin I cast every time someone smiles at me or when I feign interest in conversations; all of it's an act. Even with my new therapist Cristy, I've been representing myself dishonestly. Ever since living out my fantasy of slaying Bo, my ability to hide has slowly chipped away, my blood lust steadily growing. *I need to stop pretending and just be who I am.*

Lightly wiping my hands across my knees, I push off them and rise to my feet. Crowds of movie goers flock all around the courtyard in crisscrossing paths like ants in the jungle. Scanning around randomly, I pick individual subjects to analyze their facial features and movements. Watching this chaotic scene, strangely, isn't irritating. I feel outside of their world now. It's almost as if I'm above them, watching through the glass of a terrarium. *These aren't people.*

My connection with society has previously been tenuous, but now standing here in this public square, it's nonexistent. I hold no emotion for them, these ants marching along, oblivious to the truth. Not only oblivious, but also not wanting to seek it or face it. If they were honest with themselves, they could see it. If they would open their minds, they could easily sense it. If they came too close, they would physically feel it. The truth. The truth is…they are living blissfully in the presence of a killer.

There they all are, carrying on with their happy lives, thinking everything is perfect, ignoring the real world that's looking them right in their eyes in the form of a twisted, sick killer, living right there on their own doorsteps. Closing my eyes and lifting my face to the sky, I recall visions of fire consuming me. The sensation of my flesh melting causes my heart rate to increase, but not from the pain or panic. It's exhilaration. Spinning within the inferno, I laugh, extending my arms to the side. Faster and faster, the light molds into a solid wall of red, then…smack! As if hitting a brick wall, I abruptly stop and find myself staring into a mirror. Within it, the truth shines out.

***

"Bo? There ya are, ol' buddy. I missed you."

Bo stands before me with fire raging all around him. Touching his face and waving his arms to reflect mine, he mimics every move from within the mirror. His haggard skin bears scorch marks all over, deep black holes where his eyes used to be, and a solid flesh-colored band of crust replaces his mouth.

"Do you see what you have created? Do you see who I've become?"

His slow, single nod almost seems remorseful.

"Well, it's time to accept who I am. I've been fighting it for far too long. I just needed to see you one last time to say *fuck you* for doing this to me! Anyway, you're gone now. I've got rid of you. So now, I can move on."

I say it but don't mean it—not the 'moving on' bit. Something as simple as killing someone doesn't let you move on. You move on when your mind decides, if ever. And slaughtering someone just makes it less likely for your mind to let you forget it all. Standing motionless, it almost seems as if he is contemplating a response. Even if he does want to speak, he can't. Instead, he hangs his head down, turns away, and wanders off into the sea of flames.

~ 74 ~

"I'll be seeing you soon."

***

On my way to the car, it feels like I'm leaving a spa after a two-hour massage. Every muscle in my body relaxes to the point that my arms feel heavy. I have shoved all the stress of pretending out of me like toothpaste, except a curious feeling still clings to the sides of the tube. It's a desire. A desire to…still pretend. There's no chance to break away from it. This fucking fakery. I've spent my whole life faking normal so that I can try to be 'normal', instead of realizing that there is no such thing, and that everyone fakes who they are to get what they want. So, the ones we see as normal are faking it. That's what I should have been doing all along. It's never occurred to me that I could be doing what everyone else was, instead of despising them for it. Be who I am on the inside but project who I want people to see on the outside, just like the man in front of the cinema.

My neighbor Hans and his wife Leah are out front washing their car when I pull in. These guys are always there, as if they live on that front patch of grass or on their driveway, watching the neighborhood and just waiting for suckers like me to pull in so they can waylay them for a talk about the friggin' weather. As if I give a shit. Well, usually, I rush into the house to prevent any contact, but I'm eager to see if I can play out my new strategy. Today, I'm going to try something new, see if it helps any.

"You're off early today!"

"Yeah, took a week off. Taking some time for myself for a change."

Stepping into their yard for the first time since I moved here five years ago, it's such an occasion that they both stop working and approach me.

"Nice, man. What are you going to do with the time off? Hell, you should always find time for yourself. I could never work the crazy-ass shifts you do."

I have never spoken to his wife before, so when she speaks it's almost surprising to me. She points to Hans.

"He worked nights for about two weeks, and he was so irritable that, I swear, he could have strangled everyone. And to be honest, I could have strangled him as well."

The assertion makes me grin. At first, I assume it's my typical response to seeing someone smile, but quickly realize it's just the irony in the statement. My reaction is surprisingly sincere.

"Tell me about it. I can think of a few people I'd like to strangle right now."

They both chuckle, but I don't understand the joke. I am perfectly serious. They clearly expect me to fall about laughing. I don't, just standing and staring at them with a fixed gaze. There's that look on their faces again, the one I know so well. The one that says *there's just something not quite right about this guy, don't you think? He's a bit weird.* The confused look on my face instantly creates that familiar uncomfortable silence.

"Well, I'm gonna get a shower. You guys have a good day."

The nervous look on their faces triggers a sarcastic smile from me, and they seem just as eager to end the conversation. I swear they're giving a look to each other.

"Yeah, you too."

The walk to my door feels different than any instance previously. It isn't the normal scurry to get inside and out of sight, more of a saunter with pride, and the feeling is familiar. They look a bit—concerned, let's say. Or worried. Or scared. Just a bit. My feeling now is close to how I felt on leaving Bo's house after killing him. Arousal, excitement, power. *Holy shit! It's the fear.*

These sensations have always been so alien and unrecognizable to me before Bo; no one has ever feared me, you see. I have always been timid and non-confrontational around others, avoiding contact with people as much as possible. The feeling of overpowering someone and causing terror has spawned these new emotions, and I want more.

After a long hot shower, I lie in bed thumbing through my memories to relive them. Like flipping pages in a book, I scan for the moments I have felt most stimulated, replaying them over and over. Each event brings only minor pleasure though, some sort of barrier being between me and the recollections. Although I remember every experience in graphic detail, I'm numb to them now. What do memories matter in the grand scheme of things? Whatever that even means. See, that's fakery again. People say stuff, such as 'the grand scheme of things' without the faintest idea of what it means or whether it even has any meaning. What grand scheme? My concentration ebbs and flows through past experience until I become irritable.

"Okay, when's the last time you felt it? The neighbors? No, that was just a little bit. The theater? Hmm, not even close. The woman at the rest stop? I already tried that one. Wait!"

I visualized what happened in that car, which had no effect, but I'm reminded of when I used my imagination to see what *could* happen, of when I fantasized about what I wanted to do.

"There it is."

*****

The stimulus sends tingly shock waves through my brain as I delve in feet first. Falling down an endless hole, the wind rushes past me. The deeper I plummet, the cooler and more humid it gets. I close my eyes to a jolting blast of air. When I open them, it's dark and calm. *I remember this.* I had a dream where I was stuck in this black abyss with Bo, only this time he would not be joining me. The shimmering within the darkness begins and I wave my hands for the light to present itself to me. From a single point, it grows until the room fills with a soft yellowish glow.

Fragments begin falling in like shooting stars. The millions of puzzle pieces snap and lock into place. The outer edges remain unfinished when the shower stops, like a jigsaw with the center all completed, but around the edges, it's vague, unfinished. In the partially completed scene sit the man and woman who were in front of me in the theater. I take my seat behind them and listen intently. The obnoxiously loud sounds coming from them are incoherent and distorted, making them even more aggravating.

I slowly remove the belt from my waist, taking an end with each hand. Staring at the back of his head and gritting my teeth, I toss the leather strap around his neck and pull hard, my feet pressing into the seatback. His hands clutch at his throat, his body lurching from side to side. The woman seated next to him doesn't react, seeming oblivious to what's going on, even when he begins gurgling loudly. The more frenzied he becomes, the greater my pleasure and the harder I pull, until…crack! His neck breaks backward and dangles over the seatback, his glazed eyes staring up at me.

"All you had to do was shut up. You did this to yourself."

***

Taking in a chest full of air and letting it out slowly, I open my eyes.

"That felt great! We're gonna have to do that again before bed."

Normally, I sleep during the day, so I find it hard to get any rest during the night. I spend a few hours watching old reruns, swiping through Facebook feeds, sipping on Scotch.

"Fake…Fake…Fake."

It amazes me how many people post on there as if their lives are so perfect and full of only great things happening. A thousand posts of 'look what I did,' and 'see this amazing meal I just cooked', 'see my beautiful kids,' and worst of all, 'look at my stunning house that I've just bought' which of course means, 'see how I've spent all this money you just don't have'. Boasting. *Look at me syndrome*, I call it. Like kids in the playground, all vying for the teacher's attention or for the most popular kids to come over and beg them to be friends.

Fake, fake, fake, heavily filtered selfies. A smaller nose. Fewer freckles, a darker tan. Fewer wrinkles, bigger muscles, bluer eyes. All that shit that everyone could see right through if only they bothered to look. No one is truly happy with themselves if they need to digitally alter their photos to be comfortable enough to share them. Continuing to scroll through the feed, I see a familiar face prompting me to stop.

"What the… Roy… *fucking*… Lopez! I don't believe it."

Roy was one of the many bullies who made my life hell when I was a kid; he was by far the most brutal among them. Just the names Roy or Lopez have since made me shudder and want to puke, even though these people won't have any connection to that asshole. But I once had to live with a broken rib for weeks after he and his friends beat me. Taking the last drop of Scotch down my throat, I turn off the television and walk down the hallway to my room, staring carefully at his photograph. I want every feature of his face engraving into my mind for this. For what's coming next.

"All right, Roy. Here I come. And remember, you did this to yourself."

Perception of Prey

The chiming of my cellphone rouses me. Inching one eye open, I see the clock reads 11:00 a.m. and I wonder who it could be that calls me at this time. Anyone who knows me knows that I work nights and sleep during the day, so it's got to be one of the frequent scam calls I have been getting recently. Blearily trying to focus on the screen, the letters make no sense to me. It reads 'TCSO Terrell Co.'

"Fucking scammers, man!"

Immediately after swiping to answer, I launch into berating the would-be swindler.

"Don't you have anything better to do, man? Why don't you get a real job like the rest of us, instead of stealing from—"

"Uh, sorry to bother you. I'm trying to contact Mr. Matt Ellis."

"Oh Yeah, sorry. That's me. Thought you were one of those scammers that keep calling me."

"Haha, no sir. I am Deputy Flores, with the Terrell County Sheriff's Office."

"Oh, shit. Then I really am sorry about calling you a scammer. Haha."

My heart is suddenly right there in my mouth, and my lungs want to hold onto the only gasp of air they seem capable of holding. I can't inhale. Can't exhale. That's how it feels. My sore lungs cling onto the air, and they hold it, hold it, hold it, until I speak with a breathy tone as if heavy breathing. *Hell. Heavy breathing on the phone to the Sheriff's Office—that's going to go down well.* But I can't exhale or breathe again. My voice must sound nervous. *Take it easy, man. Don't show how you feel. It's all fine, all good.*

"No worries, Sir. I'm calling to inform you that your uncle Bo was killed a few days ago."

A ball tightly forms in my throat now, producing a raspiness in my reply.

"Yeah…my cousin, Crystal, called me yesterday and told me about it. It's shit. What kind of sad fuck could do that to another person?"

The phone goes quiet for a moment, but I hear faint scribbling against paper.

"Well, to the point, Mr. Ellis, I'm contacting anyone who knew him. I'm trying to find out if someone might have an idea of who could have done this."

My mind clutters, trying to remember the perfect reply I have practiced so many times before. I have it to a fine art, don't I? Well, I did. But right now, it's all gone to pieces. I see the words, but they are all entangled and mashed together. I try to place them in order, but—

"You there, Mr. Ellis?"

"Sorry. I was just thinking if I knew anyone who coulda done it. Yeah, I…I don't know any of his friends. Don't know much about him these days. But it's a bad world."

I'm trying my best to sound empathic, as if I feel for the guy being brutalized like that.

"How about anyone who wasn't his friend? Maybe someone he owed money to?"

Suddenly, my rehearsed response stamps back into my memory and my anxiousness subsides.

"Sorry, Deputy Flores, but I haven't seen that dude in thirty years. I was fifteen the last time we spoke. Hell, I assumed he was already dead from all the drugs by now. Is he—was he—still doing the drugs? Have you found out about all that? It was his Achilles, Deputy. Everyone used to say it was the drugs that'd kill him, though not this way. Just an overdose…"

"Yeah, we're following leads in that direction also. I have just a few more questions if it's not too much trouble."

"Sure, I'm already awake now anyway. I work nights, you know. I was still asleep."

"Aww, I'm sorry about that. I didn't mean to wake you. Let's make it one last question then, so you can get back to bed. When was the last time you saw your uncle Bo?"

He already knows the answer to that, and it's easy to see that he's trying to get me to counter my statement. I don't feel he's doing it because he's suspicious, but because he's so used to attempting to get people to incriminate themselves, that he can't help this line of questioning.

"As I said, it's been over thirty years, man. Helluva long time. I feel guilty now, thinking about it. Suppose I could've given him a bit of support; I mean, drink and drugs are big health problems, aren't they? But you know how it goes. You're young, you don't want that shit. Then after a while, it gets too hard to go back and see someone. You always think, 'next month, I'll go'. But it never happens. Hell, I haven't been back home to Texas in over a decade."

"Ah, that's right. Your cousin said you're living in Arizona these days. How far of a drive would you say that is?"

I've driven the route many times before and know that it never takes more than fourteen hours, but there's no way I'm telling him that. I drive flat out, rarely stop except for gas. But for most folks, it'd take them way longer. Way,

way longer. I want to put myself as far away from Texas as possible without providing an excessive time. If I say that, they'll soon find out because it doesn't take much to assess real travel time. Mr. Google knows everything, after all. Mr. Google is everyone's friend.

"Geez, it's been so long since I've driven there instead of flying. I don't know. Somewhere around eighteen hours, I think."

I listen quietly as he jots down my statement, wondering how well I've played it off. The quiet gives me time to be concerned about whether eighteen hours is enough to omit me from the suspect list. Just as I open my mouth to ask if he has anything else, he finally breaks the silence.

"All right, Mr. Ellis, think I have everything I need, for now. Please let me know if you think of anything that may help us out. Do you have a pen and paper to take my contact info?"

"It's okay, it's shown up on the caller ID. I got it right here. I'll be sure to save it, so I don't think you're another scammer next time you call."

I give a little chuckle though my chest's still tight and airless.

"Sorry to have disturbed you, sir. I can tell you're struggling a bit. You all right?"

I have no idea what he means. Must be the breathy sound, the raspiness too.

"Oh, yeah, thanks, Officer. Just that my sinuses play up till I've been up and about a while. It's very dry in Arizona. But you'll know that already."

"Okay then, you have a great day, sir."

"Thanks, I will—and you too. Have a great day."

The second I hang up, the conversation begins replaying. Picking through the discussion, I analyze every word in search of any that may have come across as deceptive. Apart from the sudden hoarseness, I can't think of anything that could implicate me.

"Well, that pretty much went as well as it could have. Nothing I can do about it, at this point."

My plan for the day was to relax and daydream about dealing vengeance to anyone who had wronged me but being contacted by the homicide investigator has put me in sort of a funk. Instead, I decide to return to my normal habits. My usual routine on days off is to eat a late breakfast at the diner down the road, wearing headphones and watching videos on my phone. I always order the same thing. Bacon and eggs, over medium, and white toast. All the servers know me and don't bother asking me what I want anymore. They just bring me the order and check. No communication. Exactly the way I like it.

Today is different though. As I sit down in my usual booth, a waitress I've never seen before starts walking toward me. The closer she gets, the more agitated I become. Three years ago, I made it known that I'd leave a large tip if they would just bring me bacon and eggs with white toast and leave me be. I haven't had to speak to any of them since. It's been a great arrangement. Staring at the table as if there should already be a plate in front of me, the waitress approaches.

"Can I start you off with something to drink?"

I don't respond or make eye contact.

"Sir, do you need a menu?"

I could use this interaction to fake being ordinary, but the years I've spent building an understanding of what I wanted as a customer here, stops me. In my mind, they should already know, and I shouldn't be forced to say it.

"Oh no! Carol, I know what he wants! I'll put in the order for ya!"

The waitress, confused, slowly paces away. I hear her and the other server softly talking about the confrontation.

"Okay, that guy is fucking weird."

"No—well yeah. He just doesn't like talking to people. 'Doesn't come here to make polite chit-chat,' that's what he said and fair enough. It's his choice. We just take him his food and check at the same time and leave it. Trust me. You'll be okay with it when you get your tip."

"Seriously?"

"Yeah, easiest twenty dollars you ever made."

"Well, shit. All right then."

Back to focusing on random YouTube videos, I notice the clock on my phone reads twelve-fifteen and realize that I am here three hours earlier than usual. Most of the staff here, at this time of the day, have never seen me before, much less know what I want to order. Regardless, it's not enough for me to feel any remorse for the unpleasant incident.

Ten minutes later, from the corner of my eye, I watch as the plate and bill are placed delicately on the table. Without turning my head, I glance at the waitress walking away, then try to imagine what I could do to her. All the colors bleed down like raindrops on a window during heavy rain, leaving behind only monochrome gray in its wake. My sight contracts and vibrates slightly but won't allow me to become immersed in the fantasy. Squinting and spiraling my head in small circles, I try to force the illusion, but the harder I try, the more reality forces me out.

"What the hell? Do it! Why can't I…? All right, let's try something."

My mind effortlessly diverts to the fantasy of killing Roy Lopez last night, then I force myself back.

"Okay, that was easy. Now back to the waitress."
Once again, I can't make it past the initial phase into the illusion.

"What the hell is the difference? Why can't I do this?"

Mining deep into my emotions, I realize that I don't hate the woman. I feel nothing when thinking about her because she's not guilty of hurting me or anyone else, for that matter. She hasn't done anything to merit my wrath, so my mind won't even let me imagine it. The insight is relieving.

"So…I'm crazy as shit and want to kill people, but somewhere in there is a conscience. I guess there's at least one redeeming quality left in me."

After finishing my food, I arrange my dishes neatly and wipe the table clean, then begin flipping through the bills in my wallet. Recalling how I tried to imagine tormenting the innocent waitress causes me to pause, and I feel…something. The emotion isn't regret or sorrow. It's…unexplainable. *I should leave her a bigger tip.* She's already walking toward the table to clean up as I'm moving to the door.

"Holy shit! He left me fifty bucks!"

"I told you. Just give him the food and shut up. Haha."

Hearing that, I know she won't make the same mistake again. I'm tempted to come back early tomorrow, just to make sure. Driving home, I'm determined to get my fix, which by this point has been over twelve hours. The list of people from my past I use to feed my addiction is getting so thin now, that I'm having a hard time finding new ones. I flip through the pages of my mind like a yearbook, searching for my next imaginary victim.

"Who the hell can I kill?"

Driving down the road, images stream across the windshield of almost every person I have ever crossed paths with. It's an interesting thought when you try it. Try and remember every person you ever met in your life. How many would it amount to? How many would you like to strangle? How many would you choose to disembowel now if you met them again? The problem is, I honestly can't remember that many. I wish I could. I wish I could draw up a long list, ranking them in order of 'killability' to feed my desires. I get to about thirteen, then my brain gives up and I start repeating names, unable to recall which ones I said already. Anyway, none of the ones I can remember jumps out at me as worthy. An abrupt glimpse of a red light causes me to slam on the brakes and screech to a stop in the middle of the crosswalk.

"I need this! Give me something, dammit! If you don't give me something—"

Bam! Bam! Bam!

I almost jump out of my skin at a man banging his fists against the hood of my car. As he walks through what's left of the crosswalk, he locks his eyes on me. Returning the gaze, I take in his every facial feature. Long, matted brown hair, with small plastic beads tied to the ends. Elongated nose and emerald, almond-shaped eyes. His face is dirty, sunburned, and aged. Physically, he can't be more than forty years old, but his face tells me that he's been homeless for a very long time. Constant exposure to the sun has caused his skin to become leatherlike and crumpled.

"You'll do. Don't worry, I'm about to get my payback."

The excitement of finding a new target to fantasize about is so overwhelming that I'm forced to pull over in the parking lot of an apartment complex to begin. I lay my seat back and let out a long hum.

"Here I come."

***

Transported to a theater, the scene presents itself to me as a stage, partially concealed by heavy red curtains. The faint sound of circus music emanates from above. Looking around the room, I seem to be the only one in attendance for the show. The music plays louder and louder until the crescendo erupts into a dozen spiraling strobe lights on slowly parting drapes, followed by a voice over the loudspeaker.

"For your entertainment! Tonight, we have a special event. Something no one has ever shown on stage before!"

Applause and cheers fill the room, although looking around, I still see no one else.

"Tonight…We give you… Death!"

As the curtains separate fully, a bright white light falls from above, illuminating the homeless man strapped to a chair.

"Who will be our first participant? You sir, in the first row?"

Another smaller strobe illuminates me and I raise my hand over my brow to block the light.

"Uh, I've already done the chair thing. Kinda bored with it."

"Ahh, we have a veteran at this game I see. Well, there's no way you'll be bored with this little addition!"

He snaps his finger, and the man and chair are instantly balancing on a platform over a ten-foot-high tank of water.

"You choose. Life or death. As easy as throwing a ball. Actually, that's exactly what it is. Just throw the ball from your hand and you can end this pathetic human's life right now. Put him out of his misery."

Looking down, I find a red softball clasped in my hand.

"Can we let him decide?"

"Only the man holding the ball decides. He can beg for his life if that's what you mean."

"Well, no." I *know* he's going to beg for his life. Anyone would."

"Choice! He has none. *You* hold the ball. *You* hold the power. Now choose!"

Looking up at the homeless man, I can't help recognizing the sadness in his eyes. Not because of his current dilemma, but because his life has been full of suffering. This is freedom from his pain, and he welcomes it, much like Bo before I set him ablaze. No longer driven by hate but pity, I approach the release lever.

"You're hurting, aren't you?"

"Yes…"

"I was angry at you for hitting my car, but now I know you didn't have a choice. Like a lot of the things I'm driven to do now, you're not in control of yourself. You're the first person I ever wanted to kill as mercy. Regardless—"

I drop the ball onto the floor and watch it slowly roll away.

"So, you choose life?"

"No… I choose to take life with my own hands!"

I slap the metal plate with my hand, and he instantly falls into the vat of water. His body sinks down and rests in an upright position facing me, and I watch as he looks around for an escape. I know he has no choice but to accept it, so I patiently wait. His eyes dart wide open, instantly followed by a massive gulp of water. He begins thrashing his head from side to side with his hair trailing his movements. The torment finally ends with two erratic thrusts of his jaw, then the light on the stage dims.

***

Wiping my face with my hand, I return expecting to feel euphoria, but instead, it leaves me not only unsatiated but hungrier, needing more. Envisioning isn't enough to satisfy my addiction, although it has never completely fulfilled me to begin with. *The only way I can get the emotional high back is to kill again.*

Piercing the Veil

Matt's Story

Running late, I opt to make my own breakfast this morning, because my appointment with Dr. Ruiz is less than an hour away. One of my many idiosyncrasies is that every obligation to which I agree must be honored, which is why I hate to make more than one at a time. Although I believe today's session will be as fruitless as the last, I'm still interested to see Cristy again. After putting the dishes away, I tuck my polo shirt into my jeans and check my breath.

"Holy shit, do you like this woman?"

I'm confused. I've never liked anyone before—hell, I don't even like myself—so there's no reference for me to look back upon. The only measure I have is *can I tolerate them or not?* Taking that into account, I would say tolerance is about as close to liking as I have ever gotten.

"Bah, get your shit together, man. This is the last time you're gonna see this woman anyway."

There are only a handful of veteran patients in the waiting room when I arrive. A light, but noticeable smell hangs in the air when I check in for my appointment. The source of the musk becomes apparent the moment I sit down. Next to me is a man in his late fifties, with a bald crown and tinted glasses. His flannel shirt and tattered jeans look as though they haven't had a wash in weeks, and his light brown hair is matted to one side.

"Mr. Davy?"

"Yeah?"

When he opens his mouth, the foul stench of decay causes me to turn my head away. Reprieve from the vaporous assault is short-lived when he walks past me to the counter.

"I'm sorry, we can't find your records anywhere. Are you sure it was this clinic? You don't have any sort of identification that we can use?"

"No, I told you someone stole all my stuff when I was camped in Reid Park last year."

A decade ago, Reid Park was a lush area where you would see families barbequing and playing football. Now, it's full of homeless camps as far as you can see. His unpleasant smell now makes sense. It's probably been years since he's seen a toothbrush or bar of soap.

"Matt?"

"Yep, coming. How ya doing, Cristy?"

"It's been a long day. How about you?"

"I just woke up. Haha."

"Oh yeah, you work nights. I remember."

She guides me to an examination room, different from the one previously, but almost identical. When she reaches out to open the door, I notice a sizable scar on the back of her hand.

"That's a pretty nasty scar on your hand. What did you do to get that?"

She brings her hand up to her face as if she's reading the time on a watch, then puts it back down without even acknowledging my statement.

"So…?"

"So what?"

"Did you try what I asked? Envisioning a happy place?"

As before, she's clearly analyzing my reaction while I'm contemplating how much to disclose.

"Yeah, it worked."

"Really?"

She takes notes from my simple reply of, "Yeah, it worked." Amazingly, they take a whole two minutes to write down, making me question whether she has already seen through the mask. Surely, she must have as it can't take anyone two minutes to write a note saying only *yes*. She puts greater emphasis on her last period, stabbing her pen into the pad as if she feels angry at it, then looks up with her deep blue eyes and pauses.

"How's your anger?"

"I'm still angry."

"Do you think about hurting others?"

"Same as before. I wish I could slap the hell out of some people for being assholes, but other than that, not really."

She glares at me as if wondering whether to believe me or not. She probably doesn't want a load of wisecracks, just accurate answers. But that is one of the problems with being antisocial; I have always tended to hide behind a façade of jokes. I think she's trying to read signs of deception from my eyes, but I hold them on her anyway.

"You know… So, I have a client, and you remind me of him a little in that he is always very angry too, but he is unable to control himself. He was recently court ordered to see me after he beat his wife so bad that she was hospitalized, about three years ago."

"Oh wow, that's terrible."

"Yes, it was. What's worse is that he was only in prison for a few years. After two months of consulting with me, he'll be allowed to go back to his normal life.

"I saw him walking through Walmart a few weeks ago with his wife and two kids."

"And did she look okay?"

"No, far from it. It was obvious he was still beating her."

Searching in my vault of emotions, I can't find the one that I am supposed to be portraying, so instead, I give a blank stare. I know it's a look I carry off well; at least it's sincere.

"So, he lives around here then?"

"Yes. Green Valley. The point is, you and I need to work through your emotions to make sure you don't escalate into harming someone just like my other patient did. Well, does.. You and anger are the worst of enemies and eventually, one gives up the battle and lets the other just get on with it. That kind of anger can really ruin your life, Matt."

"I think I get what you're saying, but I don't have anyone in my life to release my anger on. And besides, I can't imagine my life being much worse than it is now."

She looks shocked.

"Really? I'm surprised to hear you say that."

She stares as if she expects me to elaborate. It's what normal people do; they just wait for you to say more, to create a conversation out of a throwaway comment. But I'm way better at the throwaways. Conversation isn't my strong point, and I don't even wish it were. What is the point of it when it only leads to talking about the weather and where you're going on holiday? Or what a nice house the neighbors have and how so-and-so just died? But Cristy's different. There's some part of me that wants to make more effort. God only knows why; before long, no doubt she'll be irritating the hell out of me.

"Don't get me wrong, Cristy, It's not that my life is worse than anyone else's. In many ways, I'm sure it's better. I'm pretty free to do as I please. But if this makes any sense, there are no high points in it either. Maybe that's what frustrates me a bit if I'm honest."

She nods. I expect her to frown or to look confused like a normal person would. She doesn't behave like a normal person; she acts like a therapist. She nods at me so much that I think her head will fly off.

"That's what I'm getting at, Matt. Can you imagine what that guy—that client of mine—would be doing if he didn't have his wife to take his anger out on?"

I now know where she is going with this. She thinks if I had a person in my life, I would be abusing them and since I don't, I am prone to taking my anger out on others. Because I am a volcano ready to erupt sometime soon. Well, she's not completely wrong, but I'm not here to be fixed anymore, so…

"Yeah, that crazy bastard would be out killing people, I bet. But they're weirdos, killers. Not every guy who gets angry is going to go out and kidnap someone and dismember them."

My mouth's running away with me again. Maybe I am seeking to shock her.

"But don't you also think there's some degree of correlation, Matt? Not necessarily just the anger as a solitary factor, but when we look into the psychology of killers, especially serial killers or those who perpetrate the most heinous of crimes—they are loners. Think about all those interviews where the neighbors say, 'he just kept himself to himself'. It's a fine line between having a degree of social phobia and then beginning to get angry and wrathful at society per se. If you keep to yourself and see no value in anyone else because you don't let anyone close, then why not kill? Hence, a lot of the mass shootings."

Shit. She has a point. Is this what is happening to me? If I had firearms, would I be gunning people down because I have no one who matters?

"So, if we could help all the angry people and the loners, the crimes would reduce?"

"Exactly! And I really wished I could help my patient and therefore, help his wife. The poor woman. But I can't. It's way too late for him now. I want to help *you*, Matt."

It's too late for me, also. I don't need help anymore but it's too difficult to tell her that. The only reason I'm here is because of my pledge that I would attend. Still, our conversation has been enlightening and fascinating, but also dispiriting. At least I now know that I'm not the only person like this. There are others. But she doesn't realize I can't hurt a person that I don't hate. I can be angry but not hate.

I imagine the beatings of that innocent wife by the angry husband and wonder what she could possibly have done to deserve such brutality. It doesn't take me long to compare him to my grandmother and realize that the woman probably hadn't deserved it. He's likely just been dispensing suffering to her, the same way my grandmother used to do all those years ago. I can't make her pay because she's dead now, but he is here and worthy. I can make him a representative of all those who give out suffering and punishment to the innocent. He will be—Cristy leans in, gazing at me up close. She rests a soft hand on my forearm.

"You okay, Matt?"

I don't know how long I have sat here in deep thought, but it was long enough to merit a checkup, apparently. She is keen to bring me back into her presence.

"Sorry, I think I drifted off, thinking about that bastard. Sorry for the language."

"Just be yourself, Matt. I officially give you permission to swear."

"Yeah, I just feel so bad for that poor woman. I think that guy should be strung up by his heels. He doesn't deserve to be alive."

"Well, that's pretty extreme, but I don't disagree. Do you think you could do that? String someone up by their heels? And if so, what would they have to do to deserve it?"

Almost as obvious as Deputy Flores's attempt to get me to contradict my statement, I know she's trying to get me to show capability and intention. I grin at the notion but play it off as absurd for her to even ask.

"Seriously? No, I don't know how anyone could do something like that."

"Good."

She makes a few more notes on her pad, then places it on the desk next to her.

"Are you comfortable talking about your childhood? I promise I won't write any notes concerning anything you disclose."

The thought of telling her about the atrocities I endured as a child creates a mild trembling in my legs. Not because it bothers me to remember them but because I fear she will be able to see me. The true me. Her whole career has been based on getting into the minds of people and breaking down their emotional barriers. I must tell her something that will pacify her inquiry, but not trigger a volley of follow-up questions.

"There's not much to talk about. I was beaten a lot. Never enough to be hospitalized."

"Do the memories of those instances trouble you now?"

"Never think about it. I worked through all that stuff when I was seeing the therapist before, so… nope."

"Who was the person or people physically abusing you?"

Here we go. Exactly what I was afraid of. Even when I say it doesn't bother me, she's about to tell me why it does. This is the beginning of a cascading list of follow-up questions that needs to stop. I need to give her a simple reply, omitting the many offenders from my past.

"It was just my grandmother. We lived alone. I don't think that has anything to do with my current problem. As I said, I worked through all that years ago."

"Okay, fair enough. Well, do you have anything you would like to discuss before we end today's session?"

"I can't think of anything offhand."

"All right then. I'm hoping we can meet again. How does Monday sound?"

"Work's been incredibly busy lately. Can I just call to make an appointment when I'm free?"

She seems disappointed as she gets up to open the door for me.

"Of course. Just let the front desk know that you're my patient. I can usually get you in by the next day."

"Great! Thank you, Cristy. Have a good rest of your day."

"You too."

Getting into my car, I think about the session, and anxiousness begins to churn in my gut. Baffled by the sudden physical change, I ponder the cause and realize…*I miss her*. She is the only person I have spoken to extensively in years and although I don't want to talk about my past, I do enjoy our interactions. It's like a game of chess trying to figure out what she wants from me and coming up with ways not to give it to her. The conversational ballet is a dangerous game to play with her though, which makes it even more stimulating. *Maybe I'll go back to see her next week, but first I have some research to do.*

***

Seated on my couch much later, I begin inputting search terms into the browser on my laptop. *Man arrested for beating wife. Woman hospitalized after a brutal attack. Husband attacks wife. Woman almost slain by partner.*

Hundreds of pages worth of article results come up for each. Too wide. I need to narrow the search criteria. *Hmm... She said he was from Green Valley and that it happened about three years ago.* So off I go again, searching, searching, trying to narrow it down. *Green Valley domestic violence woman hospitalized.* Sifting through the results isn't encouraging. There are still over fifty pages. I skip past any articles older than three years and ones that don't mention a wife.

"Good God! The town isn't even that big. Why are there so many domestic violence cases? Wait…cases. He was arrested. There would be an arrest record and mug shot!"

Clicking the 'images' tab along the top of the browser, I see too many pictures to count, but only one immediately stands out. It's a mug shot showing up over and over throughout the screen. I select one of the photos to enlarge it and it leads me to an article. Within it, I read about a man arrested for beating his wife with his bare hands and then strangling her until she passed out. She was hospitalized for three days, then released, no doubt back to the same abuser who put her there. I suppose she didn't want to press charges, didn't want to see him get into trouble for it. No mention of the outcome, but it doesn't matter. I know he's free now and a perfect candidate to satisfy my needs.

"All right, who are you, guy?"

At the bottom of the editorial, it reads, 'Jeremy Biggs was taken into custody and is currently awaiting arraignment in the Pima County Detention Center'. Finally, the tingly feeling I have been looking for prickles down my spine.

"Jeremy Biggs, you son of a bitch. I'm coming for you. You'd better lock all your doors and windows, you spineless coward."

Choosing the Path

Matt's Story

It's late in the night, and my eyes are straining to focus. I've been searching the internet for hours, looking for any information that could lead me to Jeremy Biggs. So far, all I have found is that he works for a building contractor named Archer Construction, and he placed fourth in a local car show a few years ago. His arrogant smirk in the article photo detailing the event creates an irritating twitch in my right eye. I slide my fingers across the screen. Just thinking about what I'm going to do to him sparks a glow of excitement on my face.

"Let's see what your smile looks like when I find you, you piece of shit. Maybe I'll start with those teeth. Mess up your face like you did your wife's. Face…Facebook! Holy shit! Why didn't I think of that before?"

It only takes seconds to locate his profile among the dozens of Jeremy Biggs' profiles.

"There's that shit-eating grin. I'd recognize that anywhere. What do you think is so important in your life that people should know about it?"

His posts are full of rants about the government being corrupt, along with Chevy truck and hunting memes. Every comment he makes on people's timelines is overtly aggressive and laden with profanity. It's easy to see that he is the same angry man Cristy had tried to help years ago. It doesn't matter at this point. Even if he had changed his ways, I committed to teaching him a lesson, and I always follow through with my promises—especially when they are to myself.

As I scroll through his photo albums, I notice a common theme. None of the pictures include his wife; not even one. In most of them, he is posing with dead animals and rifles.

"He has guns. I need to get him away from his house and have my Ruger with me, just in case. Oh, wait! What do we have here?"

A bunch of pictures of him posing in front of a bar gives me the lead I'm looking for. I've been to the Whiskey River bar before and know the area well, having worked for a small aircraft maintenance company about two miles past it. It's outside of town in the desert with no other businesses or homes nearby. In my book, that makes it a pretty good place to find him. Good for him, and good for me.

"What are the odds you're there on a Wednesday night? Well, I got nothing better to do."

It's 1:20 a.m. when I pull into the parking lot. The bars in Arizona close at two, so I won't have to wait long to find out if he's in there. Lying back in my seat, I begin sketching out plans in my mind.

"Don't get ahead of yourself, man. We aren't ready yet. Just need to find out where he lives."

My heavy eyelids slowly creep closed, and in the darkness, specks of light burst into rays that dart through and around me. In pulsating waves, each explosion pulls me closer. *Boom…Boom…Boom.* As I lurch nearer to the source, I hear a familiar voice from my past. I know where that shit's leading me. *Finally. Let's get this over with. I've been expecting you for a long time. Tap…Tap…Tap.* I'm startled up.

"Could you step out of the car, please?"

Groggily opening the door, I am met by two police officers.

"There ya go. Keep your hands where I can see 'em, please. Have you been drinking, sir?"

"No, sir. I was waiting to give my friend a ride home."

"The bar has been closed for over an hour. Your friend either found another ride home, or he doesn't exist. What's his name?"

I'm only half awake. The other half is still in the void, making it hard to establish which one is real.

"Uh…John."

"John, huh? Does John have a last name?"

Panicked, I spit out the first person I know named John.

"Early."

"John Early? That's your friend's name?"

"Yes, sir."

His partner hasn't said a word yet. He's just watching the encounter with his arms crossed.

"How much have you had to drink tonight?"

This again. I don't know how many people fall for the self-incriminating questions, but I have nothing to hide. Well…as far as alcohol consumption is concerned.

"None. I told you, I'm the designated driver. I consent to a breathalyzer and blood test and anything else you feel you need, right now."

He looks over at his partner, still holding his arms crossed.

"Don't look at me. This is your evaluation. I will give you a hint, though. Do you suspect a crime has been committed?"

The officer stands quietly, contemplating the situation.

"How far do you live from here?"

"Less than ten minutes."

"All right, you're free to go. Just get home safe, okay?"

"Will do. Thank you, sir."

The drive home is so quick that I barely have enough time to process what's just happened. In my driveway, with the car engine still running, I try to make sense of it.

"I swear I wasn't even asleep at the bar. I could still hear the music and people talking the entire time. Even when I was on my way to—"

The sounds of my father's voice faintly repeat in my head.

"I'll come see you soon, Matthias. I swear."

"And then you'll take me away from here?"

"Yeah, you'll come live with me, here in Dallas."

That day never came. He left me in that house in the woods to fend for myself. All of my childhood of abuse could have ended if he had kept his promise and taken me away. Instead, he would visit for a few hours every few years. The amount of time I spent with him was so minimal that I can't even recall what he looks like. If I had made it fully into the void, there's no telling what would have been waiting for me.

"Probably best to leave that one alone. Let's get some sleep and try again tomorrow."

***

On the way to breakfast, I'm in an unusually good mood. Bobbing my head to the music and tapping my fingers on the steering wheel, I lip-sync to Tom Petty's 'Free Falling'. Now that there is a face to my anger, I have a purpose again.

"Jeremy, soon you'll be free…free fallin'!"

Outside the diner, I watch through the window for the waitress from a few days ago. I've come here early just to see how she'll respond to seeing me again. It doesn't take long to see her and figure out which section she has today, but it's currently filled. Patiently waiting, as soon as she's clearing a table, I hurry to the door. She's still wiping it down when I slide into the booth.

"Can I get y—"

She quickly stops herself with a startled yet confused expression. I can tell she's trying to figure out what to do. She isn't done wiping the table off and is most likely wondering if it will irritate me if she continues. I can't help but smile at her reaction before looking down at my phone. In my peripheral, she's spreading her arms wide toward the other waitresses.

"Yes. Just finish."

She hastily wipes the rest of the table and then rushes back to the counter. Even the small amount of power I feel from the interaction is satisfying. Ten minutes later, I receive another little jolt when the plate is delicately placed on the table in front of me. Chopping up the fried eggs with my fork, I eke out a smirk. Exactly how it should be. *She's learned.*

After taking the last bite of bacon, I neatly stack my dishes and wipe the table clean, then flip through my wallet. *Bah, fuck! I forgot to get cash.* Oh well, twenty is still more than enough. The problem is that my habit patterns are based on positive results. Once I've done something and I like it or it turns out the way I wanted it to, I have to continue doing it. That's why I eat the same breakfast every day. I can't stop eating it until I don't like it anymore, until I've had so many eggs and strips of bacon that the mere sight of it makes me want to throw up. The fact that I had given the woman fifty dollars last time and it resulted in me getting what I wanted, means I can't let this go. I drop enough to cover the bill on the table and then walk toward the door.

"I'll be back."

I hear the whispers of confusion behind the counter. Most of them have never heard me speak before, so hearing me say, 'I'll be back' may be interpreted as a threat. Stopping short of the door, I turn back again.

"I have to get cash for your tip."

I almost feel their relief from hearing the clarification. The bank is just across the street, so it only takes minutes to retrieve the cash that I need. All the servers watch me intently when I walk to the counter and place the fifty-dollar bill down.

"Have a good day."

No one replies. They quietly stare at me as I turn back toward the door with a bigger smile than I had earlier. A gratifying outcome.

"I'll be back."

There, I said it again, just to keep them on their toes. At least this way, they remember who I am each time I show up. From the diner, I head straight to Walmart for supplies. I already have an idea of some of the things I need, but not enough. Tape, zip ties, pliers. That's as far as I've thought through. As they are a few of the items I used on Bo, I've already proved them effective. Walking through the labyrinth of products, I search for inspiration, talking to myself.

"Bat?"

"No."

"Golf club?"

"No."

"Aww, a machete?"

"Hmm, they're all a bit too bulky. I need something I can conceal."

"Are you going to do this or not?"

I notice a woman watching me from the end of the aisle. She appears to be waiting for me to leave so she can get something from the area where I'm standing, and it makes me curious.

"Is that woman afraid of me because I'm talking to myself? Honestly, these days, people latch onto any old excuse to be scared of you."

"But then again, off course, she is, you idiot. Wouldn't you be scared of some weirdo having conversations with himself? Sure, you would. So, stop doing it. You're *still* doing it. Good Lord, Shut the fuck up!"

I slap my hand against the side of my head, then look back up. She hastily walks away.

"See? You scared the lady."

With a careless shrug, I continue my search.

"Just get a knife. It's light, easy to conceal, and you can do anything you need with it.

"That's true."

The endless choices of shiny sharp toys make it hard to decide. As I examine the blades, I find fault with each.

I'd run my finger along the edges if I could, but annoyingly, almost all are shrouded in plastic, and even underneath the plastic, they have blade guards. I can't see what I need to see, only able to rely on descriptions in some cases. I stick with the ones where at least I can see the blade through the plastic.

"Too small. Too big. Too flimsy. This one's not even sharp. Oh, look at this one. Cuisinart eight-inch chef knife. It's perfect! Dude, we could chop down a tree with this thing."

"Right?"

Waiting in line to check out, there is a small section of dog supplies next to me. I lazily scan the items until my eyes lock onto a row of shock collars. I've been hoping to tape his mouth shut, but the idea of controlling him without covering his face is too irresistible to pass up. I grab two.

A few hours later, I'm packed up and ready for my second stakeout attempt. It won't be dark for another two hours, but I want to get there a little earlier, so I can get the parking spot with the clearest view of the front door. Approaching the bar, the lot is already half full and I'm reminded that Thursdays, they have a live band playing. Knowing this gives me hope that he will show up tonight since he seems to be a regular, judging by his profile. I mean, if there's any night he should show, this one ought to be it.

"He's gonna show. I know it."

"And then what?"

"We follow him, dude."

"Is that it? Then why did you bring all that shit with you?"

"Fuck, I don't know. Just in case."

"Yeah, okay. You do realize I'm in here too, right?"

Hearing that makes me pause. I only now recognize that I have been talking to myself this way for the last few days. It hasn't been confined to the instance at Walmart earlier. Revisiting the conversations, I don't feel as though it's even another person I am talking to. It's just me talking to, well…me. Maybe I've started doing it because I've grown so tired of not having anyone to talk to, even without realizing it. Maybe this is what loneliness is like. Well, old people do this, don't they? They talk to themselves all the time, so that proves my case because old people often don't get enough visitors. Hell, they even walk through the shopping malls talking to themselves. That's plain weird. *Ah. That is what I just did, except it wasn't a mall.* But there's no point in being negative, is there? There must be other possibilities. Maybe it's a voice of reason.

"Do I sound like a voice of reason to you?"

"No, you sound just like me."

"That's because I am you. You're talking to yourself again, dumbass."

"Am I? Well, I wouldn't if you didn't keep asking me questions."

The insight into my situation becomes clear to me. I don't need or want to talk to anyone else, so I've created the only companion I could stand to be around. Myself.

"Oh, shit is that him?"

"Holy shit. It is him. Where did he come from?"

"Seriously? You gonna ask me stupid questions? How the hell should I know if *you* don't?"

"Oh, right."

He's just appeared out of nowhere. My target. That bastard I'm looking for. No headlight approaching or car door slamming; there's been nothing. It's obvious he's already been drinking from the ungainly way he's walking, and I worry that he won't be able to drive home.

"Well, now we wait."

Only an hour passes before he comes stumbling out the door, almost tripping himself up on the uneven ground when he steps off the short concrete slab. He looks as if he needs a cane. I watch closely as he scans around looking for his car then staggers toward the road. He looks as though he's going to plummet off the sidewalk and break his skull open right there and bleed to death. I don't want that, don't hope for that. It'd be all too easy, like a pedophile dying of a heart attack before they put him in jail where he'll die from being eviscerated by the other goons. I want him alive—so I can torture him. And kill him.

"Okay, don't follow too close. He's drunk, but he can still describe my car."

"I don't see taillights. Where the fuck?"

I manically circle the parking lot, looking for any car he may have gotten into, but none of them stand out. Annoyed, I let out a prolonged groan, then give up the search. I stop at the exit, ideas of where he could have gone assaulting my mind.

"You know what? Let's check this way."

I turn right onto the road instead of left, which is the direction of my house. About a mile down the road, a man is walking. I slow the car to a crawl.

"Is that…?"

He throws his left arm out with his thumb upright, still facing away. He looks kinda desperate, as if he's been drinking and walking for hours on end. There are positives and negatives to picking him up. If I give him a ride, I can find out where he lives, but he could be linked to me if someone sees us. If I don't, I could be following him for hours. I need to decide before another car comes by. I push my foot on the gas as the choice becomes clear.

"What are you—"

"Look, shut up. We may not get another chance. Let's go for it."

Crashing the front bumper into him, my car propels him fifteen feet through the air, before his limp body slams and then slides down the roadway. He remains lifeless on the road in front of me. The light from my headlights cast a small shadow next to him.

"Is he dead?"

"Fuck, I hope not."

He remains motionless when I approach and kneel next to him.

"Hey, you okay, man?"

His barely perceptible groan is reassuring.

"Ah, whew. Thank goodness. Okay, this is what's going to happen."

Inevitable

Matt's Story

The wind lightly blows from the east, sporadically carrying barely observable clusters of sand with it. Cricket mating calls crowd the barren lands, otherwise tranquil silence. Within the warm yellowish glow of headlights lies the blood-spattered body of a man. His six feet tall, lean build appears tiny, curled up on the ground. Deep, oozing gashes litter his face and arms, and his left leg rests at an awkward angle. Absorbing the scene is so titillating that I want to drink it in all night but worry that he won't last much longer. His breathing labors already, and he's lost quite a bit of blood. I'll be lucky if I can even wake him from his trauma-induced slumber. *Damn, he's not looking good.*

"Hey, Jeremy, can you hear me?"

Grasping his shoulder, I shake him forcefully.

"Hey, wake up. It's time to start. I need you to be awake for this."

His initial, intermittent moans are difficult to detect, but grow louder with each breath, until he rouses, confused.

"What…What happened?"

"There ya are. A car hit you, Jeremy. I was beginning to worry that you weren't going to make it."

"Do I…know you?"

"Nope, but I know you. I explained who I was earlier, but think you may have been out of it, so I'll give you a brief recap."

I casually take a seat on the ground in front of him, so he can see my face. Then I lean in slightly.

"My name is Matthias, and I brought you out here to show you something. You see…people like you have a hard time noticing the evil within themselves and the people around them suffer for it. My goal is to make you pay for what you have done to people."

He doesn't respond.

"You're wondering how I'm going to do it, right?"

He still says nothing, can barely keep his eyes open.

"I'll do it by showing you the evil inside me. And that might help you out."

He shrieks as his attempt to move is immediately followed by excruciating pain. His scream cuts short when the two shock collars I have strapped tightly to his neck surprise him with more agony. Like a dog stunned that their bark suddenly causes pain, his eyes widen and bulge.

"Holy, what the fuck was that?"

"Those are shock collars around your neck. Pretty painful, huh? Also, you have a severely broken left leg, so I wouldn't move it too much. I didn't mean to break it, but it's kind of a win for me since there's no need to bind them now. You ain't running anywhere on that thing."

"Why are you doing this to me?"

"Really? Are you even listening to me? I'll make it simple. You hurt people, so now I'm going to hurt you. I have the same uncontrollable anger issues that you do but hurting innocent people doesn't really do it for me, so here we are. Lucky you! You are the chosen one!"

Taking in his soft whimpers provides the feeling I have been yearning for; to be feared. His suffering is thick and savory. I marinate in it for a few moments then run my hand gently down the back of his head.

"Did your wife cry like that while you were beating her?"

"Wha–what? Do you know my wife? Did she get you to do this to me?"

"Shh-shh-shh. Calm down, man. I have never met your wife, and no one gets me to do anything I don't wanna do. The person responsible for your current predicament is you. *You* did this to yourself."

"How the fuck did I do this to myself?"

His ignorance and tone are infuriating.

"You're not fucking listening! I'll *make* you fucking listen."

I slowly pull the eight-inch blade from my leather bag, then slide closer to him and run the back of the blade across his cheek.

"Are you listening now?"

His body trembles while he closes his eyes and turns his head partly away.

"Ye–yes."

"Good, because I'm not going to explain again. What did the people you hurt do to deserve retribution?

"I...I don't understand."

"Did your wife do something to deserve all the beatings, being choked almost to death?"

"I guess not."

"You guess not? Well, at least you're getting closer to understanding. Okay, so you were punishing her for no reason. Correct? You do bad things to good people. That makes you a bad guy, right? And you know what happens to bad guys?"

He sullenly stares up at me through blood-encrusted bangs like a boy caught doing something wrong by his parents.

"The answer is yes and guess who deserves punishment? Say it with me…bad guys."

"Hel—"

"Ouch, I bet those hurt. No one can hear you out here, Jeremy. I only put the collars on you for fun. Well, and because I wanted you to be quiet as I talked. I don't say much but when I do, I hate being interrupted."

He turns his face into the sand and weeps heavily, rocking his head from side to side. I stick the knife into the dirt next to him, then reach back into the bag and retrieve a hammer and chisel that I had purchased for work years ago but never found a use for, until now. It's clear why hoarders get into the mess they do, because things will always have a use if you hold onto them for long enough. I'm glad I kept these items. I can enjoy them now.

"Let's get you rolled over. Sorry about the zip ties. I pulled them way tighter than I needed to, but there's no way to loosen them so…"

Delicately pushing on his torso, his breath grows rapid and heavy through clenched teeth.

"One…Two…Three!"

"Fuck. Fuck. Shit."

He wails and then halts repeatedly with each shock from the collars when I heave him onto his back. It's hard to tell how much of the liquid flowing down the sides of his cheeks is tears and how much is blood. In the darkness, there is only a glistening wetness, though perhaps looking thicker than mere water but I can't be sure.

"What are you going to do to me?"

"Well first, I'm going to ruin your smile. You don't deserve to smile. After that, you'll see."

He rocks his torso as I position myself on his chest, my knees along his cheeks.

"What are you—please don't. I swear it'll never happen again. I won't do it again. I won't."

"That's funny. I used to say the same thing to my grandmother as a child. It didn't work then, and it won't now. I'll tell you another bit of wisdom I learned back then. Just take it like a man.

"It's what my uncle used to say to me, Uncle Bo. You kind of remind me of him a bit."

His lips tightly clench when I bring the chisel to his mouth. It takes little effort to part them and rest the tip of it on one of his front teeth. I compress his head between my thighs to stop him from moving and bring the hammer a few inches above the chisel. His manic protests cause the collars to zap him repeatedly.

"You're going to feel a little pinch. Let me know if it becomes too uncomfortable. Get it? Like the dentist always says. Wow, tough crowd."

Clank!

The chisel punches through like a coin into a slot machine. His repeatedly interrupted screams feed my craving like a drug addict's first hit after a relapse. The sensation surges higher when he chokes on, then spits out a generous amount of blood along with what I presume to be tooth fragments. I give him time to regain his composure.

"Don't worry. I don't want all of them. Just the middle four, then we can move on to the next thing."

"God, please no. Please, I'm begging you."

"There's no one out here to help you, Jeremy. Do you wanna know why I brought you out here? You can't see it, but there is an abandoned mine shaft about ten feet, over there. There are hundreds of those things around here. I found this one about ten years ago, looking for land in the middle of nowhere to build a house on. All right, enough storytime. Let's finish getting those teeth out."

He watches with his mouth tightened when I begin guiding the chisel toward him. The instant it touches his lips, he swings his head to the side, knocking the tool from my hand, then spits a mouthful of diluted blood into my face. I calmly wipe the warm fluid from my eyes.

"You remind me a lot of the last guy I killed. He was defiant too, at first. Do you wanna see what I did when he pissed me off? This!"

I slam my fist repeatedly into his face. His crimson red droplets feel like a warm shower sprinkling over me. It takes eight strikes before his head finally goes limp and falls to the side. After taking a few moments to catch my breath, I pull the knife from the ground with my right hand and grab his upper lip with my left. Like carving fat from a medium-rare steak, the flesh is easily removed in one motion. It doesn't take him long to revive and begin choking on his fluids. He's heaving and gasping now.

"Here, turn your head back to the side before you drown. It's pretty hard to spit without an upper lip ain't it? Do I have to tell you that you made me do that?"

Then I see it. Surprisingly, the sight of a defeated man. He lies there motionless, calm, and silent, blood slowly seeping from his mouth. It all gets a little boring, how these people just give up after such a short struggle. Even a fly caught up in a spider's web does more fighting for its life than either this guy or Uncle Bo. Honestly, I can't work out what's wrong with them. Don't they want to live? Is that it? My next action relies solely upon his response to my next question.

"Are you already there? Do you welcome death to end the pain?"

His eyes scan back and forth, seemingly processing the consequences of answering no to the question. If he's smart, he knows that what he's been subjected to so far is only a fraction of what I am capable of. Still, I will let him decide his fate. One ends in death, but the other ends in more pain, and then death.

"Yes."

"Wow, I'm surprised you came to accept your fate so quickly. Well, you did get hit by a car and I'm pretty sure that you have quite a few broken bones in there, so it's probably helped to speed things up. I'll tell you what. I won't torture you anymore if you eat this. Prove to me that you really are ready."

I lay the two-inch slab of flesh on the dirt in front of his face.

"That's your upper lip. Eat it and I'll free you from the pain."

He concentrates on it for a few minutes, and I become impatient.

"There's a time limit on the deal. I have other stuff still planned for you and wanna get to it."

The instant he decides, it shows in his eyes, a look of focus and determination. A look of acceptance. It's the exact moment I have been waiting for and seeing it causes my heart to thump heavily. He slowly cranes his neck out and takes the dirt-covered flesh between his teeth. Holding it there for a few seconds, he begins panting rapidly, then suddenly throws his head back and takes the piece down his throat whole.

"Holy shit. I gotta say, man, I didn't think you had it in you. That was gross, but you made a good choice. I was going to torture you a lot more, then lower you into the hole where you'd suffer until you eventually bled out. Instead, I'll make it quick."

Scrolling through the playlist on my phone, I find Tom Petty's 'Free Falling', and hit play. He starts sobbing heavily when I grab his shirt collar and begin dragging him.

"You'll be free! Free fallin'! I love this song, don't you?"

He's already shown me that he's accepted death, so I have no reason to prolong his demise. As soon as I reach the edge, I thrust him into the six-foot-wide opening and listen. Three thuds against the rocky walls, followed by a loud smack, inform me that he's reached his destination.

"Tell Bo I said hi."

Gathering my supplies, I take one last check of the area and then get into my car. Before leaving, I close my eyes and let the experience replay in my mind one more time. Although I gain extreme satisfaction from the event, one thing still bothers me.

"I wish he would have let us do more."

"It worked out. We got what we wanted, and he got what he deserved. Don't get greedy."

"I know. It's just—"

"Just nothing. You have plenty to keep you satiated for a while. Enjoy it."

I put the car in reverse and press the gas pedal.

"You're right. It was fun!"

Unexpected Encounter

The sliver of daylight creeping through heavy black curtains wakes me earlier than I'm used to, but I dart out of bed with more energy than ever before. There is a slight skip in my step and my pace is more that of a man happy to start the day. This isn't the normal me, but I like it. My reflection smiles back at me in the mirror as I brush my teeth.

"That's a handsome guy right there. What you gonna do today, handsome guy?"

"Make some breakfast and relax with some television."

"That there…is a great plan. I couldn't come up with a better one myself."

After dressing, I flip the tv on, then immediately turn toward the kitchen. I don't care what's showing because it's only on for the background noise. I gather the usual breakfast supplies, then begin my preparation routine. Once the pan is hot enough, I throw on the bacon, pushing the slices to the side and cracking in two large eggs. As it's popping and sizzling, I flip the bacon constantly for an even cook each side.

"That's right Carol, officials say. His wife reported him missing early this morning. A few patrons of this bar right behind me say they're sure he left at around 8:30 p.m. last night and hasn't been seen since. It's as if he left this bar and disappeared into thin air."

The spatula falls from my hand as I rush to the living room. On the screen, I see a man in a suit, holding a microphone in front of the bar I was at last night.

"No way. This is so cool!"

What I'm feeling right now vastly overshadows any pleasure I have gotten from torturing. My arms tingle with goosebumps, and my heart hammers within my chest. I'm glued to the screen, absorbing my indirect notoriety with an eerie grin, lapping it up. *This is me. It's all about me! Except, they don't even have a clue. They think it's about poor Jeremy. But it's not. It's all about me. Haha!*

"There are no leads at this time, but authorities have said that he would have been seen either walking or riding with someone."

"Oh! Oh! I know this one! He was walking! Final answer!"

"If you have any information on the whereabouts of Jeremy Biggs, we ask that you please contact the Pima County Sheriff's Department."

"Yeah, I won't be doing that. Thanks for the suggestion, though."

"Up next, KGUN 9 will show you an inside look at—
"

I'm startled by the fire alarm and rush into the kitchen to find that my food has burned to a crisp. Scrapping the charred remains into the trash, I don't have the typical reaction of anger. Instead, I am relieved and a little excited.

"Well, no bacon for me. Anyway, it looked like Jeremy's upper lip. I don't want to eat that. Plus, I'd rather not cook for myself today I'll just go see my friends at the diner."

"Friends?"

"Come on, you know what I mean. Don't be a dick."

The diner is almost empty when I walk in. A woman and her daughter are sitting in the corner booth to the right and a man in a flannel shirt and ball cap is seated at the counter. I opt to take my normal seat in a booth to the left. Judging by the lack of customers and the fact that there are only two servers, I assume that they are typically slow this time of day. A cursory glance assures me that they both already know what I want because of the order slip dangling from the kitchen window. I scroll through articles on my phone, looking for any regarding Jeremy's disappearance.

"Hey, you! Strange seeing you here."

My face draws a confused posture when I look up to discover the person speaking is Cristy.

"Uh, no. It's strange seeing *you* here. I eat here almost every day."

"Really? I bet you eat the same thing too."

"How'd you know that?"

"Matt, I'm a psychiatrist. My job is to know things. Comprehend people's emotions and thoughts and transform them into something tangible."

I don't know how to process what she has just said to me. It almost seems as though she's said it just to get my reaction. What does she mean by 'tangible'? I thought 'tangible' meant something you could touch. How can you touch emotions and thoughts? But that's the thing about people who profess to delve into minds. They're madder than I am.

"Are we in a session? Why are you talking that way?"

"Haha, no. Sorry, I always talk this way. I don't mean anything by it. Mind if I sit with you?"

I can't shake the strange feeling that she's purposefully come here to see me. I've lived in this small town for over five years and have not once seen her before, then suddenly after meeting her a week ago, she shows up randomly. Or could it be that now I kind of know her, she's stood out? I guess that's possible. I must have seen a thousand people in here and never noticed a single one before. But still… I look around. This hardly seems like the kind of place a doctor would come. I thought all doctors were into health. A psychiatrist is still a doctor, right? She's not going to stay healthy by coming here. I also don't pretend that I will.

"Matt?"

"Oh, yeah. Sorry. Um…sure. Have a seat."

It's weird seeing her dressed so casually, in a tee-shirt and jeans. Not that I expected her to wear a lab coat everywhere, but by her classy and professional demeanor, I assumed she would dress in at least a blouse. That detail isn't the most intriguing though. Where are her glasses? Does she only wear them at work to give the impression of a typical therapist?

"Do you come here often?"

"Not really. The first time I came here was just last week. The food was good, so I decided to try it again. Well, you know what the food is like; you eat here almost every day. Why here?"

Even though it's obvious she intends her question to pick into my psyche, I can't help but entertain the conversation.

"They leave me alone."

"They? The servers?"

"Yeah, I don't like talking to people much. They know what I like and just bring it to me."

"Wow, that's interesting. You know it's strange that I became a therapist because I don't like talking to people either. That's why I don't date or go out. Just work and home."

It sounds like she's describing me, and although I already knew and accepted it about myself, hearing her say it elicits a genuine look of sympathy. So, this is weird. Here we are, two self-confessed social phobics claiming to hate talking, oddly talking to one another anyway. Choosing to sit together, moreover. Bizarre. Why are we doing this? But then again, I didn't choose to sit with her. She's chosen me.

"Can I get you something to drink, ma'am?"

The waitress's eyes don't sway from Cristy as she slides a plate onto the table before me.

"Oh, he already has his food, so I'll probably just head out. I'm not that hungry anyway."

"You're not going to eat?"

"Nah, I won't impose on your peaceful breakfast. Oh, hey. Before I go, would you like my number? I know you're probably not coming to the clinic again. But I'd love to keep in touch."

A woman has never given her number to me before and if they had, I wouldn't have known what to do with it. Although I suspect that her reasoning isn't for that sort of relationship anyway, the deep enthused stare she has while waiting for my answer is confusing. Looking into her alluring blue eyes, I see no harm in having her number. It's not as if she'd be forcing me to contact her. And if I do take her number and contact her, what harm can she possibly do to me?

"Yeah, sure. You can just put it in my phone. Here."

"Great, feel free to call or text whenever. It doesn't need to be about therapy or anything. I just think you are an interesting guy."

An "interesting guy" is not a description anyone has ever used for me before. I give her a toothy smile from the perceived compliment.

"Thank you. I think you are an interesting woman too. I'll be in touch."

Watching her leave the diner, a quiver begins in my gut. It intensifies when she waves through the window as she walks by.

"Ah, you sly dog. I knew you liked her."

"No, I don't. I just think she's…I don't know. She's *interesting.*"

"Haha. Yep, I like her too."

Back at home, I search incessantly for news coverage about Jeremy Biggs. Every report I come across says the same thing. A man has been reported missing. No one's seen him since last night, and they most likely should have seen him walking from the bar. For hours, I'm glued to the screen waiting for any information, until finally, there comes a live video of the area from which I abducted him. In the background of the reporter is a large area marked off with police tape. Dozens of officers are walking around in the desert.

"So far, all they are telling us is that he has not been found yet, and they are investigating this as a potential homicide. As you can see behind me, a large area of the road has been marked off, and there is what seems to be dried blood on the pavement. It's not implausible to think Mr. Biggs may have been involved in a vehicular collision. But the question remains: where is he?"

"Wow, that's very disturbing, Jerry. Is there any indication that he was able to make his way off the road and into the desert? Are there any marks to show that he walked or—"

"It's what officials are hoping to find out today, Chuck. But I've heard that some involved in the investigation believe Mr. Biggs was taken from the scene."

"Well, let's hope that he was driven to a hospital and is being treated for any injuries he may have sustained in the accident."

Psh, accident, my ass! I turn off the television, annoyed. There is no way that they believe it was an accident. That's just how those newscasters talk, to give people false hope so they won't panic. That's what the police tell them to do. Besides, none of the ants out there can handle the truth, so they block their senses from it. The cops know what happened. Well, some of it. It's impossible for them not to since I basically told them.

***

Lying on my side with my head nestled on my clasped hands, I feel the house shake. The wood frame creaks and cracks, the room slowly dimming. When the last speck of light dissipates, I hear a click, and a dark road becomes illuminated. Simultaneously, I am speeding down the path so fast that the trees are blurs of yellow and green. I extend my foot to push the brakes, but nothing is there, except the yellow stripes of the road flashing by. Strong winds lash at my face and I'm afraid to take a breath from it. My velocity increases and with it, sharp stinging on my skin.

The sensation of piercing needles shifts to searing hot pokers the more I accelerate. No longer able to handle the pain, I open my mouth wide, projecting a bloodcurdling scream. The motion and pain abruptly stop, and I find that I am at the scene where it all happened. There I am, kneeling next to Jeremy's bloody body.

"Hey, you okay, man?"

His barely perceptible groan is reassuring.

~ 142 ~

"Ah, whew. Thank goodness. Okay, this is what's going to happen. My name is Matt, and I'm here to make you pay for being an evil bastard. First, I'm going to put you in my trunk, then take you somewhere special. That'll be nice, won't it? Somewhere you've never been before, and that will give you lots of memories."

He lightly groans once again.

"There, I'm going to take your teeth out, cut your fingers off, then probably do something crazy painful with your tongue. Teeth because you don't deserve to smile, fingers because you used them to beat and strangle your wife, and tongue because I've seen how verbally abusive you are on Facebook. Any questions before we get going, Jeremy?"

A stream of blood marks the road in the wake of his body as I drag him to my car. Before putting him into the trunk. I place two dog collars tightly around his neck, then forcefully zip-tie his arms behind his back. Once I lift him into the trunk, I notice his left leg is bent unnaturally at the knee.

"Fuck man, I think your leg is broken. I'm sorry. That wasn't part of the plan for tonight. Hitting you with my car wasn't either, but we need to be flexible with this stuff. Ya know? I didn't mean the flexible comment as a joke about your broken leg. That would be fucked up."

I delicately position his leg out of the way and slam the trunk lid closed, then walk back to where his body was on the road. There is one large pool of blood with three smaller pools trailing from it. With white spray paint, I draw an arrow aiming at the larger puddle. Then below the arrow, I daub 'Evil'

.

The twenty-minute drive through the maze of dirt roads is peaceful with a slight chilly breeze. May in Arizona is hot during the day, but the temperature drops to around sixty most nights. I let the cool wind flow between my fingers, pulling up to my destination slowly.

"Here we are, Bo! Shit! Sorry, I mean Jeremy. Your name is Jeremy. I knew that."

He moans as I struggle to maneuver him from the trunk of the car. Once he's out and on the ground, I grab him by his belt and then drag him to the front.

"Hey, Jeremy, can you hear me?"

Grasping his shoulder, I shake him forcefully.

"Hey, wake up. It's time to start. I need you to be awake for this."

***

My eyes open to a now dark living room. The sun has gone down while I was in the void. Even though it feels as though I've been in there for only a few minutes, over two hours have passed. I rise from the couch and scratch my head, walking to the light switch.

~ 144 ~

"Wow, time's crazy in there. Jeremy was fucked up, man. I kinda feel bad about hitting him with the car."

"Are you serious?"

"Nah, screw that piece of shit. I'm hungry. Got any ideas for dinner?

"How about the diner? I hear your girlfriend likes it there."

Thought for Food

Matt's Story

I spring out of bed early, in a cheery mood and with vigor, just as I did yesterday. I don't know why I have been so energetic and enthusiastic at the start of the day lately. Maybe it has something to do with killing Jeremy. I do feel a little jolt of energy every time I think about it, but I notice each time it's a little less potent. After a long hot shower, I wipe a line through the layer of mist on the mirror and make eye contact with myself.

"Last day off work. You gonna make the best of it?"

"You know what? I am. Let's get out today and get some sunlight and fresh air."

After breakfast, I hop in the car and drive fifteen minutes to Anamax park. When I was married, I used to take my kids there to play. While my kids were there to run around and make new friends, I mostly spent my time people watching. Even back then, I disliked interacting with them but would expend hours of my life analyzing their actions. Traveling along the narrow path shaded by a tree line, ants skitter all around me. Walking, running, and riding their bicycles with blank stares, they appear to be drones traveling with no destination or purpose. My slow gait ends at a sturdy metal bench covered in paintings of Arizona flowers and cacti.

Years ago, this was where I preferred to sit because every part of the park was in view. Today though, the view to the left of the bench is partially obstructed by a ten-foot-wide sign that reads, 'Coming soon' with a concept drawing of future additions to the park. Still, I sit down and scan the neatly manicured field across from me. It's Saturday, just before noon, so the park is full of visitors. A group of kids playing tag. A few couples are holding hands, and there's what seems to be a birthday party over at the picnic tables. Off in the distance, a baseball game is taking place and the kids' parents cheer them on.

A child's frantic scream draws my attention back to the field nearest me. A hundred yards out, I can only just make out the child and a woman. She looks to be striking the child and he or she lies curled on the ground, crying. The mother is yelling, but I can't make out what she's saying. My eyes well up with pressure and begin to fill with tears. The anger…the true anger that I haven't felt in a while boils to the surface. I clench my fists and close my eyes tightly, shaking uncontrollably.

"You fucking bitch!"

***

My body shoots across the field, leaving behind tidal waves of grass in my wake. Like a train at full speed, the people passing by are distorted flashes of color. The woman grows larger in my sight until *smash!* She goes limp as she slides across the still moist ground. Before she comes to a stop, I jump into the air above her and slam my clasped fists into her chest.

"Why would you do that to a child? They did nothing to deserve you! You are a horrible mother!"

She is unconscious with her head lying to the side, so I reach down to bring her to face me. A chill travels down the back of my neck when I see that it is my grandmother. Her pale wrinkled skin has the texture of the outside of a cantaloupe, and her thin lips are pursed and imperceptible. Suddenly, her eyes dart open. The surprise sends me flying backward and, in an instant, I'm shoved from the void.

***

Looking back across the field, the woman and her child are no longer there, but my anger remains.

"Would you have hurt that woman?"

"No, why do you think we have the void? I need a place to imagine it without actually doing it. If I were going to do it, I would just plan it and do it. Wouldn't I?"

"True, but still weird that you think about it."

"Would you rather I not have an outlet?"

"That's strange. Didn't Cristy mention that she was worried about what you would do if you didn't have an outlet?"

"Yeah, she was pretty on the nose with that assessment. Oh well, let's go home; it's getting hot out here."

Rising from the bench, I notice on top of the overflowing trash can, a folded newspaper. When I pull it from the pile, there's a picture of Jeremy on the front. Reading the article coving his disappearance, I find it intoxicating. It states that the case has officially been labeled as a homicide and that currently, no suspects have been identified. The picture they used I remember seeing while trying to hunt him down.

"Your smile doesn't look like that anymore, does it? I'm keeping this."

When I get home, I carefully cut out the article, then place it into the back of a photo album of my kids. I lightly run the tips of my fingers across the thin plastic sleeve, focusing on the area over his face. Each pass generates a tiny, barely noticeable static shock, along with a tingling in my spine.

"You'll be safe in here."

The idea that what I did was significant enough to be televised and printed in newspapers, is feeding my addiction more than accomplishing the act. Instilling fear and causing suffering feels amazing, but it wanes so quickly. This is an even greater high that I can feed on for longer. The best part is it gives me time between meals.

"I'm hungry. Let's get something to eat."

"You should invite Cristy."

The idea doesn't seem half bad. I do enjoy her company and when I'm around her, calmness sets in. I told her that I would keep in touch so I might as well ask her. She's probably too busy anyway. Searching through my contact list, I find that her name has a heart next to it. How did she do that and what does it mean?

"She likes you, man. You are an 'interesting guy', after all."

"Whatever, let's just get this over with."

I opt to text instead of calling her because it's easier to ignore her reply if I don't like it. *Would you like to have lunch in about thirty minutes?* The short notice is meant to dissuade her from accepting my invitation. To my surprise, she responds almost immediately. *Sure. I'm free. Where would you like to meet?*

Taken aback, I don't know what to do. I hadn't planned on her saying yes, and other than at the diner, I only eat fast food. I explore my recollection of eateries I have passed in the area and recall a nice-looking Mexican restaurant by the Taco Bell. *Mexican restaurant by the taco bell?* I hardly have a chance to hit send when she replies. *Sure, see you in 30.*

I wait at the entrance for Cristy as customers pass in and out of the restaurant. The smell of seared beef and sautéed vegetables wafts by me every time someone opens the door. It's been thirty-two minutes since her text accepting my invite, and I begin worrying that she isn't coming.

"She's only two minutes late, man. Calm down."

"I said thirty minutes. That means—"

"Hey, I was worried you wouldn't keep in touch. Were you just talking to yourself?"

"What? No, I was singing a song I just heard in my car."

"Ah. I hate it when you can't get a song out of your head. It just keeps nagging and nagging in your mind until you finally just give up and sing it aloud."

"Yeah…That's what happened."

The restaurant is busy, but not overly crowded. A week ago, being in a place like this would have pushed me over the edge, but at this moment, it feels as though Cristy and I are the only two people here. We take seats at a table in the back and immediately, the waitress brings chips and salsa.

"Have you ever been here before?"

"Yeah, a few times. They have great fajitas."

I'm glad she says that because I have no clue what I'm going to order. I sense she would not be impressed if I ordered bacon and egg. But then again, why would I want to impress her?

"What were you doing when I texted you?"

"Just case notes and stuff. Boring crap you don't want to hear about. More interestingly, what were you doing? I was surprised to hear from you."

"I was at Anamax Park, just walking around."

"Really? That sounds like a nice relaxing time."

"It was until I saw a woman beating her kid. Not spanking. Beating. It was brutal and yes, it made me angry. Before you ask."

"I wasn't going to ask you that. I was going to say that it was terrible and that I hate people like that. You have every right to be angry about what she was doing."

So, there she goes with that therapist-speak again. Telling me I have 'every right'. *Gee, thanks! I'm glad you give me permission because I really wasn't sure I was allowed!*

Nevertheless, the stillness in her eyes tells me that she's being sincere. I lock onto them, and she seems to know that I am trying to read her. Her smirk says, 'you're out of your league', then she turns to her menu. Flipping the pages, she continues the conversation.

"So, what happened to the woman at the park?"

"Nothing. I looked away for a moment and when I looked back, she was gone."

"It's so sad the poor child has to go through that. I hear about those things all the time and it makes me angry that they can get away with it. Even in your case. I don't want to bring up bad memories or anything, but it's amazing that you made it out of that house with everything your grandmother and uncle did to you."

What did she just say? Did I tell her about that stuff? I recall our two sessions for every discussion we ever had and not one time did I mention a house or my uncle.

"How did you know about my uncle?"

"Oh, sorry. I read your book. I just wanted to know more about what you went through so I could help you. I'm sorry if that makes you mad, but I figured since you told me about the book, it was okay for me to read it."

"I'm not mad. I just wish you would have told me."

"Look. You're not my patient anymore and I'm not here as your therapist. When I read your book, it was when I assumed you would still be coming to see me. I'm sorry."

So, as my therapist, you can poke your nose in? I thought, incensed. Then I realized. *Hell, I published the thing. It's hardly her fault I put my inner thoughts on the internet.* I exhale, letting go of the pent-up breath.

"It's fine, really. That was the past. I told you I'm over it. Anyway, what's with all these people getting away with doing that shit to a child?"

The timing was bad for the question because I notice the server standing quietly beside our table. I look over at Cristy, embarrassed.

"You go first."

"I'll take the steak fajitas, well done, and a side of guacamole."

"I'll have the same."

"All right, I will have that right out."

We hand the menus to the server, then Cristy reaches into her purse and pulls out a small bottle of lotion. After squirting a small dab into her palms, she begins rubbing her hands together.

"What were we saying? Oh yeah, I think these people get away with it because the kids are too scared to say anything. These predators have a way of intimidating the kids into silence."

"I know what you mean. I felt that way as a child."

"Matthias, are you *sharing?*"

"Haha. No, just trying to be polite. I'm just saying, I know how the kids in those situations can feel pressured into staying quiet."

She's still rubbing her hands together, watching me. When she stops, she has a look of seriousness I've never seen on her before.

"There was a guy in Twin Peaks who was molesting his kids a few years ago, and that bastard is already out of jail. Gerald Watson or Wallace or something. Either way, he only did like two years for that. The system is so fucked up."

"I think the judges in those cases should do time for being too lenient."

"Right? Oh, here comes our food."

While eating, we talk about random likes and dislikes, and again about how much we hate talking to people, yet here we are…talking to one another as if we're close. I'm comfortable with her. I feel as if I can talk about anything, and she won't judge me for being weird or creepy. Still, I'll only let her see a select part of me. There is no way I'll let her know everything. She can't be allowed to know the evil within me.

"Well, it was really fun. Maybe we can do it again sometime?"

Again? Did I just have a date? Are we dating?

"Definitely. I had a great time too. I'll text you when I'm free."

She hugs me and whispers into my ear.

"I hope you do. Have a good night."

A curious feeling shrouds me as I watch her walk away. It's not love or lust, but closer to a temporary quelling of loneliness.

"She totally likes you, dude."

"You think?"

"Come on. She basically made out with your ear."

"That's true, but we could never be a couple. She would find out our secrets. We can't let anyone find out or we'll have to stop and I'm never stopping."

Dilemma

Matt's Story

Curled up in a soft microfiber blanket on the couch, I alternate continuously between the three local news channels, waiting for my fix. The coverage of Jeremy's disappearance is more intermittent than yesterday and less extensive. His allure is quickly fading from the minds of the public and the media appears to be following suit.

"Do you think we should give the cops a clue, so the story gets back in the headlines?"

"Are you crazy? No, we ride this one out and lay low for a while. Leaving clues? That's the dumbest idea I've ever heard. Let's get some sleep."

"Yeah, you're right. It was pretty dumb."

***

The next afternoon, I awake well-rested, and in what now seems a typical, energetic mood. It's a good thing since I'm due to be back at work today. One thing is perplexing though; I can't remember if I dreamed last night. I have vivid dreams every night and can usually recall every detail of them. Today though, my mind is drawing a blank. No doubt Cristy would say I was suppressing—or repressing—some tormented inner emotion when my mind refuses to remember them. I shrug it off and continue my daily routine.

When I arrive at work, I'm relieved to find that an aircraft already sits parked in my assigned bay and is well into its maintenance plan, so I won't be on panel duty tonight. The supervisor is at the assignment board, but it looks as though he's already handed out the orders to the crew.

"Matthias, welcome back. How was your vacation? You feel better?"

"Thanks, Mike. Yeah, I feel a lot better actually."

"Good to hear. You look well. You wanna start on the cable rigs?"

"Sure, who do you have me with?"

"You can have Tim or Doug. They both need more practice with rigging."

For some reason, I prefer to work with Doug tonight. Tim's an alright guy, but I've only worked with him once, for about an hour. Although he doesn't talk as much, he's also way slower at getting things done. At least I know what I'm getting into with Doug. Plus, I can tell him to shut the fuck up if I need to, like last time. There's no sense in being over-polite around people like that. I tried the gentle hints and those didn't work. So, from now on, if I need him to cool it, I'll be straight. I find him at the tool counter, checking out hydraulic testing equipment.

"You might as well check that back in. You're with me on rigging tonight."

"Really? Mike said I was going to be on gear checks."

"Nope. Tim's going to do that and you're with me."

He pushes the equipment back to the tool room attendant and turns to follow me.

"Welcome back, man. You okay?"

"Yeah, I'm great. Just needed to relax for a bit."

"I hear that. Did you get drunk when you were off?"

Why would he ask me that? Does Doug see me as an alcoholic who drinks so much that I needed to take time off to do it? Or that I drink so little because of work, that I feel a need to take time off to do it…? It could be either way. There's not a lot of sense in trying to see inside his mind. But my confused glare prompts an immediate clarification.

"Oh, I didn't mean anything by that. It's just…I swear I saw your car out front of Whiskey River the other night."

I'm reminded that our shift is from Sunday to Wednesday. He lives out in that direction and would have been off the night I abducted Jeremy. I need to end this before the questions become too specific.

"Wasn't me, dude. I only left my house to eat and get groceries. Spent all that time on my couch. I felt like shit."

"Oh, well it looked like your car, that's all I'm saying.'

"Do you know how many black chargers there are in this town?"

"Yeah, you're right. Let's get on with it, then."

The confusion on his face says he's still not convinced, but he continues to gather his tools anyway. Prepping the flight controls for rigging, he's quieter than usual. Normally by now, I'm ready to pull my hair out from his incessant yammering. He's thinking. I need to divert his mind from whatever he's obsessing about. I definitely don't like the look on his face.

"How was your weekend, man?"

"What? Oh, it was good. My mom came to visit with my little sister. I took them down to Madera Canyon for a hike. It's pretty down there. Have you ever been?"

"Yeah, it is pretty."

The Doug I'm used to comes back in full force. Virtually constant, for eleven hours, he assaults me with random discussions but I'm going to try and put up with them, so I don't set him back to thinking about seeing my car. That's the problem. If I shut him up, I'm afraid his mind will spring back to that in the silence.

He took his family to the county fair. He told them about his new job. He's thinking about getting a motorcycle. He bought his niece a new bike. He planted roses in the front garden. This is unbearable, but I just smile and nod at every word. At least he's not thinking about me being at the Whiskey River bar anymore.

At the end of the shift, I'm packing away my tools for the day when I spot Doug looking at me awkwardly. Now that he's no longer busy, he seems to have time to go back and process all his latent thoughts from earlier. Pretending not to notice, I casually close and lock my toolbox, then walk toward the hangar door. Doug quickly follows.

"Hey, you know a guy came up missing from the Whiskey River bar that night?"

"Oh, yeah? What night?"

"Thursday. The night I thought I saw your car there. Apparently, he was hit by a vehicle or something."

"If he was hit by a car then how is he missing? He's not going to get hit by a car and then get up and walk off, is he? Well, maybe he could. I dunno. Never been hit by one."

"I dunno either. The whole thing is weird. The news said it was a hit and run and that the person driving probably took the body and dumped it, so they wouldn't get in trouble."

"That's ridiculous, Doug. If he was leaving Whiskey River then he would most likely have been drunk out of his skull and if someone hit him, then it would have been an accident because the dude was probably stumbling all over the place. Anyway, he'd have brought it on himself."

"True, it's just strange, that's all."

His steps match my cadence to the parking lot. Once through the security gate, I notice he's parked in the front row. I've parked in the back, yet when I pass by his car, he continues to follow. *What's he doing*? I open the car door and turn around to see him casually inspecting my front bumper. Now, I'm incensed.

"You're fucking kidding, right? Think I hit some random dude with my car and then dumped his body in the desert? Seriously, you are starting to piss me off, kid."

He springs erect then cowers from my tone. His face is that of a disappointed child. Sluggishly dragging his feet, he moves toward me.

"I'm sorry, Matt. I watch too many crime shows. It's just, I could swear it was your car I saw. Please don't be mad at me."

"So, your plan was to solve the big case by proving that the only guy willing to be your friend is some killer, murdering random people with his car? Did you see any evidence up there, Sherlock? Want a closer look? Want me to drive it into a garage so you can order a report?"

He lowers his chin and then slowly shakes his head.

"Okay, so then are we done here? Can I go home and get some sleep without worrying that the cops are going to be busting down my door any minute?"

"Yes. I'm sorry, man. Will you please still teach me how to rig the flaps tonight? I promise I won't bring it up again."

"We'll see how pissed off I still am tonight. Maybe I'll just go out and run another random guy over. Maybe I'll drag his mutilated corpse into the back of the car and go home and eat it."

His face is a sight for sore eyes. He looks terrified, probably at the anger in my tone more than at my words. I already know that guy watches enough horror and police shows to outsmart anything I might throw into the scenario. "I said, are we done then, or what?" He vaguely nods but his eyes speak volumes. His eyes say, *go, go... please go.*

I slam the car door and then rev the engine loudly before speeding out of the parking lot. In the rearview mirror, I see him still standing in the same spot, watching me. All the way home, my heart is racing. That's the closest I have come to being caught and I'm not even sure that it's over yet. It would be terrible for the cops to catch me right off the bat; some killers can get away with it for good. Some for years. And some for just a few months or weeks. It surely can't be all over for me after such a short time, can it? It was a location in the middle of nowhere. It's just not possible.

And then if the man I work with spotted me and reported me, that'd be real bad luck. He's so certain I'm the one who did it, yet he's risked his life just to prove it by saying so as he's standing right in front of me. Anyone with that level of confidence won't give up so easily. But then again, if he stands right in front of me, maybe that means he *doesn't* believe it could've been me. Maybe he was standing there to confirm it *wasn't* me. If he sees my car's intact, then he knows it's not me, right?

This is way too confusing. But anyway, I've decided: he knows it wasn't me. So, he can just go home and forget all about it. Otherwise, wouldn't he just be terrified? Too terrified to stand there and more or less weigh up whether I did it? No, he knows it wasn't me. Plus, wouldn't he think that if he confirms to me his thoughts that I'm guilty of it, then I'd kill him before he can tell the cops? *He definitely doesn't think I did it*, I think.

"I need to handle this."

"Handle? You mean kill? You're gonna kill Doug?"

"What else am I supposed to do? Just let him go to the cops?"

"He has zero evidence. If he keeps digging, *then* we can kill him. See how it goes."

"Hmm. Well, I don't know. What do we do, sit outside his house? Do surveillance on him?"

Really, I didn't know the answer. I had meticulously cleaned my car after leaving the desert that night. It was the very first thing I did after getting back to the safety of the suburbs. That's when the police catch people when the criminal thinks they'll leave this or that till morning. Not so with me. I was straight onto it. I always knew there was a reason for buying that particular car. It was tough, didn't show a scratch as far as I could make out. With a flashlight, I'd given it a good inspection. Then I looked again before leaving for work in the morning. When he was inspecting my front bumper, I already knew there wasn't so much as a scratch for him to find. The trunk has no carpet, so it was easy to wash that down with bleach and water.

The tools I disposed of in a trash can at the end of my street, and the can was picked up the next day. The only evidence I have is the newspaper clipping I've put in the photo album at home. *I'm not getting rid of that.* But even so, a tiny niggling voice in my head is saying, *what if the cops see that clipping?* But I just can't bring myself to get rid of it. Such a small thing—I can get rid anytime, flush that thing down the toilet if I have to. If it comes to someone banging on the door…

Inches away from putting my key in the door latch, I receive a text. *Hey, haven't heard from you. Are you off work yet?* It's Cristy. What's she doing texting me at seven in the morning on a Monday? I debate texting her back but instead put the phone back into my pocket.

In the shower, I hear my phone beep two more times and know it can only be her. What does she want? Still wet, I retrieve the phone and check the messages. *I wanted to see if you were free for breakfast. I know you usually eat later, but it might be good to eat before you go to bed.* Why isn't she at work or at least getting ready for work? *Aren't you working today?* I put the phone on the bathroom counter while I dry off and receive a reply while hanging the damp towel on the rack. *Haha! Memorial Day. We regular people get it off.*

Oh wow, she's right. I forgot today was Memorial Day. I don't get holidays off at my job. We work four twelve-hour days every week, regardless of holidays. I never eat before bed but now that I think about it…I am a little hungry. *Sure. I'll meet you at the diner in 30.*

It strikes me as odd when I feel my lips curve up. Usually, I hate anyone bothering me this time of day—or any time of day, come to that. But for some reason, I let her off. *AWESOME!!! See ya then,* she texts.

She's already seated in my usual booth when I arrive. Her face lights up with a big smile when I sit across from her.

"So, how was your night?"

"It was work. Boring, except for my coworker who was annoying as usual. That dude will not stop talking. Is there a psychiatric condition that might explain that?"

I'm mostly kidding but at the same time, maybe there is.

"Try being a therapist. Everyone I meet won't shut up. But on the other hand, there are times I tell someone to open up to me about everything and they barely say a word."

We both laugh at her fairly clever joke. Then I frown a little in case she's referring to me.

"How about you? Did you do anything fun last night?"

"You know me, always working. I've been seeing a girl for a few days now who's had a rough life. She was addicted to drugs and became a prostitute. Anyway, she's been clean for a while now and wants to get custody of her daughter, but I have to clear her first. Spent most of the night going through a foot-high stack of files on her."

"Good Lord, that's a lot. So, do you think you *will* clear her?"

"I don't think she'll ever be well enough for that. When they took her daughter away, she was only five years old, and they found her locked in a closet covered in her feces and crying. Any person who could do that to their child will never be normal. You know what I mean?

I know exactly what she means. I have only recently come to terms with the fact that I can never be a normal person because of my past. I've spent decades fighting it, only to realize that this is who I am. The last-ditch effort was to erase the person most responsible for my condition and when that caused even greater internal turmoil, it forced me to concede at last.

"Hey, you know what I mean?"

"Yes, sorry. I was just thinking about something else. Sorry!"

"Where do you go when you trail off like that?"

"What do you mean?"

"Sometimes, you get a blank stare on your face and don't say anything for a while. It's like you're stuck in limbo."

"Void."

"What? Did you say void?"

"Void? No, I said *boy* as in, 'oh boy, where is this going?'"

Why did I even say that? She's a psychiatrist and a damn good one. She would know exactly what I meant by 'void', instantly knowing how crazy I am.

"Seriously though, I'm interested. What's going on in that fascinating head of yours?"

"I don't know. I just think a lot. Sometimes when I hear something, it makes me think. There's nothing particular that I think about. It's always different. For instance, that time I was thinking about how you said she would never be normal, and it reminded me of how I always wanted to be normal and will never be."

"Normality is subjective, Matt. You are who you are, regardless of what other people perceive as normal."

The waitress slides two plates of food onto the table. Both plates have bacon, over-medium eggs, and white toast. She holds her focus on me and doesn't acknowledge the server at all.

"If you like your food delivering to you without talking to anyone and the people are okay with that, then it's now normal. And a lot of the things people say are normal just don't suit anyone. For example, in some countries, it's normal to not cross the road until the green man walks, even when you can see it's a massive, long road and no traffic. In Germany, for example, they do that. They won't cross a road unless they have the green man because it's abnormal. In other countries, their normal is to say *the hell with it, I'll dodge the traffic and cross.* See what I mean? Normality is whatever people accept."

How can she make me feel so comfortable around her? The way she talks is so accepting of who I am or at least who she sees me as. Even after I sense she's psychoanalyzing me, I feel all right, knowing I can tell her stuff and that whatever I say, it's safe with her. Well, relatively. At our first session, she did state that one caveat: *as long as I don't feel anyone will come to harm, this is between you and me*. And regardless, I like it.

Anyway, as I am not her patient, I trust even that caveat doesn't apply anymore. Hopefully, she likes me enough now on a personal level that she won't freak out at whatever I say. Not that I am about to tell her anything that could incriminate me. Her grin reveals that she knows she has said something that's just made an impact on me.

Outside, we uncomfortably stare at each other for a few moments before she breaks the tension.

"You had a good time, didn't you? Come on, you can say it. I won't tell anyone."

She leans in as if we are sharing a secret. That's the thing; she knows I like to keep to myself, and we have fun with that. She isn't trying to change me, just to go along with whatever works.

"Yeah, you're okay. I kinda like hanging out with you…kinda."

"Whatever! Don't make me start calling you Mr. Ellis again!"

"Mr. Ellis was my dad, but you can call me Daddy if you want."

She playfully pushes on my shoulder and turns away.

"I'll call you Mr. Pig because you're a dirty little piggy! Haha!"

I'm parked in the opposite direction, so I stay where I am, just watching her walk away. She stops, turns, rushes back, then grabs my face and kisses me on the cheek.

"I'll see you later… *Daddy*. Go get some sleep. Haha!"

Does this woman like me? She's acting as if she does and not in a friend sort of way either. The way she is frolicking to her car makes me consider that she is, in fact, into me.

"We have to figure this shit out."

"Figure what out? She's obviously into you, man."
"Yeah, but we can't have anyone in our life right now, especially a psychiatrist. That woman could pick us apart. Why now? After all these years, why the hell did I have to meet her now?"

Getting into my front seat, I glance across the parking lot to see Doug crouched in his car observing me. Has he been following me all morning, even while I was at home taking a shower? He is never going to let this go, is he? And there was I, thinking I might have to watch Doug. That would be funny. Doug watching me watching him. Who'd be the first idiot to realize that we're just heading around in circles? For the briefest of moments, the thought amuses me. Then it doesn't. "It's not funny. It's serious."

"Okay, now I agree. We have to take care of this."

The Itch Scratches

Matt's Story

Doug patiently waits for me to drive away, but I sit for a few minutes in my car, contemplating what to do. The more I think about it, the angrier I get until my eyes close, and I release a long sigh. The calm before the storm, I pause in silence, waiting for the darkness to take me, but nothing happens. The frustration builds to a boiling point when the visualizations fail to emerge. Abruptly, I leap out of the car and rush toward Doug with my fists clenched.

"What the fuck are you doing here, Doug!"

The terror in his eyes only feeds my determination as I stomp closer to him. His mouth is open, but he can't find his words among the fear.

"I–I–I don't—"

"Bacon breakfast burrito with no cheese, and a side of hash browns?"

A woman approaches from my left holding a white paper bag and I'm immediately mortified by the situation. He takes the bag with his quivering hand, focusing on me with wide eyes. I reciprocate with a much softer gaze. Ashamed, I turn back to my car and begin walking.

"Sorry, Doug. My mistake. I'll show you how to rig the flaps tonight."

Lying in my bed, thoughts of what could have happened crowd my mind. What if the waitress hadn't brought his take-out order at that exact time? What if I'd attacked him? What if, in a fit of rage, I killed him? The constant what-ifs hinder my hope of getting any sleep, so I decide to go to the living room and watch television. But the thought flits through my head that perhaps all these serial killers didn't even start out intending to be serial about it. But soon enough, you get paranoid about someone noticing what you've done. Then you have to kill that one as well. Then someone gets onto you about that or says that your behavior's been weird lately. It gets you suspicious of them too, so they have to be the next on the list. Or maybe someone just reminds you in some way of the first victim, driving you to insanity so you have to end them too. It's endless.

Hours go by with no mention of Jeremy. In less than seventy-two hours, it appears his disappearance isn't newsworthy anymore. In a way, that ought to be good for me because it means the public will be less inclined to think about anything they may have seen. But it's not good, not at all. It means I can no longer get the emotional stimulus that I need to be content. I already feel the hunger creeping in.

"I need to find someone. Someone deserving of me. Someone the world's better off without."

I begin searching for wrongdoers within my area, comparable to a person shopping for a new dental provider. Every promising candidate I find takes hours of research to exclude. They are either in prison, moved away, or I can't track them. Discouraged and irritated, I slam the laptop shut, shoving it off the table and onto the floor, then I begin pacing the room.

"I need something to settle this urge. Give me something. I don't wanna hurt an innocent person, but I won't have a choice for too much longer."

"Hey, just breathe. There's no need to make such a drama of it all. We'll figure this out. You know there are a bunch of homeless men downtown?"

I stop pacing and throw my hands up.

"That won't fucking work! Don't you remember the homeless man we imagined killing the other day?"

"Well, what about the woman you saw beating her kid at the park?"

"Really? Let me guess, you know her name and where the hell she lives!"

"Oh, right."

"Or what do you suggest we do, just sit in the park and wait for her to show up again? Should I put up a tent? Relocate there, living in the bushes?"

"Sorry, sorry. I guess you know best."

"Yeah, just shut the hell up and let me think!"

I crouch to my knees with my hands wrapped around my head, humming loudly. Who are you? *Where are you at? What the hell did you do to deserve…me! Who was that person that Cristy mentioned the other day? Some guy in Twin Peaks. A Gerald Wilson or Walters or something. Oh, right. You don't fucking know. Think. Think!* I hop up and start to pace the room again.

"Come on. What the hell was his name? I know it was Gerald and something that starts with a double-u. Gerald…Fuck!"

The alarm on my phone abruptly interrupts my frantic episode, going off all of a sudden. Disappointed, I silence the siren, then lazily make my way down the hallway to get ready for work. My reflection in the mirror isn't the cheery, *ready to start the day* one I have been seeing lately. It's fatigued, irritated, full of hate. He looks malicious and as if he's had enough. Locking eyes with him, I feel myself feeding on the rage in his stare. It pulls me closer, inch by inch, until my forehead rests against the glass. Unable to escape his grasp or turn away, I watch as a raging fire consumes his eyes. Bright white light and heat flash into my face, followed by darkness.

***

Now, a new voice assaults my ears unexpectedly. A familiar voice, yet certainly not one I expect to hear right now, and not here.

"It's so sad the poor child has to go through that. I hear about those things all the time and it makes me angry they can get away with it. Even in your case. I don't want to bring up bad memories or anything, but it's amazing you made it out of that house with everything your grandmother and uncle did to you."

"What the…?"

Cristy! That is exactly what Cristy said to me. Her voice sounds muffled and resonates around me, but there is nothing except darkness everywhere I look. My feet anchor in place, my arms feeling as if they are pushing through water when I try to move them.

"Hello… You there, Cristy?"

A shimmer on the floor below me catches my attention. I wave my fingers through it, causing ripples and swirls of colorful light. Back and forth, the colors and voices become clearer with each pass. When I stop, there is a hazy view of two people at a table. The one on the right is Cristy. I can tell by her impossibly blonde hair. But who is she talking to? Squinting, I try to focus through the blur, but it only makes it worse.

"Haha. No, just trying to be polite. I'm just saying, I know how the kids in those situations can feel pressured into staying quiet."

Although it sounds slightly off, there is no mistaking the voice as my own. I even recall saying those exact words, the same as I recall Cristy's exact words too. But what am I doing here? A dark cloud accumulates over the hazy couple, making them even harder to recognize.

"There was a guy in Twin Peaks…"

"Oh, shit. This was the conversation. This is where she—"

"Molesting his kids a few years ago…"

Her words keep fading in and out, trailing off into echoes.

"Who is it? Tell me!"

"Bastard…Gerald…"

"Gerald who?"

"Gerald Wat… Wattle? Watkiss… Ah, Wallace…"

My eyes spring open, but I am still pressing my face to the mirror. *No, still not the right name,* I think. *It's not Wallace. But it's something like that.* When I pull back, a large red circle fills my forehead. Lightly rubbing it with my fingertips, I begin repeating the name in my vision.

"Gerald Wat or Wallace, something like that. Wat. Waters? Waiters? Watson? Wait—Watson! That's it! Gerald Watson or Wallace!"

The instant I solve the question, my enthusiasm to start the day returns. Looking back at the mirror, an eager yet ominous grin greets me.

"There you are. I've been looking for you."

There's no time to search for Gerald right now, so I plan to start researching in the morning when I get home. I clock in to work with only seconds to spare, then begin gathering the tools I need to rig the flaps. Doug doesn't seem to be around tonight, and it makes me wonder if it has something to do with our altercation this morning. I wouldn't be surprised if I scared him off.

"Hey, Mike. Who do you have helping me with the flaps tonight?"

"Still Doug. He should be around."

"Hmm. I haven't seen him."

"Check the cockpit. He said he was gonna get everything prepped for when you got here."

As soon as I walk past the bulkhead, I hear Doug cursing, his head and torso underneath the control structure and legs flailing around.

"Just go on, you piece of shit. Crap. Why the hell won't you go on?"

"Hey, Doug? Sure you have the right collars? The controls for the flaps have larger stops on 'em."

His body relaxes and I hear the metal collars fall to the floor.

"Jesus. Now you tell me."

Muffled grunts and huffs follow as he worms his way out from the small bay. Once he's clear, he stands up, dusts his pants off, then stares at me.

"I want to apologize about this morning, Doug."

"No reason. I understand. Want to say something though, without you getting mad at me."

After what I put him through, it's the least I can do, to let him get out his frustrations about how I've overreacted.

"Okay so, I know that was your car at the bar that night. I didn't want to tell you, but I saw you in it. I only wanted to ask you how it felt. That's all, man."

A white-cold fear shoots down the length of my spine, a lightning bolt of horror. *No, no, no, no… no! Oh Jesus. Fuck.* My brain is pounding so hard that every word he utters shoots a sharp pain into the back of my eyes. I can't breathe, can't react, only managing to stare blankly.

"You don't have to say anything. I just want you to know that I'm not planning on telling anyone. This morning, you were right when you said you're my only friend, and I know it was probably an accident and you didn't want to get in trouble. You did what you had to do. I hope one day, you'll tell me how it felt though. I'm kind of interested in that stuff."

'That stuff'? What stuff? Murdering people or doing hit-and-runs and driving off? What is he on about? And more to the point, what do I do about it? He walks past me toward the exit.

"Good."

Stopping short of the doorway, he turns and smiles, then scurries down the stairs. There is something liberating about him knowing now that he's told me. And *because* he's told me, I know he can't go telling someone because he'll always wonder if I'll come after him next. He said it was *probably* an accident. He doesn't know for sure. Doug will always have that element of doubt, hounding him.

So, it's all good. Finally, a person in the world who knows who I truly am, what I am capable of. The one among the millions of clueless ants to open his eyes and see the truth. His acceptance of me, even when faced with the knowledge that I've just killed a man, is both relieving and terrifying.

"Can we trust him?"

"I don't think we have a choice."

"There's always a choice."

"Let's give him a chance before we decide on that route."

The night doesn't move along ordinarily by any means. Every few minutes, I catch Doug staring at me with an awkward grin on his face. When he sees me notice, he doesn't turn but instead evolves into a toothy smile. I've always known Doug was strange. After all, it takes one to know one, but this is well beyond his typical level of oddness. What is he thinking about? The way he's acting brings the familiar cramping and twisting in my gut that I had a little over a week ago.

God help me if what I've done might send him on some crazed killing spree of his own. The way he looks at me seems to say he just might, that it's triggered something in him, same as it did in me. He's looking at me almost with adulation, with a huge admiration, with reverence. I think he's beginning to idolize me now. The problem is, if he does something like it himself, he probably won't hide it well and then the police will ask why he did it, and he'll say it—he'll tell them. *Shit, maybe I do have to get rid of Doug. I'll have to see how things go.*

At lunch, he sits across from me. He always eats by himself in the corner just listening to music, so I know this is going to be another addition to the weirdness. He sits where he can also see me at all times, so that when I move, he gives me that inane grin again as if to say, *we have a secret, you and I.* He takes a bite of his sandwich and then leans in, but I pretend not to notice.

"Hey, did the guy scream?"

He whispers as if we were in a library. Placing a chip into my mouth, I ignore his question, staring into the bag. He leans in closer and then looks around the room. The grin comes again.

"Hey, did the guy scream when you hit him?"

I exhale angrily, crumple the bag of chips in my fist, then walk out.

"I'm sorry, man. Don't be that way. I'll stop asking."

The rest of the night goes by quickly because Doug gets reassigned to do a job on the aircraft three bays over. When the shift ends, I know he will try to follow me to the car, all the while inundating me with questions.

"Hey, Mike? Mind if I cut out fifteen minutes early? Everything's wrapped up on my end."

"Sure. Do me a favor, though. Check that right tie-down on your way out. It looks loose."

"No problem."

After pulling the tie-down strap taut, I hurry to the door. Pushing the knob, I glance over to bay five and see Doug glaring at me. I politely wave goodbye before passing the threshold. The relief from getting out with no further contact is swiftly replaced by concern. Doug holds my life in his hands. He has power over me and at any moment, could choose to use it.

"We may have to take care of him."

"One project at a time though. Let's get done with Gerald first, then we can figure out how to deal with Doug."

Sitting on my couch, I start the hunt for Gerald but it's immediately evident that I'm too tired to focus. I haven't slept in two days, making the simplest of thoughts difficult to process. Rubbing my achy eyes and yawning deeply, I decide to put the search on hold till this afternoon. The instant my head hits the pillow, I receive a text.

"Come on, man. I just wanna sleep. I can't come have breakfast with you, Cristy."

Checking the message with one eye closed, I'm relieved to discover she's not inviting me to breakfast. *You probably had a long night. I just wanted to say sleep tight and uh...wow it's bright.* I don't know why, but her horrible rhyme makes me laugh out loud while replying. *I'm already in bed. BTW, you're a doctor but no Dr. Seuss.* I know the instant I put the phone down she'll text, so I wait. *HAHAHA!* There it is. Now, I can get some sleep.

My head barely has time to sink into the pillow before I'm drifting off. My body floats along seamlessly and unabated. No sound, no light, and no surface to touch, just an endless sea of nothingness. I open my mouth, but no words come out, not even the sound of air rushing from my lungs. My arms and legs flounder about aimlessly with no resistance. Is this place peace or purgatory? Maybe it's both.

My alarm jars me awake. I slept so hard that my muscles are aching, and my neck is stiff. I rise from the same position I lay down in this morning, having not moved even an inch. The joints in my arms and knees creak and pop, struggling to climb out of bed. When I finally get upright, I stretch my arms to the ceiling and exhale a long raspy yawn.

"Yeah, that was purgatory. I feel like I've had my ass handed to me and now we get to deal with Doug's bullshit all night. I shoulda hit his ass with a fucking car instead."

The Descent

The sky is filled with dark clouds and the wind is intermittently gusty. Debris drifts across the road in front of me on the way to the diner and little specks of rain randomly sprinkle my windshield. A storm is coming, and it looks to be a big one, which excites me. I have always loved rainstorms; the heavier the rain and the louder the thunder, the better. Among the chaos of howling wind, the deluge of water, and rumbling heavens, I always get the most restful sleep.

Feeling slightly better but still sore, I roll my shoulders forward and back to loosen them up before walking into the diner. Once I enter the doorway, I stretch my neck from side to side then stop unexpectedly. To my surprise, Cristy is waiting in my booth with two plates in front of her. Her lashes flutter when she sees me.

"Are you going to eat all that? What were you gonna do if I hadn't shown up tonight?"

"I know you have to be at work by six so I figured if you weren't here by five-thirty, I would be forced to be a little piggy like you, except this piggy can eat."

"You sure are fit for a so-called piggy."

"Why, thank you."

Throughout our conversation, I can't help but find it strange that she assumed I would be here tonight; then again, I did tell her that I came to eat here almost every day. Although her being here without knowing for certain that I would show is peculiar, it's also endearing. She is assertive but in a good way, and she's trying extremely hard to spend time with me, something I have never experienced before. While I do like it, my ever-suspicious nature will not let me drop my guard. What does she want? What does she stand to gain from someone like me?

"Hello…you there, Matt?"

"Uh…yeah. What's up?"

"There you go, off into la-la land again. I was asking if you had anything fun planned for the weekend."

I sure do. I plan to hunt down, torture, then kill a really bad guy to feel excited about causing pain and fear in another person. Then I'm going to sit on my couch and eat popcorn, watching the media trying to figure out what happened to him. But I can't exactly tell her any of this, can I? Rolling my eyes toward her, I see she's awaiting my answer.

"Not really. You know my life is boring. I hate being around people."

"Do you hate being around me?"

"Of course not. You hate everyone too, and you're different. I like hanging out with you…kinda."

"Oh Mr. Ellis, you sure know how to charm a lady. Haha. Well, I'll let you get to work. Have a good night."

"You too."

The walk from the gate to the hangar is a dreadfully mixed soup of emotion. Whatever Doug has in store for me, I know I won't like it; it will take an incredible amount of concentration to keep myself from attacking him, but I must endure it if I want to get to Gerald. I have to focus on one thing at a time and currently, Doug is harmless.

Doug stares at me with adoring eyes, in a warped way. If I hadn't done what I've done, I'd find him creepy, stalkerish. But as I have done what I've done, it kind of makes sense. I can only guess he's never had a role model before. Now, he seems to think I'm it. I have to just keep Doug on my side, keep him quiet while I do what comes next.

My goal is to feed the urge and that means Gerald has to be first. After it's done, I'll worry about what to do with him. Doug approaches from the side while I'm getting my assignment from Mike, then stands there silently.

"I need you to take 721 out to the run pad and do all the engine and system checks, then tow her over to pad 'A' for delivery. Don't forget to bring me the checklist before you leave today."

"I know."

"I have to remind everyone, Matt, because of what happened last month. It looks bad on us when we can't deliver a plane on time all because we didn't turn in the paperwork."

"Wasn't me, but I get it, boss. I'll have it for you when I'm done. Who's my copilot seat?"

"Doug's right there. Just take him."

Exactly what I hoped to prevent. Annoyed, I amble to my toolbox with Doug in tow.

"Hey, I didn't get a chance to say goodbye this morning; you left so quick."

"I left early because I didn't sleep yesterday. I was exhausted."

"Oh, that must be why you were so irritable."

What did he just say? The seething scowl I cast onto him is palpable. He's pushing things now, pushing them way too far. The wheels are visibly turning in his head, trying to figure out what he had said wrong. I close the already short distance between us, firmly grasp his right shoulder, then project my eyes into his.

"I was irritable because you keep bringing up stuff that I don't want to talk about."

His shoulder trembles within my grip and his gaze cowers toward the floor. I hold him, hostage, for a few more moments then gently release him.

"If we can stop all this shit, then we can still be friends. Deal?"

His face still drooping, he nods in agreement.

"I don't want to hear another word about it, right? I hope we understand one another."

His eyes are wide, showing too much white. But even then, he seems to wear that look on his face that says, *I really can't believe what you've done* in an admiring way. I don't know what I'm to make of it. I also cannot believe what I've done. He nods again with vigor. We shake hands and I slap his back.

"Hey, if you two are done making out, I need you both to get this bird ready for final check and delivery."

"You got it, Mike. We're on it."

I look back at Doug.

"Right, Doug?"

"Yes, sir. We are on it."

It's almost as if the storm is waiting for us to pull the aircraft outside before it releases its wrath. Within minutes of chocking the wheels of the plane on the test pad, the sky opens and releases its deluge. After Doug and I get everything secure, we climb into the cockpit, then start our checks. This is his fifth delivery check with me, so he has it down pretty well. Thankfully, he needs very little guidance which is a relief since I sometimes feel like I have to tell him every little thing.

"Good. Okay, now right engine, eighty-five percent."

The plane shakes and the engine whines as I push the throttle lever to eighty-five percent power, holding it for five minutes. All the systems show good, so I pull it back to idle. Jotting down the results on the checklist, I notice Doug staring at me from my peripheral.

"What's going on, Doug?"

He continues to stare but doesn't reply. When I turn to face him, it's clear he is thinking very hard about what to say. He is mulling something over in his busy head, stewing and brewing, locked in an inner world as he does so. His silence is maddening, but I hold back on the assumption that he may be scared to say anything after our short altercation earlier, so I reassure him.

"Tell me what's going on, Doug. I won't be mad."

"I just want to know what it was like."

"This shit again?"

"You told me you wouldn't be mad. I mean, I promise I won't say anything if you tell me, but if you don't, I may have to tell the police what I know. That's the problem."

The blood in my face starts to boil and my hands shake uncontrollably. He continues watching me, undeterred by my obvious state of rage.

"You blackmailing me, Doug?"

"No. Well, yeah, I guess. Kinda."

"You know what? Fine! I'll tell you what happened, then I'll tell you what's going to happen."

His eyes gleam from the thought that his burning questions are finally about to be answered, but immediately dim once I begin.

"I killed him! I tortured him then murdered him because he knew my secret and threatened to tell the cops. In other words, *I did to him exactly what I'm going to do to you, Doug. That's if you don't watch your dirty mouth. So, now what do you say"*

The blood drains from Doug's face and his jaw slackens slightly. I give him time to process what I've just told him before turning my body toward him and leaning in.

"Do you wanna know my secret, Doug? Do you still wanna tell the cops what you know?"

He sits there quietly petrified so I decide to speed things up by showing him the four-inch Gerber knife I always carry in my pocket. I open it repeatedly, humming an eerie tune, then stomping my foot onto the floor.

"Well, do you!"

"N–no, sir"

"Good. Because the last guy's missing his entire upper lip. If I get so much as an inkling that you might blab, I'll remove both your fucking lips and make you eat 'em. Now remove the chocks and straps so we can finish these checks. And don't talk about this shit."

The sentence I have to keep repeating in my head like a fucking automaton. *Don't talk about this shit. Don't talk about it, Doug. Fuck you, Doug.*

He rushes out into the rain to do as I've told him, without uttering a word. The rest of the night he says nothing unless I ask him a question and even then, he won't make eye contact with me. When the shift ends, he's out the door before I can say goodbye.

"You think he'll stay quiet?"

"I don't think he'll ever speak again, but who knows?"

"Think we better watch him? Tail him?"

"I don't think so. And anyway, that'd be impossible."

But I'm somehow not even scared. From the way he reacted on the plane, something tells me that I have nothing to worry about. I debate texting Cristy before I head home, but I'm still in a bizarre mood and don't want her to see me this way. Instead, I'll head home and see what I can find on Gerald.

Back home on my couch, I enter as many variations as possible of Gerald, Watson, Wallace, and child molesters, with no luck. When I try to narrow it down to Twin Peaks, endless results present themselves. There are dozens of places around the country called Twin Peaks. In Arizona alone, there are multiple places and trails with the name, but no actual town.

"This is ridiculous. This was supposed to be easy. Well, maybe not easy, but at least easier than the last one."

"You aren't going to be able to just hit a button and all the bad people will be listed out for you to choose from. It's going to take some digging."

"Yeah, well I'm tired. I'll dig some more tomorrow."

A few hours after dozing off, a text awakens me. I know it's just Cristy, so I ignore it and try to fall back asleep. Less than a minute after, I receive two more text alerts.

"Jesus Christ, you know I sleep during the day, woman."

When I read the messages, it jolts me fully alert. It's not Cristy at all. It's my cousin Crystal. *Hey, Matt. You there? They found Bo's killer. It was some guy he owed money to. Real nasty dude. Anyway. Call me.* I know deep inside she knows I won't call because I don't give a crap about Bo. I would feel bad for the guy they arrested for his murder instead, but according to Crystal, he was a 'real nasty dude' anyway, so screw him.

It's evident I won't be able to get any more sleep, so I begin my day. Drying off after a shower, I try to think of new avenues to pursue that could lead me to Gerald. The only person who knows where he lives is Cristy, but I can't just come out and ask her; that would be too obvious. I wish there were some way of getting the information without directly asking for it.

"I bet she has his info in a filing cabinet somewhere at her house."

"I'm not breaking into her home. Especially the home of a woman who lives alone. That's a list you don't want to be on, man. Oh, my God!"

I rush to the computer without putting any clothes on and type 'sex offender registry' into the search bar. A website comes up with multiple search options, including an interactive overview map. Starting from my current location, I widen the search area and check all the blue dots that appear. Each one gives me a picture, a name, and a link to a list of their offenses. I'm astounded by how many people are within a fifty-mile radius of me and grow angrier with each click.

"No… No… No… Holy shit!"

There he is. Jerry D. Watson of Marana, Arizona. I zoom into his location, and it shows me a white square to indicate his house with an address in the top right corner of the screen. Scrolling out to research the surrounding area, the name of his neighborhood pops up.

"Twin Peaks Estates. Are you fucking kidding me?"

Twin Peaks wasn't even a town. It was the name of a small group of homes west of Marana. I write down the address, then click on his profile link. The picture that pops up is his mugshot with the booking number and height. It says he's forty-six years old with brown eyes and brown hair, but he looks closer to sixty. The top of his head is bald and the thin silky strands on the sides are grayer than brown. His face is slender and emaciated with sunken eyes and his nose is long and thin. A bushy reddish-brown beard blankets his jawline and chin. He's the archetypal sex offender, the one you can pick out in the street. So I like to think, anyway. He's not someone I'd choose to live next door to.

"I'm going to start with that beard. I think he needs a trim."

The alarm on my phone cuts short the pre-planning as it starts to chime, alerting me that the day has begun.

Getting dressed, a feeling of disappointment fills me that I haven't heard from Cristy. Maybe she's finally decided that I'm not the person she wants to be around. Or maybe she's simply tired of trying so hard to get through my armor. Either way, deep inside, I know it's best if she stays away.

From outside the diner, I see that she is not at my booth, then feel a cramping sensation in my chest. I don't know why it bothers me that she isn't in there. I don't even know why I care. My best guess is that she is the only person I can stand to be around, other than myself. And maybe it's just nice to be liked. To have someone who seems keen to see me. I can't deny it's given me an ego boost lately.

When I walk through the doorway and turn toward the table, a single plate is already there. Confused, I look around the restaurant. Maybe they haven't cleared it yet. That won't do. They know to keep my table clean for me. As I approach, I notice that it's my usual meal, and still hot. I sit down and scan the room again, looking for anyone to protest. Trusting that the food has been put there for me, I take the fork and start to eat then notice the corner of a page sticking out from underneath the plate. When I pull it out, it's a note from Cristy.

'Happy Friday! Well, Wednesday for you. I'm sorry I missed you. I hope you enjoy the food.
And don't worry; I got the bill.

'Little Piggy.'

The cramping in my chest is replaced by a heavy pounding and my eyes begin to swell with pressure. This is a bizarre new emotion, one that's unfamiliar. What is this? A warm bead of liquid slowly travels down my cheek, and I recognize it… A single tear. I forced myself to never cry again many years ago as a child, to never shed a tear in sadness. I made that promise to myself. But the unintended consequence of being successful at it was that I would never shed a tear in happiness either because I would never allow myself to be vulnerable…to love.

"What the hell is she doing to me?"

Near Miss Mystery

Matt's Story

I stand outside the hangar door for a few minutes, dreading what crazy drama Doug's got lined up for me. What am I going to do if he brings it all back up again? How can I ensure that he'll keep his mouth shut? He's on a knife edge. Almost literally. There's not much further he can push me. Then it'll all be over for him. But we're not that far yet. I don't feel he's a threat, just an annoyance. I put my hand in my pocket to make sure I've remembered to bring my knife, just in case, then walk through the door. The hangar is empty, which can only mean one of two things; either the incoming aircraft's late, or we won't be getting one tonight. I cross my fingers and hope that it's the latter. Mike is prepping the assignment board when I approach.

"Which one is it, Mike?"

"Won't show till tomorrow, Matt. You can either pick up a broom or take the night off."

I'm already slowly backing away from his desk in anticipation.

"Screw that broom. I'm outta here. Did Doug leave already?"

"Nope. Called in sick. Told him we didn't have a bird anyway, so it doesn't need to count as a sick day. Have a good weekend. I'll see ya Sunday."

"Yep, see ya Sunday, boss."

Doug called in sick. I don't think so. Only Doug and I know the truth about why he isn't here tonight. I only hope he's curled up in his bed scared and he doesn't get the nerve to go running to the police. I know if I push him too hard, he'll think I'm leaving him with no choice but to go to them for protection, so I'm trying to give him a little breathing room. Just not too much. There's no time to worry about that right now, though, because I have a date waiting for me. Akin to a child rushing to get in line at a carnival ride, I race to my car. If I hurry, I'll have time to scout Gerald's house and maybe have some fun, if I'm lucky.

I briefly stop at the store to pick up a new knife, then head home to gather my other supplies. Rummaging through my garage, I find that I have run out of the large zip-ties and only have a package of the smaller ones left. Using more of the smaller ones will be as effective as fewer large ones. I put them in the bag. The air is cool but not nearly as chilly as it will be in a few hours, so I bring a black sweater, just in case. Taking the go-bag over my shoulder, I make my way to the door. Packed inside are a knife, tape, zip-ties, and a three-pound hammer.

"Oh shit. I almost forgot."

I retrieve the phone from my pocket, then etch his address into memory. Finally, I place the phone on the kitchen counter before walking out. Standing on my front porch, I take in a deep breath of the cool air, close my eyes, then hold it for a few seconds before blowing out, opening my eyes simultaneously, then striding to my car. On the highway, I try formulating a plan, but don't know enough about the area.

Although the target only lives an hour away, I've never had a reason to travel that far north until now. The aerial map shows that the neighborhood is made up of four separate editions, resting on the edge of a desert preserve to the west. Maybe I could get him out there somehow.

"Just kill him in his home. You can always clean up the evidence after."

"What if he makes too much noise?"

"That's why we have the hammer, dude. You could knock out a rhino with that thing."

"So, we somehow knock him out, then bind and gag him before torturing him, then kill him. Afterward, we remove any trace evidence. Sounds simple enough. Let's try that."

It's nearly nine o'clock when I pull over, parking across from where I suspect he lives. There are around fifty houses in this section of the community, all looking identical. But it's my lucky night. Someone has painted all the addresses on the curbs in front of all the homes, so I'm fairly certain that I am in the right place. Few other cars stand parked on the road at this hour, but I'm not worried about being spotted because the streets aren't illuminated, and the moonlight isn't breaking through the clouds.

For hours, I stare attentively at the front window lit only by the glow of a television. No other rooms in the home show any sign of habitation. Shortly after midnight, the window abruptly goes dark, my adrenaline starting to flow.

"Not yet. Let's wait a little bit before getting a closer look."

Time slogs by, waiting for exactly one hour to pass. Every minute feels like a goddamn hour in itself. I stretch my legs, pushing back the seat as far as it will go. I lean back, close my eyes, try to relax. Impossible. I can't imagine it would take much longer for him to fall asleep. It's so unnervingly quiet around here that my ears continuously create a ringing noise that pulses with my heart rate. Every so often, the sound of a car door closing in the distance followed by an alarm horn cuts through the silence, reminding me there are other people around.

Finally, the clock shifts to twelve and I slowly make my way up to the house. Delicately twisting the doorknob, unsurprisingly, I find that it's locked. Well, it is my lucky night after all; work did not need me, giving me the night off, and then some sucker painted the numbers on all the curbs. Two amazing coincidences. Two pieces of luck. Good things come in threes, right? Because of that, I think he'll surely have left a window unlatched or open. A lot of people in Arizona leave their windows open on cool nights such as this. I creep to the side gate leading to his backyard with slow, careful steps because it's landscaped only with gravel. Every movement creates a crunching and grinding sound beneath my feet. Following the path along the side of his home, I use the wall that separates his yard from his neighbors for balance. Halfway down the path, I hear rocks shuffling in the neighbor's yard followed by a low growl. I pin my back to the brick wall and freeze. The growls build in intensity and duration and with it, my heartbeat. A single bark causes me to flinch and squeeze my eyelids shut.

"What is it, boy? Hear something? Where's it at? Show me."

He shuffles and barks just inches from me, separated only by the block wall. I hear a snap and watch as a beam of light casts back and forth over my head. My chest tightens and aches. I dare not move or even breathe.

"Well, I don't see anything boy. Let's go inside."

After they are gone, I can't force myself to move. I'm petrified in place, thinking about how close I came to someone catching me. *Just breathe. Relax and get your shit together*. It takes close to ten minutes and dozens of deep breaths to finally calm down enough to move my feet and although it's almost sixty-five degrees outside, I am sweating profusely. Inching forward little by little, I finally make it to the back entrance, a double-paned sliding glass door. With two fingers, I firmly pull the handle, and with a small pop, it smoothly slides open.

Inside, the home is surprisingly organized and clean. Other than a few dirty dishes on the counter, there is no obvious clutter. There is a noticeable hint of alcohol in the air and an empty bottle of off-brand whisky on the coffee table. I don't see a glass nearby, which leads me to believe he was drinking straight from the bottle. Maybe he drank himself to sleep. The carpeting is thick, making it easy to travel around the home without making any noise and the single hallway has only a few small plugin lamps to light it. It's dim.

I peek my head into two of the bedrooms to find they are both decorated in pink lacey curtains with teddy bears and clouds painted on the walls. There are no beds or furniture of any kind in either bedroom. Only a single pink and white rocking horse sits in the corner of the room to the right and a full black garbage bag remains in the middle of the room to the left.

Upon entering the master bedroom, the aroma of alcohol strengthens greatly, causing my nose to furrow. On the bed is a man lying on his stomach above the blankets in boxer shorts, snoring faintly. I stand over him, watching, imagining the things he could have done to his children. My rage intensifies. I gently open the bag, retrieving the hammer. Then I place the bag on the floor. Without hesitation, I swing the head of the hammer down into the back of his head, scattering red droplets in every direction. His arms and legs jerk upon impact but lie motionless afterward. I forcefully shake him to be certain. Seems I knocked him right out.

I had no chance to play with him first, no chance for torture and torment. It's fair to say I'm a little disappointed. But at least he's out and pliable for what I need to do. It's only sad he passed out so easily and quickly, no suffering. Aren't they all supposed to suffer, these abusers? I wish they would. Never mind. When he regains consciousness later, I'll make sure he gets what's coming to him then. I just hope to get the chance.

"Hey, you awake?"

He doesn't move or make a sound; he's even stopped snoring now, so I check his pulse to make sure he's still alive. It's faint but it's there, so I continue with preparation, tightly wrapping the tape around his mouth and then binding his feet together. I use the same roll, before moving on to his hands. The tape is exactly the right amount, almost down to the bare cardboard in the middle. I have more in the car, but it's good how I knew exactly how much to bring inside for now. Well, I have always been meticulous. In part, I suppose that is why I chose the job I do. It is no different when preparing someone to transport them safely and securely. I've learned the hard way that it's easier to move someone with unbound hands first and then bind them when they are where I want them to be.

Pulling his outstretched arms, I drag him into the living room and roll him onto his stomach, then force his arms behind him and strap three zip-ties around his wrists. They fit perfectly; a sense of relief washes over me as I can now shelve the anxiety about having no long zip-ties.

"All right, I think we are good now. We'll start in a few minutes."

I no longer know who I'm talking to. To myself or to my captive. Either way, this time, I get no response which is a little dispiriting after all the effort in such careful preparation. I turn on the lights to get a good look at him on the floor. It's strange seeing his appearance now. He has to have gained at least thirty pounds since someone took the picture that I saw. His face is rounder, his cheeks fuller, and his thin long chin is now wide and sagging. He has flabby jowls. If I had passed by him on the street, I may not have even recognized him. This time, I'm not sure I'd immediately pick him out as a dirty pervert, but there you are. It just shows how we can walk among them and never know. I realize the same applies to me. People pass by me and don't recognize me for what I am either. Oddly, it delivers a sense of pride. Something about having such an alter ego is satisfying.

The grandfather clock chimes loudly, begging for me to begin. I don't think I could wait any longer, even if I wanted to after hearing it. Each bell ring is a countdown, drawing me closer to inevitability; when the last strike fades off, I roll him onto his back and take my usual position atop his torso.

"Hey Gerald, you awake?"

Using the back of my fingers, I caress his cheek repeatedly. The carpet below his head is saturated with his blood and the pool is slowly expanding, worrying me that I may have hit him too hard and have little time left. The air is thick with the stench of iron, the smell that can only come from human blood—a lot of it. It assaults my lungs and sinuses with every breath, making me heave.

"Wakey, wakey, sleepy head!"

I draw my hand away from his cheek, extend my fingers, then slap him across the face. After a few seconds, I strike him again. Raising my arm for a third blow, I'm thrilled to see his eyes fluttering behind his eyelids.

"There you go. Come on out, Gerald. We got things to do, big boy."

Lightly pinching his left eyelid, I pull it open to examine his eye. It's shaking frantically from side to side, but his pupil constricts to the light, so I know he can still see. Watching the eye jump so crazily is fascinating; I could do it for hours. The show comes sharply to an end when his other eyelid bursts open, and he locks them both onto me.

"Finally, you were so out of it, man. I think I hit you just a little bit too hard. Really sorry about that. I'll note that for next time, though. You see, I try to learn stuff from each experience. I'm still sort of a novice at this."

He thrusts and slides his hips to get free, attempting to scream. He flails and writhes, bucking his body. But he will be limp soon. It's inevitable; the tape and zip ties have him so tightly bound, it will be exhausting to move and he's not young. I move my body along with his until he tires and stops with an angry huff. Only resting for a few seconds, he begins the irritating tirade again, until I bring the knife to his throat. His body grows rigid and his breathing rapid and shallow.

"Do I have your attention now?"

He nods in acceptance.

"Okay good. So, here's what's going to happen. Now please bear with me because I haven't worked out every detail yet. First, I want to trim this nasty ass beard. I mean come on, man, it's gross. Second, your dick needs to come off; seeing as it's done most of the damage, it should be the first thing, don't you think? Hmm, maybe we can do something with it afterward. I don't know, we can play that one by ear. Are you ready?"

He jerks and pulls when I grab a fist full of his beard and draw the knife up from under his chin. The frenzy grows more intense with the initial incision and it's becoming harder to keep him down. Like riding a bucking bull while trying to fillet a fish, the cut is inconsistent and jagged. Once I get to the front of his chin with less than an inch of flesh to go, I hear three snaps in quick succession, then find it difficult to breathe. My veins are bulging, head getting hot. In a panic, I drop the knife and reach for my neck, but his meaty hands are in the way. Peering down, I see his arms are free and his hands are grappling around my throat.

His evil eyes gaze right into mine as I feel myself fading into the darkness, and I can't help but wonder in my last moment if he sees the same evil in mine. I accept that this is my fate, although I deserve much worse, and relax for the end. I never expected this; life is full of surprises. Here comes purgatory. Here comes perdition. Everything goes black.

***

"Cough-cough. Cough."

There is a light at the far end of the darkness, growing in size and intensity. By the time it makes it to me, it's so bright that I can't stare directly at it. Through barely parted eyelids, I search for a way out but can't move. The more I scan, the more my eyes acclimatize to the blinding light, until an image begins to appear. Fuzzy, brown, and curly. And with random bits stuck on its surface. *What is that?* I open my eyes wider to focus and recognize that it's carpet. Confused and weak, I lift myself to the couch, take a seat, and bury my hands into my palms.

The memory of what happened slowly comes back and fills my gut with pain. I know the police will be here any minute to arrest me and they will no doubt connect me to Jeremy's and maybe even Bo's murders. This is it; this is my last moment of freedom. I'm not going to spend it in this piece of shit's house though. I'd rather they take me from my own home, so I rub my eyes with my fingers and stand to leave, but I'm stopped by an unbelievable sight. Lying before me is Gerald on his back, my knife sticking out from his chest. I examine the room for clues as to how this may have happened, but everything is as it was before I passed out. The front door is still locked, but the back sliding door is wide open.

Did I leave that open? Did I close it? I have no idea. Regardless, something bizarre is going on because I know I'm not the one who stabbed him. There is a large puddle of blood under and around his body and a long streak of it leading to the door. It's apparent someone has dragged the poor fucker from the entry to where he rests right now, all the way along the carpet. It wasn't me. I know it wasn't my doing.

What's not apparent is how the knife ended up four inches deep into his chest. What the fuck is going on? Was there someone else here? Why would they do this and where the hell did they go? Will they soon come for me too? I know I have been prone to daydreams and acting out in them, but this is far beyond anything I have experienced. The last thing I remember is choking in the exact spot where I woke up. There is no way I would have done all this, then returned to lie on the floor to fall asleep.

It would be a bad idea to stick around too much longer to figure this out; the person might still be around. After all, they probably saw me on the floor and assumed I was already dead. I grab my bag and kneel briefly next to his body. Pulling the knife out is harder than I thought it would be. I have to wiggle it back and forth before it breaks free. Using the knife, I cut the tape off his feet and face and remove the broken ties on his wrists, then toss everything into the bag.

Once I'm certain there is no more evidence in the home, I walk to the door, but I'm afraid to open it. What if there is an army of police officers out there waiting on me? Worse yet, what if whoever did this is out there?

"Screw it."

I open the door and peek outside. It's as quiet and eerie as it was when I arrived, but much cooler. Stepping over the streaks of blood on the floor so I won't leave shoeprints, I quickly look around the corner, expecting someone to be there, but there is no one. I close the door behind me and with my back to it, glance around, waiting for something to happen. I listen carefully for any sounds that would alert me to the impending assault, but there is none; only the mating calls of crickets fill the air.

When I finally gather up the courage to run to my car, it feels as though I am running from something; not just the crime scene, but from someone… Someone just like me. The hunter may have become the prey.

"What the hell did I get myself into?"

New Dilemma

Matt's Story

I step out of the shower and wipe the fog from the mirror. The face before me is unrecognizable. My neck is swollen and bruised, and my eyes are lined with ruptured blood vessels. It's hard to speak; even breathing feels like burning needles on the inside of my throat. I place my palm over my battered reflection. *What have you become? Is this where you want to be?* I slowly slide my hand down the slippery glass, turning away before noticing his sadness.

My heart hasn't calmed since leaving Gerald's house two hours ago; my mind will not let it. There are too many unanswered questions and any of the answers to them would be liabilities for me. I was scheduled to be at work, so there's no reason for anyone to suspect I'd be planning to travel an hour away to kill someone tonight unless they followed me. Then again, how would they have done that? Were they waiting in front of my house for me to leave? If they were, did they know what I was on my way to do? It was pitch black outside. I would have seen their headlights from a mile away.

Every attempt to figure out an answer only results in more questions piling up in an ever more perplexing maze, comprised only of dead ends. Pacing the dark bedroom, I repeat the questions in my head, to no end. Who could have done it? Why? How did they know? How…how…how? Exhausted, my body reaches its limit and can take no more for tonight, so I abandon my thoughts where they are. After some rest, I'll have to figure this out in the morning. Tossing in my bed, sporadic questions keep popping into my brain, preventing me from passing the threshold into sleep. I'm stuck in limbo between awake and out cold when I receive a text.

Already tired and irritated, I snatch the phone off the table angrily. *Hey, you wanna have breakfast?* I look at the time and see that it's six-fifteen, the time I would normally be on my way home from work. *Sorry Cristy but I'm not feeling well at all. Throat hurts. Maybe this afternoon after I get some rest.* There is no way I'm in any condition to eat right now, even if I wanted to; I can barely even speak. *Aww, okay. Well, feel better. Let me know.* I put the phone back on the table without responding and bury my head back into my pillow.

The receptors fire in my brain so energetically that my hair follicles tingle. With my eyes closed, I follow the movements of the questions across my eyelids, like a canvas. They cascade from all directions, flying in and then trailing out. Eventually, I relax and let my thoughts fade into oblivion.

The alarm wakes me at four, but I don't want to get up. I feel as though I have been rolling down a rocky slope all night. Every muscle and joint aches and spasms when I struggle to move. Eventually, I force myself to climb out of bed and into a steaming hot shower. The pulsating hot water relaxes and eases my body, leaving me still sore but able to move more freely. Brushing my teeth, my stomach grumbles, cramping from hunger. The swelling in my throat has gone down slightly and although raspy, I can speak now, but I'm not sure I could endure the pain of eating. Still, I should try. I debate inviting Cristy, but I still look really rough and don't want her to see me this way. Who knows what questions she would have for me, seeing me in this condition? I grab my keys and open the front door to find a package waiting for me. I find a plastic container full of soup and a note when I open it.

'I'm sorry you aren't feeling well. Here's some soup. Just microwave it for two minutes.

'Cristy.'

The delightful feeling from her amazingly kind act is swiftly replaced by frustration and confusion. How the hell does she know where I live? Has she always known? I can't move past it and need to know immediately, so I text her. *Thank you so much for the soup, but how did you know where I lived?* I close the door and put the soup in the microwave as I wait for her reply. Almost in sync, the phone and the microwave both ding at the same moment. *Your address is on file, silly. I read it weeks ago when you first came to see me. I actually used to live in the house at the end of your street. Small world.*

House at the end of the street? That house hasn't been for sale since I've lived here. Maybe she left there before I moved in. *Ah. It was just strange to find that you knew where I lived. It was a bit of a shock. You know how private I am, so it wasn't what I expected!*

She's a psychiatrist, so surely to God there's no way she doesn't understand how bizarre this is. *I'm sorry. I just wanted to do something nice.* I hear the sad tone in her text, and it makes me feel bad for even bringing it up as an issue. She went out of her way to do something nice for me and here I am questioning her like a criminal. *Oh no, I'm sorry. I was only wondering is all. Thank you for the soup. I'm going to get some more rest. Have a good night.*

I sit on the couch, careful not to spill any of the steaming hot soup on the floor, then turn the television on. Maybe there will be news about Gerald's death. I would love to feel excited about seeing the coverage, but technically, I'm not the one who killed him, am I? If anything, I am nervous about what they might report because it's I grim reminder that there is someone out there like me who knows me, and most likely knows where I live…*Where I live.*

"Where I live! Cristy knows where I live!"

"You're kidding, right? You were doing this before you met her, and she hasn't got a clue that you've been killing people."

"That's true. Plus, why would she do this? She has no reason to."

Motive. That's what I should be focusing on. Who would gain from following me to Gerald's house? Is it a coincidence that this happened after I killed Jeremy? The only person who knows about me killing Jeremy is…

"Fucking Doug. You slick crazy bastard!"

He's probably been spying on me since he saw me at the bar that night. All the questions about how it felt and did he scream; he's a psychotic killer in the making. Well, now an active killer since he's killed Gerald. The thought of him standing over my lifeless body on the floor sends chills down my spine. I wonder what he was thinking, staring at me, seemingly dead. It probably made him feel good, powerful even. He's done the job that I couldn't, and I lay there marinating in my own failure, while he stands tall as the ultimate predator among us.

Envisioning it causes my eyes to fill with so much pressure that my sight blurs. My anger reaches a climax as I pound my fist onto the table, spilling the still-warm bowl of soup onto the floor.

"Not today, Doug. I gave you a chance. You chose this. You chose me."

I spend hours trying to get into the void to imagine torturing Doug, but I haven't been able to go there for over a week. Something is wrong. Maybe it was my way of dealing with things in the past and now that I have a new way of coping, I no longer need it. My anger and lust for pain have been free to flow for a month now. Over that time, I have needed to use the void less and less. I only want to see what it would feel like to have my hands wrapped around his throat, to see the look on his face when he realizes that his actions have put him in my path of destruction and pain. If he would have only left it alone, he would be out there living life. Instead, he gets to look into my apathetic eyes as I squeeze the life from him. Because he got in my way, took the glory from me, robbed me of the opportunity to rob Gerald's life. The frustration is driving me crazy. I slap the sides of my head repeatedly.

"Fucking do it already. Take me there. I wanna kill this fucker for what he—"

I understand what's happening now. I had lost the taste for harming innocent people in the void weeks ago. Since then, I have had other things to keep me satisfied and haven't had a reason to revisit. I can't go there with him because he hasn't hurt me or anyone else that wasn't deserving. Currently, Doug is still not worthy of me, at least in my conscious. Even though he has killed, it was an evil person and it needed to be done.

"So, are you going to let him live then?"

"What? No, he still needs to die. I just won't torture him, and I'll feel bad about it this time."

Although my mind won't let me imagine killing him, my body is more than capable of doing it. He hasn't proven to be an evil person yet, but I still have to do it because I warned him, and he disregarded it. I always follow through with my promises, even if I may feel bad afterward. I receive a text that redirects my attention. *Breakfast?* I look at the clock: eleven in the morning. *It's Friday, don't you have work?*

My right eye is still red and faint bruises line both sides of my neck. I'm nervous about her seeing it. *No more patients today. Come on. I'll meet you in 30. I'll buy!* In the mirror, I inspect my face meticulously before I decide. What am I going to say happened? A fight? *Okay fine. I'm on my way.*

When I arrive, I'm not surprised to see her already seated in my booth, even though I'm fifteen minutes early. She smiles and waves through the window as I approach the door. My pace is sluggish and timid to the table.

"Oh my God. What happened to you?"

"I got into a fight last night."

"A fight? Weren't you at work?"

A detail I hadn't thought about.

"Uh, yeah. It happened at work. Some guy I work with attacked me. It's fine now."

She turns her head slightly to the side like a dog trying to understand its owner. When she squints, I hear the wheels turning in her head, trying to decide if I'm being truthful. Her eyes narrow. She is assessing me, the 'interesting person' that she said I was.

"That's crazy. What was it about?"

I've only been here ten seconds and already feel like she's interrogating me. It's been a long twenty-four hours and I'm not really in the mood to answer questions. I know she's just trying to be sympathetic, but the best way to sympathize with me right now is to leave me alone.

"I'd rather not talk about it. Let's talk about you. How was your day?"

For a split second, she seems to be thinking about asking a follow-up question. She quickly reconsiders.

"Uh…yeah, okay. So, I saw that girl I was telling you about the other day; the drug addict."

"Yeah, I remember her."

"She was my only patient today. Anyway, her in-laws got custody of her daughter and she even lives with them too—the mother does, not just the child. It's a pretty dangerous situation because I can see her kidnapping her own kid. It would be so easy since she's right there, ya know?"

I don't care about any of this. She's reminding me of Doug, that incessant chatter about something and nothing, and certainly not about anything I care to listen to. I'm not sure why I even accepted to come out today. I feel like shit. My head is pounding, and I just want this meeting to be over with, but don't want her to be mad at me either. She has been nothing but sweet to me and doesn't deserve a rude response. How can I end this irritating conversation without being mean?

"You there, Matt?"

"Yeah, sorry. Is there any way you can influence the judge to reconsider?"

"I wish, but the Brewers are pretty well off, and according to the judge, they are a stable family for the baby."

Brewers? I know a Brewer. My interest in the conversation is now peaking. I swing my shoulders upright and look intently at her.

"Did you say, Brewers? Is the father of the little girl Doug Brewer?"

"How did you know that?"

I can barely hold in my astonishment at how coincidental this is. What are the odds that we would be talking about the family of the man I am planning on killing right now?

"Uh, I work with the guy. He's a weird dude."

"Yeah, I know."

"I never even knew he was ever married. Why didn't he get custody of his daughter?"

"They were only married for a short time, and I can't tell you. Doctor-patient confidentiality."

"He was your patient?"

"Oh…I guess not. His ex-wife was, so I guess I can tell you. He was abusive to her. A very angry man."

That is a side I have never once seen from Doug. He's always been so standoffish and awkward, timid really. Maybe he only shows his true side in secret, like me. Wait…is that why he's always talking to me? Does he think we are the same? He thinks we are kindred spirits, apparently.

"The courts won't let him have custody because he beat his wife?"

The rarely seen serious gaze from Cristy punches through me like a lightning bolt.

"He's pretty much been disowned by his family because he attacks everyone in his life. He hit his ex-wife, his mom, and his dad. The police have arrested him like five times, but his family keeps bailing him out, in hopes that he'll change. They feel bad for his ex; that's why they let her live with them. She doesn't pay rent or anything."

That slippery bastard. This is just another example of how every single person I have ever met is a liar, all of them, including myself. I have worked with that kid for two and a half years and not once did I know he had a child or was aggressive. I don't know why, I just imagined him as some lonely weirdo who sat on the couch watching tv or playing computer games. Hell, I can't even imagine him having a sex life, let alone a daughter. He's played the role of a helpless new mechanic for so long and so well that we were all fooled.

"He's such a timid kid at work that it's hard to believe."

"Listen, Matt. People hide behind layers and only show the one they want at any given time. The layer you got was what he needed to show at the time. His core is what the people who know him best get."

I understand exactly what she means because I have been breaking down people that way for over a decade. She is only getting the layer of myself that I want to show, and I hope that she will never have to see my core.

"I know what you mean. I already knew there was something strange with that guy but couldn't put my finger on it. Now I can."

I look at the table and then around the diner.

"Hey, aren't we going to eat?"

"Eat? No, I already ate. I thought you were sick, so I have soup in the car for you to take home."

"But we've been sitting here for so long."

"They know it's our table."

"Oh, my God! I love—"

I stop myself short of a colossal mistake. How could I even let myself go down that path?

"Did you just say—"

"No, let's go."

We both slide out of the booth and Cristy drops a fifty-dollar bill onto the table. We hadn't even eaten anything. When we get to her car, she opens the passenger door and pulls out a box similar to the one she left on my porch yesterday. Inspecting her car, it looks so familiar.

"Black Beemer huh? Looks like we are both dumb enough to have black cars in Arizona."

"Haha. Well hard to see black at night…you know, for the cops."

After a laugh, we both hug goodbye, but this hug feels more personal, full of energy and emotion. We pull away slightly and stare at each other for a few moments. She seems to be waiting for me to say or do something.

"Oh, good Lord!"

She grabs my face with both hands and pushes her lips to mine. My heart pounds through my chest feeling her warm, moist lips against mine. When she pulls away, her magnetic attraction pulls me with her. Falling one step forward, I'm interrupted by her outstretched hand.

"Whoa boy. Let's not get ahead of ourselves. One step at a time."

Her smile makes me grin awkwardly. She senses my embarrassment and moves in close
.

"We have time."

She pecks me on the lips and hops into her car. I stand to the side and watch her drive away. She is so amazing. I want to be with her, but can I diverge from the current path I have chosen? Can I change and choose to live a normal life? And does it even matter if I do change—since I might be locked away soon anyway?

"Let's kill Doug first, then we can settle down and have a life with Cristy."

The Final Solution

Matt's Story

With outstretched arms and a long bellowing yawn, I awake from the first good night's sleep I've had in almost a week. I scrape the morning crust from my eyes with my fingertips and walk lazily to the bathroom, where I smile at my reflection. I'm relieved to finally recognize myself again. The swelling is almost completely gone and only a small red spot remains in my right eye.

"I haven't seen you in a while. You're looking a lot better, my dude."

Now that I am well-rested, I can focus on my next target…Doug. The details of the previous day's conversation are a bit fractured, at first, but are slowly coming together as I grow more alert. Cristy had said that Doug was an aggressive and abusive man who has attacked multiple family members. Hard to imagine, but if Cristy believes it, then it must be true. Regardless, I was going to kill him anyway; the fresh information only adds to my reasoning and removes any remorse I may have felt.

Back into my routine, I plop onto the couch with my freshly made breakfast and flip the television on, hoping that there is coverage of Gerald's murder. It takes little time to find a news station that's reporting from the scene.

"Officials say he was found dead this morning in the living room of this home right behind me. It's believed the attack occurred sometime Wednesday night. They won't say how he was killed, but they did mention that it was an exceptionally gruesome scene. He was found by a postal worker who says that the door was partially open when they walked up to the porch and saw a trail of blood, followed by noticing what looked to be a man's legs on the floor. They immediately called nine-one-one."

I recall when I left the home. I know for a fact that I had closed the door completely before leaving. My heart flutters in my chest, trying to guess what may have happened after that.

"Holy fuck. Was Doug still in the house when I left?"

***

My eyes are glued to the screen, concentrating on the front of the house. I see myself on the porch with my back to the door, looking around. In the right bedroom window, I make out a shadow peering through the blinds. Sliding to the floor, I begin crawling closer to get a better look, almost able to make out who it is, if only I could get even closer. I bring my face right up to the glass, expecting my forehead to hit it but instead, my face passes freely through, and I'm surrounded by white noise. I keep pushing forward unhindered until the bright white and black static give way to a midnight sky.

I'm on the porch of Gerald's home, standing in the exact position I was in a few nights ago. Inside, I hear the muffled movement of someone shuffling their feet as they walk around. I try to open the door but my hand phases through the knob in a wisp of air. My chest grows heavy staring at the brown wooden door, envisioning what's happening on the other side. In a slow build-up, my breathing increases in tempo as I clench my fists.

"You did this to yourself, Doug!"

Jumping through the door, I'm startled by the instant change in illumination. The room is brighter than I remember; scanning around, I realize why. There are no walls or floors, just endless white. The only things in here are Gerald, me, and a shadowy figure. My body rests on the floor motionless, the shadow kneeling next to it. I can faintly hear it whispering as I move in closer. From over its shoulder, it's caressing my cheek with my own knife while talking to me.

"You see what you did to me? I suppose you think this is fortuitous. It's not! You created me and I am about to reap what you sowed!"

It raises the knife above its head and plunges it into my torso.

***

I'm immediately thrust back into my living room with my hands tightly clutching at my chest. It's hard to breathe, feeling the blade still embedded within me, and incessantly attempt to remove it.

"What—what the fuck? What was that? That's exactly what I said to Bo. Was that supposed to be Doug? Was he telling me that I made him into a monster like me?"

Over an hour passes and I still keep reaching for my chest to remove the knife. The pain has lessened, but it's still there, a dull stabbing sensation deep within. It's obvious that my mind has been trying to tell me something from the void, but I can't decipher it. All I know is that I didn't see Doug in the form that I expected. I'm too shaken to think straight right now.

"We need to relax for a bit. We can't go out there like this."

I pour a glass of Scotch and turn on the radio to calm down. Lying on the couch, I slowly sip the Mortlach twelve-year I had been saving for a special occasion, even though there hasn't been a special enough reason to open it in the four years I've had it. I argue that this may be my last opportunity to drink it since I don't expect to get away with this one. One of the major mistakes that people make is killing people close to them. Although Doug and I aren't friends, I'm sure he has spoken about me, especially since I'm the only person he talks to at work. Nevertheless, a promise is a promise; Doug must die.

Taking down the last sip of my second glass of Scotch, I hold it in my mouth to savor the smokey caramel flavor. This may very well be the last time I get to taste it or freedom for that matter. I let it gradually slide down and coat the walls of my throat, so warm and comforting that I close my eyes in tranquility and hold it for a few seconds.

"Now I'm ready. Are you ready?"

"I was ready before you were, man."

I grab my Ruger pistol before putting my shoes on. I want this to be quick and easy, with no games and no torture. This is my last party whether they catch me for my crimes or not. I just want to be in and out. Afterward, I'll either be in prison or will be with Cristy, both results that I have come to terms with. I take one last look at my scarcely furnished home before I leave. Why I would ever want to come back to such a pitiful life?

"What do you even have to live for? Look at this shithole. You are a pathetic human being."

"I am who I was meant to be. I just waited too long to realize that."

The door creeps closed with me standing in the doorway. I remain in place for a few moments when I receive a text. I already know who it is before I look. *Hungry?* She always seems to text me at the worst times. *Can't right now. A little busy.* After I respond, I realize that it may be the last time I will ever get a chance to see her again. Hell, it'll probably be the last time she ever wants to see me after she finds out what I've been doing. *Actually yes, I am hungry. Meet at the Vietnamese restaurant in Green Valley?* I consider this my last meal request before execution. *Sure, see ya in 30.*

When I arrive, Cristy is waiting for me in the parking lot, leaning against her front bumper. This is the first time I have ever seen her in shorts and flip-flops, and I like it. She looks great in comfortable attire and reminds me of a car model in the way she is posing with her BMW and beautiful smile.

"You're looking a lot better, slugger."

I run my hand across my face.

"Yeah, I was looking pretty rough, but I'm right as rain now. Ready for my next bout."

"Haha. Get over here already."

I meet her at her car and wrap my hands around her waist. She throws her arms over my shoulders and looks at me with such adoration that my legs begin to weaken. I wish that this could be my life, but time and circumstance have already determined our destiny. She senses the sadness on my face.

"Hey, are you okay? What's wrong?"

For the first time in longer than I can remember, I begin sobbing uncontrollably. Not just a single tear, but an unending supply of emotion runs down both of my cheeks. She wipes them with her bare wrist, then kisses them clean.

"Hey—hey, tell me what's going on."

The pressure builds as I find it harder to catch my breath between whines. She pulls my head into her chest and runs her fingers down the back of my head repeatedly.

"Shh. It's okay. Whatever it is, it'll be okay. You don't have to tell me if you don't want."

Her embrace feels like a warm blanket around me. I calm with the beat of her heart against my chest. *Thump...Thump...Thump.* It massages my stress and worries away with each beat until I feel like a limp piece of meat within her grasp. I slip through her arms and back away a little.

"I'm sorry. I never wanted you to see me like this. It's just been so much craziness lately."

"No, please don't be sorry. I always knew you were hurting inside. I don't want to pry, but I'm here if you wanna talk about it."

The sincerity in her eyes makes me want to start bawling again; I look away and bury my face into my shoulder. She reaches out and cups my cheek with her hand.

"Hey, let's go in and get something to eat. You'll feel better after a bowl of pho. *Everything* is better after a bowl of pho!"

I smile, not because of her compassion, but because she not only knows what pho is but also how to pronounce it correctly. She clasps my hand and leads me to the restaurant entrance before opening the door for me.

"After you, madame."

My face beams in reverence as I pass by her. The restaurant is tiny, with only six tables evenly spread within a two-hundred-square-foot area. We sit at the table nearest the door.

"Have you ever eaten here before?"

"When I was married, my wife and I ate here all the time."

"That's right, you used to be married. How is your ex these days?"

I never think about my past life anymore. There she is, delving again into areas I'd rather not go. It feels as if every conversation has to be about unearthing my past, though I sense she is sincerely interested, and I am not some kind of pitiful project in psychiatry. Maybe she's just more used to talking than I am. And maybe that's because she clearly has nothing to hide, unlike some of us—I mean me, of course. But either way, I don't want to sit here talking about my past, about the period when I was able to fake who I was to seem like the average husband and father. The loving dad who went on date nights and took his kids to their sporting events. The only reason I did any of those things was because it's what I saw other men around me doing. I assumed that it was what I was supposed to do. Five years into our marriage, my façade began to crack, and eventually, she declared she'd had enough of my unremitting depression.

"I apologize. I can tell that was a bit too personal."

"Oh, not at all. I just…I haven't talked to her or my kids in years. I don't keep in touch."

She stares at me with a slight frown. She feels sorry for me—or perhaps it's more that she dislikes me losing contact with my children—and wants to ask more. With Cristy, it's as if all her emotions display on her face. She can't hide a thing. She probably doesn't try. But right now, she holds back just a little, for which I am grateful. She looks momentarily vexed, then awfully sad at what I say. Multiple questions show in her expression. She won't let them loose. Probably, that's from her fear of causing me to get emotional again. She knows I don't do emotions very well. Oddly, I am not ashamed of crying in front of Cristy; with her, I can be myself. The last thing I want is someone else joining in or even over-commiserating!

"Can I get you two something to drink?"

I look up at the waitress who is facing me but can't get myself to speak. Cristy reaches across the table and puts her hand over mine.

"He will take water and I'll take a green tea. Also, can we get two large bowls of pho?"

"Yes ma'am. I will bring it out shortly."

Cristy's fingers begin delicately rubbing the back of my hand, causing goosebumps to appear on my arm. How could someone so caring, so beautiful, so captivating be interested in me? A man whose sole purpose in life right now is to cause pain and death. I begin weighing my options. *Do I have to kill Doug? I can stop right now and choose to be with her.* Then again, I would be living every moment in fear that he would run to the cops. I would just have begun a new life, a clean life, with Cristy. It would all be perfect. We would be settling into our harmonious bliss together, each going to work, coming home, sharing news of our days over a home-cooked dinner and a glass of fine wine. We'd be holding hands, planning our future, booking holidays, buying a car—all those things. Hell, we might even buy a home together. Big commitments, big investment of my heart.

Then, along would come this horrendous shadow from my past. It would break us. No, I can't go ahead thinking that he—Doug—might pop up anytime and destroy me. There's also the concern that since killing Gerald, he might want to come after me next or worse, Cristy. No, I have to do it if I have any hope of moving on. I must eliminate Doug for my safety and peace of mind. I roll my eyes up to meet Cristy's. My future lies in hers. She's just grinning with her left brow slightly raised.

"What?"

"Nothing. I was just seeing how long you were going to be in your little world without me interrupting you."

"Yeah? How long was it?"

"Uh, around five minutes this time."

What does she mean by 'this time'? Do I make a habit of this? Apparently so. I feel slightly aggrieved; she is always observing me, always watching me, always commenting on how I am. It's especially irritating because she's right. I have always hated that, all my life. I have always detested people telling me I am this or that, acting this way, behaving that way. Stop watching me all the time, for Christ's sake. But the weird thing is that in this case—because it's Cristy who keeps telling me these things—the irritation passes by. It's Cristy. I *like* Cristy. A lot.

The server drops off our two large bowls of rice noodle soup and a second server quickly follows behind her with our drinks.

"Can I get you anything else?"

"No thank you. We're fine for now."

She wastes no time pulling the steaming noodles from the bowl and blowing on them lightly before stuffing them into her mouth. The slurping and smacking sound she makes should irritate me but at this moment, they are the sweetest noises in the room. See, again I make allowances for Cristy. I must really like her a lot, perhaps more than I am admitting to myself. We share glances at each other as we eat, with little conversation between bites.

Once we get outside though, I notice her demeanor change. She's more serious and her body language is less relaxed, almost like a doctor getting ready to deliver bad news to a family member. This time, it's my turn to ask Cristy what's wrong instead of her asking me. I put my hand on her shoulder and turn her to face me.

"Okay, now what's going on with you?"

Her lower lip quivers as she fights back the tears.

"I need to talk to you, but not right now. I want you to promise me something."

"Sure, anything."

She grabs both sides of my shirt and pulls me to her, so close that I can feel the warmth of her breath as she speaks.

"I promise I will tell you everything if you promise me that you'll get some rest and calm down emotionally. I saw how torn up you were earlier, and it scares me."

"You're scared of me?"

"What? No. I'm scared *for* you, not of you."

If she only knew what I was capable of, what I had done, it would be the other way around. What could she possibly worry might happen to me? Maybe she thinks I'm so distraught that I'm contemplating committing suicide.

"You don't have to worry about me. I'll be fine. I just have some things I need to figure out but after that, everything will be great."

"Just promise me. I'll come over tomorrow and we can sit and talk."

I want her grief to stop. Such a beautiful face should never be subjected to sadness, so I lie.

"I promise. I'll get some rest and I'll calm down emotionally."

I promise it but with no idea how to achieve it. I feel like a little kid promising to do better at school, while knowing I am hopeless at the subjects I've failed. She examines my face, trying to decide if my response is truthful, then places her palms on both of my cheeks and presses her lips to mine. I know this may be the last kiss I will ever have, so I place my hand behind her head to bring her in tighter. I want to cry. But this time, I can't, now knowing how it distresses her. That's insane. She's a psychiatrist for God's sake. She should be able to handle people in tears. Momentarily, it feels a little unfair. But only momentarily because this is Cristy after all. For Cristy, I will try to achieve anything, even giving up my 'hobby' of killing. But just not yet. In time, after I've seen what to do about my friend Doug. She pulls away, meets my eyes, then places a single kiss on my cheek before turning away.

"I'll see you tomorrow."

"You better. You made a promise."

She waves through her side window as she passes by. I return with a tepid sweep of my fingers, then climb into my car. Once inside, I start the car and then retrieve my gun from the glove box, rocking it side to side in my hand.

"Never shot anyone. Well, I guess I can soon add it to my list of fucked-up shit I've done."

I place the gun on the passenger seat and drive out of the parking lot. Unlike all of my previous victims, this time, I know exactly where I'm going. Doug's car had broken down last year and he asked me for a ride to work. Passing by the Whiskey River bar on the way to his house, I slow down to see if I can spot the red stains on the pavement from Jeremy. They must have pressure washed it clean because I find no sign of blood.

It's almost five in the afternoon when I pull my car over about three hundred feet from his home. I sit quietly in introspection. Do I really want to do this? Is there any other choice? The truth is, I don't want to do it, but have to. This is the first time I haven't been excited about harming someone. It's not that I feel sorry for him. He definitely deserves what I'm about to give him. It's just…I have something else to fill the void. I have lost the taste for violence and gained a taste for companionship. And now, it's plain that I have trapped myself in this unholy mess, this mire that will come to haunt the rest of my days at some point. I just do not know when.

It has snowballed beyond everything I ever thought it would be. Like I said before, it's evident how serial killers become 'serial'. They probably started with just one tiny problem, same way as I did. It's as though these killings take on a life of their own, a momentum of their own. The killings become unavoidable. Like now.

"Come on. The sooner we get this done, the sooner we can move on."

Tucking the gun into my waistband, I adjust my shirt to make sure it's concealed, then casually stroll down the sidewalk to his home. His car isn't in the driveway, and I know he never puts it in the garage because when I was here last, it was packed wall to wall with junk. To be certain, I ring the doorbell and listen closely. After a few minutes, I turn the knob and I'm surprised to feel it rotating. I gently push the door open.

"Hello? Doug, you home?"

Nothing but silence. I'm surprised at the size of his home and how bright and clean it is. It has to be at least a third larger than mine, furnished from wall to wall. I'm reminded that he comes from a well-off family as I pace the hall studying his photos. His family looks like the traditional smiling groups in the photos you get that already sit in nice little frames. The people are all prim and proper in their stature and demeanor.

"Oh, hey."

I catch sight of him holding his daughter in one of the photos. He looks genuinely happy and so does she. There are dozens of pictures of them together and in all of them, she is smiling and laughing. What am I about to do to a father? *Shit.* What I do to the father, I do to the daughter. It's possible he doesn't have a close relationship with her, however. After all, Doug never even told me he had a daughter. He pries into my life all the time, but what has he revealed about himself? Apparently, next to nothing. He deserves punishing for that too.

I'm sharply interrupted by the sound of a car door closing and immediately bolt around the corner waiting for him to come in, but he stops short, then lightly taps on the door. Why would he knock on his own door? It slowly opens and I'm stricken with confusion.

"What—what the hell are you doing here?"

The Broken Woman

Cristy's Story

It's a lovely morning outside. The sunrise is chipping away at the light chill left over from last night. Dressed for work but wrapped in a light shawl, I sip from a cup of coffee and soak in the beautiful scenery, huddled on the back patio chair. Cardinals, excited to start the day, flutter back and forth through the dimly lit sky. My barrel cactuses are in bloom, covered in bright yellow and purple petals. I watch as a familiar hummingbird stops by to sample its nectar.

"Hey, Henry. Where are your friends this morning?"

He buries his long thin beak into the bloom to sample the sweet dew hidden deep within, then flutters off.

"Guess you got your fill. Come back any anytime, Henry."

I know the alarm on my smart watch is about to go off because there is only a small swig of coffee left in my cup. Turning my wrist, I cancel the alert with three minutes to spare, tightly clenching the shawl at my breast, then rising to my feet.

"Time to start the day, Cristy."

Once inside, I retrieve the lunch I prepared last night and put it into my beach tote, along with my laptop and a folder of case notes. Even though I installed a key rack by the front door, I rarely ever use it and regularly have a hard time finding my keys as a result. Each time, I tell myself, *use the key rack, Cristy!* Then I ignore myself yet again, until the next time and the next. For some strange reason, this time, I find the keys sitting in a small puddle of water on the edge of the bathroom sink. As I walk down the hallway, I'm curious as to why I would have left them there, then remember that when I got home yesterday, I needed to pee so bad that I rushed straight to the toilet. I chortle at how ridiculous I am.

When I arrive at the clinic, there are already four people in the waiting area, but I know none of them are here to see me; my first appointment isn't for another forty minutes.

"Morning, Dr. Ruiz."

"Come on, we talked about this, Carol."

"I'm sorry. Haha. Good morning Cristy."

Carol is a sweet middle-aged woman who stands at around five-and-a-half feet tall. She's slightly overweight and self-conscious about it, so she wears loose-fitting black dresses every day. I know she has an eating disorder, but don't want to tell her that I know. People act so awkward around me when they know I'm constantly analyzing them. I'll wait for her to come to me for help. She already knows I am there for her, I hope.

"Can you please let me know when my first patient arrives? I only have two today and I'd like to get them through as early as possible."

"Sure thing, Cristy."

I set my bag under the desk and begin reviewing the case report for my first patient. Line by line, I follow each word with my fingertip. *When asked about his emotional state, the patient showed visible signs of irritation and anger. I do not recommend discharge from treatment at this time.* I've been seeing him for a few weeks now, and every time he comes in, I still get nervous. My job is to help him through his anger, but our discussions never lead anywhere. He blames his victim for his actions, stating, "It's her fault I hit her. She keeps winding me up." It takes an incredible amount of self-restraint to respond to this professionally. I believe he has mother issues but it's only an assumption at this point, since he will not open up to me.

"Cristy, your seven-thirty is here."

"Great. Thanks, Carol."

I mentally prepare myself for the impending stress I am about to go through by placing my palms on my forehead and taking three deep breaths, then walking to the waiting room.

"Jeremy Biggs, Good morning, sir. I can see you now."

He has a scowl on his face as he stands and walks toward me but doesn't acknowledge my 'good morning.' As he leisurely follows behind me, I feel as though he thinks walking slower will reduce the amount of time he will have to spend with me in the room. He has successfully lessened his visit by a whole five seconds by the time he sits down.

"Mr. Biggs, how has your anger been since I saw you last week?"

"Fine."

"Have you had any thoughts of hurting yourself or others?"

"Nope."

"We go through this same process every week, Mr. Biggs. The sooner you realize that I am only here to help you, the sooner we can work through your issues. And then you can stop being forced to see me. I do understand why you find it difficult to come here, but to get better, we need to have you open up to me more. You know that, right? I can't do the work for you."

There it is. It's only been a few seconds and I already see the veins bulging in his neck. His face passes through multiple shades of red. I know what has triggered him; it's the idea of being forced to do something he doesn't want to do. He's stubborn, petulant, a natural arguer, it seems. These types never do very well in any form of therapy, always feeling they have to push back against everything.

I commit the instance to my memory because I don't like writing whenever I'm treating him. In our first session, he became so irritated that he snatched the pen from my hand. I was terrified that he was going to stab me with it. Ever since seeing the unhinged anger in his eyes, I've stowed my pens in the desk when I'm in a room with him. In fact, I made a mental note to store everything inside the desk. Stapler, hole punch, paperweight, any heavy books, all objects someone could use as missiles or attack instruments.

"You seem angry right now, Mr. Biggs. Are you?"

"Nope."

Of course, that denial says it all. It's unbelievable how he can speak such a simple word in such a way that it provokes a sense of fear in me. My mouth begins salivating heavily, so I swallow before proceeding.

"How's your wife?"

Until now, he has been staring at his hands, lightly rubbing them together. Asked about his wife, he slowly draws his eyes to meet mine with dead seriousness.

"My wife is my business, not yours. You wanna know about her, then the judge shoulda committed her to this horse shit you're putting me through."

"I'm trying to help you, Mr. Biggs. I'm sorry it's so painful for you."

"Painful, my ass! It's not painful. See, that's exactly what I mean. People like you always make more of everything. Just because I say it's shit, you say it must be pain. You talk garbage."

I feel his stare penetrating like a dagger into my heart. I grow lightheaded as it races to process the increase in adrenaline. Everyone has a natural response to fear. They either stay and fight or run in terror, and I have no doubt I'm the latter. I gather my composure, then continue.

"So, I suppose you plan on being defiant about the whole process forever? Wouldn't you rather just get it over with and get back to your normal life?"

"Oh, I'm still living one. The fact that I have to see a cunt once a week won't change that."

This is how our sessions normally end. He almost always loses his temper and says something inappropriate, then I tell him we are through for the day and remind him that I do require him to come back the following week. Staring at him with disbelief, I consider continuing. But how could I control his escalating anger? I do not feel we are making progress and as the weeks go by, he becomes increasingly belligerent and awkward, obviously on purpose. He does everything he can to stay monosyllabic and, worst of all, to belittle my profession and me.

"And that will be it for the day. Congratulations on adding another day of therapy, Mr. Biggs. I'll see you again next week."

His hoarse laugh as he's leaving causes chills to cascade down the back of my neck. The moment the security door closes behind him, I retrieve a pen from the desk and update his file with a single line. *The patient remains uncooperative and combative toward treatment.* This is my seventh session with him, and they all have ended this way. As much as I would love to pawn his case onto another therapist, I can't get myself to do it; I couldn't live with myself knowing that I had cursed someone else with that psycho. I need a little break before my next appointment, in no condition to be an effective counselor right now.

"Hey Carol, I'm gonna run across the street and grab a chai tea. You want anything?"

"Aww thanks, but I've been having some blood pressure issues. Dr. Stevens told me to cut back on caffeine for a while."

"That's some good advice. Okay then, back in a few minutes; should be before my eight-thirty shows up."

The coffee shop is an easy three-minute walk across a two-lane road. The area is mostly rural, and the traffic is light, so it takes no time to gain an opportunity to cross safely. Before I make it to the window, the woman is already typing in my order.

"Chai tea, soy milk, light ice?"

I love that she already knows what I want and gleefully toss her a smile, cupping my hands around my hips.

"Yes, ma'am."

From the time I left to the time I reenter the clinic, only ten minutes have passed but new faces have already replaced the people in the waiting area. I slide my security card into the reader and grab the door handle when I hear it unlock.

"Oh, Cristy. Your eight-thirty is here a little early. She's at the end in the crop top."

I know she can hear us talking about her, but she doesn't pull her attention from her phone.

"Miss Brewer?"

Her innocent, childlike voice melts my heart when she speaks. She looks to be in her mid-twenties but sounds closer to ten or eleven.

"Yes, ma'am."

"Hello, I'm Cristy. You can follow me."

She gathers a couple of items from the end table and nervously walks toward me, like a puppy with its tail tucked.

"I'm Madison but my friends call me Maddy."

"Madison is such a pretty name. I can't have kids, but if I ever had a daughter, I would totally name her Madison."

She grins as if she has never received a compliment before, then walks through the doorway as I hold it open.

"We'll be in here, room three. Just have a seat on the chair right there."

I study her movements and attire carefully to get an idea of what kind of person I am working with. She has a shy tone, and her stance is defeated and cowed, shoulders sagging loosely to the side, and she has difficulty making eye contact. All this points to abuse of some sort. The strange part of the equation is how she's dressed in a crop top shirt, skinny jeans, and flip-flops with freshly pedicured feet. Those are signs of confidence, not timidity. I put on a pair of glasses even though I have perfect eyesight. It makes me seem harmless and causes most patients to relax.

"All right, Madison, what brings you in today?"

Her eyes stay locked on her hands.

"Life is just so hard, ya know? I feel like it would be better if I was just dead."

My chest aches at hearing how such a sweet, beautiful, and presumably innocent girl is going through so much anguish that she would readily choose death.

"That's so sad to hear, Madison. But I do understand; many people feel like this at some point, so please don't think you're unusual or that it cannot get any better. I'm going to help you through this, all right? I promise you that. But in return, I'd like you to promise me something."

Madison nods weakly. It's clear she has opted out of life. She looks at me wide-eyed, waiting to hear what I wish her to promise me.

"You have so much life ahead of you, Madison. Are you willing to promise me that you won't hurt yourself while you are still coming talking to me?"

She nods again.

"Yeah, I can do that. To be honest, I don't think I'd harm myself like that—not as in suicide, you know? I just mean that I wish I were dead, not that I'd do it to myself."

"I see. I'm so happy you won't harm yourself. Thank you for sharing this."

"It's fine."

"Let's start with what's bothering you right now."

She sobs lightly, rubbing her hands against her knees. I have only just met her, but there's a maternal instinct to reach over and grab her in a tight embrace. My training and experience ultimately win and instead, I sit silently. After a few minutes, she calms down and begins to explain.

"I have a daughter who is five, and I've lost custody to her abusive father. We were only married for less than six months, and he told the judge that I was a drug addict and that I'm an absent mother, so they took her away from me."

"How can that be enough for a judge to grant your ex sole custody? I mean, you should have at least gotten visitation even if what he said was true."

"His family's rich, that's why. They had people plant stuff in my car and hired people to lie about me. I couldn't do anything about it. He was so abusive to me. He would hit me for no reason. Even knocked this tooth out."

She uses her finger to pull back her cheek, displaying a space where a tooth should be.

"I'm positive he's abusing my daughter. I caught him…"

She trails off and begins sobbing again. I pull a tissue out from the box on my desk and attempt to hand it to her, but she doesn't notice, so I reach over and lightly wipe it across her cheek. She looks up with overflowing eyes and clasps my hand.

"I don't know what to do. No one will help me. The cops, the judge, and everyone is against me. Even social services told me to stop calling them. They hate me calling. I just wanna die."

My eyes begin to swell and fill with tears. I swallow them like a pill and quickly wipe them away.

"Please don't say that, honey. Madison…Hey, Madison. Look at me."

She gradually raises her chin to face me. Her bottom lip is quivering, and her cheeks are soaked in tears.

"I promise you again; we will figure this out. You and I will work through this together."

Her sobbing subsides and I catch a small glimpse of the beginning of a smile. I can tell that she feels some relief in the hope that someone is willing to help her, but staring into her innocent hazel eyes, I begin to worry that I may have made a bad promise to a client, a promise that I have no way of keeping.

"Thank you so much, Cristy. For the first time in months, it's like there's a tiny bit of hope that I can get my daughter out of the hands of that monster."

What did I get myself into? I never promised that, never even hinted at that, did I? Is that how it sounded? I don't know what I'm going to do but can't let this poor little girl down. I need to buy some time while I figure this out.

"Here's what we are going to do, Madison. I want to see you again in a few days, so we can work on your emotional struggles, and you can tell me more about what happened. Until then, promise me that you won't do anything to harm yourself. Can you do that?"

She wipes her face with her fingertips, then clasps my hands between hers. Her skin feels cool and slippery against mine, and it's unpleasantly wet with tears. But I am not worried about that. She is holding onto me, and in that, I offer her some sort of a lifeline. It's what I want. Although I haven't the slightest idea of where to go from here, it's nice to see that I've calmed her down and given her hope, if only for now.

"Can you come back Friday, say nine-thirty?"

"Sure. I'll be here. Thank you so much, Cristy. Seriously, I feel a lot better. Like… like a weight's gone from my shoulders already. I don't usually have *any* hope."

"Well, it's like the old motto says, Madison! 'A problem shared is a problem halved!'"

Damn. What have I just done?

I know better than to give a patient false hope. What the hell was I thinking? This is often my problem—I take on people's issues as my own. They are *not* mine. They are nothing to do with me. Maybe I can reel back a little what I have just said to Madison, so it doesn't hit so hard when she realizes I can't do anything to help her. I begin walking her to the front door with my hand on her shoulder.

"Look Madison, you have to be patient but also understand that things may never work out the way that you want them to. I'll try my best but there is only so much I can do."

She faces me with her eyes down and softly nods in acknowledgment. Her pain is so deep that I can't help but become angry at the person causing it. When the front door closes behind her, I approach the check-in counter.

"Hey Carol, can you send out a request for the medical files for Madison Brewer? I think her ex-husband was the one who was prior military, so you may have to check private sector records."

"Sure thing. Anything specific?

"Anything that required hospitalization."

It can take weeks or even months to get records requests filled by the private sector, but it would help me understand her case greatly if I knew what she has gone through. I'm not very optimistic that there will be any records, though. If there was incontrovertible evidence that her ex-husband was physically abusive, I'm sure the judge wouldn't have given him full custody of their daughter. Carol sits typing out the request.

"Done. I'll let you know when we receive it."

"Thank you, Carol. I'm going to pack up and get out of here. I have a full schedule tomorrow, so I want to get some things done today."

"All righty, have a good day, Ms. Ruiz."

She smirks at me when I turn to correct her, so I know she's messing with me. I smile and silently wag my finger at her before walking away. Halfway down the hallway, I whisper under my breath.

"Don't make me start calling you Miss Chastain."

"I heard that!"

I giggle hysterically to my office, then pack my things back into my tote bag. Draping it over my shoulder, I contemplate where to have lunch. I prefer to eat alone, in solitude, because I get nervous around crowds.

"The park won't be busy this time of day. I bet the ducks have even returned. It'll give me some peace and quiet to figure some things out. I've really dug myself into a hole right now."

Origin of Sentiment

Cristy's Story

I'm so upset that I can't eat my lunch, so I break off little bits of bread and toss them out into the groups of pigeons. Each time, they scurry off and then rush back to fight over the fragments. My mind is muddled and heavy by the problem I'm facing; how can I help Maddy? I don't know why I care so much. She was a stranger to me until she walked in this morning, but there is something about her that reminds me of myself. An innocent, caring young woman, abused and forced to live her life with the baggage forever weighing on her. Watching the pigeons flock and disperse in rhythmic cadence, memories of my past begin flooding in.

***

I was around Madison's age when I thought I had met my soulmate, James. The first year was a whirlwind of exciting experiences and lust-filled rendezvous. When he looked at me, I could feel my heart flutter, and any fears I had of the future were comforted in his hazel eyes. We were both attending college at the University of Arizona and graduated within months of each other. I finished first and started working for a small clinic in Marana. The following months seemed to flash by, working long hours. By the time I'd get home, James would already be hanging out at the bars with his friends. The occurrences happened so often that I stopped calling to ask where he was.

The turning point happened a little over two years into our relationship on a warm summer night. I came home to find him absent as usual and decided to go to bed early. A few hours later, I awoke to him forcing himself onto me. His breath reeked of liquor and cigarettes, and his skin was clammy and hot. I attempted to push him away, softly at first, then forcefully, but he easily overpowered me. Eventually, I gave in and let him do what he wanted. I stared at the ceiling in tears. That was the first time that I had seen that side of him, but it wouldn't be the last.

From that night on, he would regularly show up inebriated and force himself on me. Each time, I would attempt to stop him to no avail and concede to his advances. I don't know why I stayed with him. I guess deep inside, I still loved him, or at least the idea of who he had been before. Looking back, my naiveté in believing he would ever change was foolish. Even worse, I thought that would be the extent of the damage he could do to me. Well, I was wrong.

One morning, I awoke with an acidic burning sensation in my gut and rushed to the bathroom. For ten minutes, I evacuated all the contents of my stomach into the toilet. After washing my hands, I looked into the mirror and knew…I was pregnant. In that instant, my stomach knotted, and I felt faint. How was I going to deal with a child that would eternally link me to him? I had to get rid of it. That same day, a doctor prescribed me two medications that would induce a miscarriage. I swallowed the first pill the moment I got into my car, to start the process. The second medication, I would have to wait two more days to take.

I constantly worried that James would see the guilt on my face, so when we spoke, I wouldn't look directly at him. If anything, it made things worse because, for the first time, he started asking me what was wrong. I would simply reply "nothing" and continue with whatever it was I was doing. When the time finally came to take the second round of medication, I felt a slight relief that it was about to be over, but it wasn't. It only got worse. At first, everything seemed to go normally with some minor spotting and cramps, but nothing unbearable.

That night, the cramping progressed to severe spasms and increased blood flow. Still, I assumed it was normal. Two days of excruciating pain passed before I realized something wasn't right but couldn't go to the hospital because James would find out about the pregnancy. My head pounding and mouth drier than it had ever been, I awoke in the hospital with no recollection of how I got there. When I turned my head to the side, my eyes were met by James's.

"When were you going to tell me about the pregnancy?"

His tone was soft yet full of hatred. I didn't know what to say. Nothing I could say was going to make what I did any better, so I just stared blankly at him. His silent fiery gaze caused a chill in my spine. At that moment, I felt as though he could easily have strangled me.

"How ya feeling, Ms. Ruiz?"

"I'm fine. What happened?"

"Unfortunately, you had a severe infection in your uterus. It seems that you may have had a miscarriage, but the fetus was never passed. So it…well, let's just say you will be okay now."

When I tried sitting up, I felt a sharp pain in my stomach and reached down with my hand to find a large bandage on my abdomen. Confused, I looked back at the doctor. His face drooped as though he brought more bad news.

"We had to remove your uterus, Ms. Ruiz. The infection was too aggressive."

"You mean I can't ever…?"

"I'm afraid not. We have a few services that may be able to help you through this emotional time if you would like."

"Uh…no…that's okay. Thank you."

That day, I lost the ability to ever carry a child again. Although it was killing me inside, I wouldn't let myself cry. I knew what they did to patients who showed extreme emotional distress, so I was not going to be one of them. I just wanted to get out of there. Even though I had just gone through major surgery and was pushed out in a wheelchair, James didn't even open the passenger door for me. He hopped in, slammed his door, then waited for me to clumsily climb in. The drive home was eerily quiet. He wouldn't even look at me.

When we arrived home, he still showed no regard for me, and rushed into the house, leaving me in the car. In excruciating pain, I carefully hobbled to the front door and pushed it open. Standing in the doorway, I saw James sitting on the couch with the abortion medication bottle on the table in front of him.

"You ready to tell me now?"

I wanted to run, but even if I physically could, I had nowhere to go, so I nervously closed the door behind me and took a seat next to him. We sat in silence for what seemed like an eternity before he finally spoke again.

"You killed my baby? Did you kill my fucking baby?"

"No, I—"

"Yes, you did, you fucking bitch!"

He instantly lunged over and grabbed a handful of my hair. When I started to scream, he began slapping me at first, then punching me with his knuckles. He didn't stop until he tired and even then, he continued to hold me forcefully by my hair. Every time I tried to move, he shook my head vigorously, to the point I could feel strands of my hair detaching from my skull. With no hope of setting myself free, I stopped trying and let my head go limp in his grasp with my wide eyes staring up at him, waiting for him to begin hitting me again. He didn't. He just stared at me like a piece of meat that he had just tenderized.

I know now that when a man strikes a woman, the first time is just a test. If she stays after he gets a taste of that power over her, she can expect more of the same. The six months following my surgery, I received daily verbal, sexual, and physical abuse from James. If I didn't put up a fight, the beatings were lighter, so most of the time I would just curl up on the floor and take it. He soon grew tired of not being able to elicit a fearful response from me, and one night, found a new way.

I was in the kitchen cooking when he approached me from behind and wrapped his left arm around my waist, breathing into my hair. I could smell the alcohol on his breath and assumed he was about to force himself on me again, so I prepared myself by putting my palms on the counter in front of me.

"I think I've been too light on you, Cristy. To truly break a horse, you first have to make it too scared to buck you. Do you think you could you buck me?"

He didn't give me a chance to respond before he plunged a kitchen knife into the back of my right hand. I let out a blood-curdling scream and he responded by cupping his hand over my mouth.

"Are you broken in yet? Huh?"

My muffled shrieks seemed to be pleasing for him to hear as he alternated cupping and uncupping my mouth playfully. The sharp pain in my hand became unbearable as I struggled to move it. In an adrenaline-fueled panic, I forcefully removed the blade with my left hand and then thrust it over my shoulder. His grip on both my waist and mouth slowly relaxed. Then he pulled the knife from my hand. I stood motionless, waiting for him to use the knife on me again but he didn't. I only turned when I heard gurgling, trailed quickly by a loud thump.

James was on the floor, grasping at his throat with the knife embedded deep within it. I knew I should have called for help, but it was the only opportunity I would ever have to be rid of him, so I waited until the last blood-filled breath left his chest, then checked for a pulse. Once I was certain that he was dead, I called for an ambulance.

The investigation following his death started off stressful, as I was obviously the one who had killed him, but once my lawyer arrived, they quickly released me without charge. The headlines labeled the incident as a woman, fearful for her life, had been forced to kill her boyfriend in self-defense. Their portrayal slightly bothered me, not because it wasn't true, but because it wasn't the full truth. But if the authorities knew I'd had every opportunity to save him after stabbing him, I would have been facing prison time. I made the right choice.

The only thing I have to show for my three-and-a-half-year relationship with James is a scar on my hand, the inability to bear a child, and multiple scars on my face. I can fortunately conceal those with makeup.

***

I inspect the back of my hand and lightly rub the scar while sitting on the park bench. I can't let this happen to Maddy. She deserves better. I toss the rest of my bread onto the ground and empty the remaining contents of my lunch into the trash, then walk to my car.

Once I get home, I take off my shoes at the entrance, then lay my case files on the kitchen table before sitting next to them. My cat, Rani, immediately hops onto the table, meowing loudly.

"I'm sorry, baby girl. Did Mommy forget to feed you before she sat down? Bad Mommy. Let's get you some food."

Rani had appeared while I was getting coffee across the street from the clinic last year. She just ran over and started rubbing her body along my leg, purring. I instantly fell in love with her. Having had no physical contact since James, I didn't think I would ever want to again, but something about her affection reminded me of how great it felt to be needed and loved. Before I knew it, my arms were scooping her up and taking her home. She was not flea-bitten or emaciated. Nor was she scared and starving. This made it necessary to wonder: did I steal her? Was Rani somebody's pet and were they crying for her?

To assuage my troubled mind, I made some tentative inquiries around the veterinarians in the area. I hoped no one had reported missing a cat fitting Rani's description. No reports. She had no microchip. The relief was enormous. I could have posted notices about a found cat in store windows and on lamp posts. I didn't. I just decided she had not had a home and so, she was now officially mine.

"There ya go, sweet baby. Eat up."

I sit down and then begin thumbing through Madison's file. I never wrote anything down during our session and I want to get everything squared away before our next meeting. *The patient shows the common signs of physical abuse. i.e., timidity, difficulty making eye contact, and slumped posture, also a defeated stance and loss of self-confidence. She states that there was abuse from her ex-husband (name unknown). The combination of trauma and the loss of custody of her daughter has led to depression and thoughts of suicide.*

I tap my pen on the paper, trying to think of anything else significant. Oh, yeah. *The patient states that the authorities, including social services, have refused to investigate despite her repeatedly informing them of possible abuses of their daughter. Attempted to get patient to elaborate on her emotional state, to establish current suicidal propensity. Patient reports she is unlikely to self-harm but sees no value in her life.* I close the file and then slide Jeremy's in front of me. Then, I open it and review the repetitive notes from the last seven weeks, wanting so badly to write in big bold letters, 'Asshole' on the front page. Instead, I write the heading, 'Session Eight' at the top of a blank page, then close the folder.

Normally, I would review every note in his file again and try to come up with ways to get through to him but today, two factors are preventing my normal routine. First, I'm mentally and emotionally done with his shit, and second, all I can think about is Madison. I put my elbows on the table and then bury my face into my palms.

"How do I help you? How do I get your daughter away from that monster before it's too late?"

Meeting Matt

Today is one of the worst days I have ever had since starting at this clinic a few years ago. My inability to take my mind off of Madison has caused me to run behind with every appointment. I sense the irritation in each patient who walks through the door to see me. At this point, I am almost forty minutes behind schedule and need to make up some time.

"Who's my next patient, Carol?"

"Uh, Matth…eye, I dunno. Mr. Ellis. The guy right there."

She points at an attractive clean-cut man with springy brown hair, looking at his phone.

"Oh, he's cute. Why is he here?"

She brings up the appointment notes as she brings her glasses down from the top of her head.

"Uh, you'll never guess. Anger."

"Oh great. Seriously? Another one?"

"If it makes you feel any better, he was very polite, even though you're running forty minutes behind."

"Really? Because he looks mad right now. Can you send him back for me? Haha."

"Sure, you 'fraidy cat."

"Mr. Ellis? Uh, Matth...eye?"

"Matthias. Yeah, that's me."

"Sorry about that. I'm really bad at names. Doctor Ruiz is ready to see you."

I rush to the bathroom to pee. I have been holding it for the last two hours and feel as if I'm about to explode. When I'm done, I rush back to the exam room to find Mr. Ellis standing awkwardly in the center of the room, as if he has no clue where to sit.

"Mr. Ellis?"

"Yep, that's me."

"Ah, Okay. Mr. Ellis, what's going on? Please have a seat."

He looks around even though I'm pointing directly at the seat I want him to sit on.

"You can just call me Matt. Well, Doctor Ruiz, I–"

I hate it when people call me Doctor Ruiz. After my father died, my mother remarried and made me take her new husband's last name. At thirteen years old, I took it very hard, but it seemed as if very little time had passed before she moved on. *Ruiz* is not me at all. But Matt looks just as uneasy. Maybe calling me by my first name will help him.

"Please, call me Cristy."

"All right, Doctor Christy."

Okay, now that's funny. I can't help but laugh with my hand over my mouth followed by a nasally snort. Any worry of a tense meeting is immediately comforted by his gaffe.

"Just Cristy is fine, Matt."

Even though I stop laughing, I can't help but hold a lingering smile. Matt's problem, as Carol said, is anger. He has been feeling 'emotionally unstable', he says, whatever he means by that. Then he adds this means anger. I watch him intently, seeking to determine if he or anyone else is at risk. Will he harm himself or anyone else? I hope not. He looks like a nice guy, a good guy. I have no idea why, but I get those vibes from him. His story already interests me. Dare I even say, it intrigues me? But it does, and I sense he really wants to be here. He craves help.

Whatever he says isn't as important as how he reacts, so I watch his mannerisms. Matt relates how he 'isn't really an angry person', but that he has had emotional issues in the past. He denies being suicidal or wishing harm to anyone despite extreme anger outbursts. It only seems appropriate to write very few notes. Unfortunately, whenever you write notes after asking questions, the patients get jittery if they are lying. He is jittery, for sure. His leg swings and his eyes dart everywhere, and in between, he shows agitation with his hands, picking at fingernails, examining his palms, actions of this nature.

I check again. Will he harm someone? Again, he denies it, so I have to accept that to some degree, despite the fact he answers with 'not really' instead of a negative. I stare at him more intensely, trying to coax out any emotion, but he sits stoically. If he does have anger issues, he's extremely good at hiding it.

"Not really? Okay, we'll come back to that. I'm interested in something you said previously. You say you've had past emotional issues?"

"Yeah, some pretty severe depression. I came here to see a therapist."

"Interesting. Did the talking therapy help?"

I link the possibility that he may have relapsed. But he is not depressed anymore, he tells me adamantly. He feels the therapy last time was a help and that he also penned a book to get his emotions down in writing. Ceasing the note taking, I raise my head to face him. I ask more, and he tells me his book is called Born into Darkness. He uses interesting words to describe it. I write in my notebook, 'about how I grew up abused and found a way to be happy.' I write down its name quickly, interested in what a person with depression and anger writes about, especially a male perspective. Plus, it could be an amazing way to understand and help him. It's a therapist's dream to have so much access to the mind of their patient.

My watch says that if I hope to catch up today, I'll have to cut this session short. But I have to see him again. He is interesting and somehow, something tells me he is on my level, that we would get along. But I have to sound him out further on a professional level too.

"I'm sorry we started so late and have to cut this session short, but I want to go back to your answer earlier. You said that you 'don't really' think about hurting people. What did you mean?"

He answers in a way that makes me laugh loudly.

"Doesn't everyone wish they could just punch people for being assholes?"

He's good at twisting his answers but there is definitely something mysterious and dangerous in his eyes, but it doesn't resemble anger. It's similar to a sociopath's static gaze. I tell him that yes, I'd like to punch some people too! Then he turns a little distant. I want to call it 'strange'. He just stares when most people would laugh at what I say. Perhaps his current state is robbing him of the ability to laugh. That wouldn't be so unusual. *Anhedonia,* the inability to take pleasure in the things we normally find pleasurable and would enjoy doing.

Including laughing. Will he come back? Wednesday would be good for me, I suggest. His blank stare bores into me again. I can tell that he's trying to come up with an excuse not to come back.

"I can come back Wednesday but can't plan anything after that until I check my schedule."

Well, I am slightly bemused! What kind of a response is this? He says it as though he's doing me some sort of a favor! As if he thinks I am pestering him. Has he already forgotten he brought himself here, and booked himself in, claiming to desperately want the help? And now, he's shying away. I can't understand that. I'm pleasantly surprised when he commits to another day. I need to make sure I book fewer appointments on Wednesday to ensure I can spend a whole session with him.

"Great! I'll see you then. And hey, if you start to feel angry, try this. Close your eyes and imagine what it is that's making you angry. Don't open your eyes to see it. Keep it in your mind, then change the event to something else that makes you happy. You think you can try that?"

"Sounds simple enough."

"Terrific! I'll see you on Wednesday."

I walk him out, expecting him to get into a low-profile, discreet vehicle, based on his seemingly insular personality. Instead, I watch as he climbs into a newer model black Dodge Charger. He is an enigma to me, and I want to figure him out, see what makes him tick. His book may well help me there, and after my last appointment for the day, I excitedly rush home to hunt it down and check it out.

"What would you like the world to know about you, Matt? Where did you come from and where are you going? Who are you, really?"

Depiction of a Psycho

Cristy's Story

I rush into the house, throw my bag down, then feed Rani, before sitting on the couch with my laptop. I have the name of Matt's autobiography etched into memory at this point. I type it into the search bar, and it pops up, the top result on the list—not because it's a top seller or anything but rather because I have searched for it specifically by name. It appears hardly anyone has read it and I can't help feeling sad for him. But perhaps I need not since it's likely he wrote it for catharsis. Maybe he isn't hoping for sales. But then again, why publish in that case?

On the one hand, he seems meek and humble. On the other, narcissistic, self-important. And that's not possible. He is one or he is the other. Humility and grandiosity are opposites. Yet he seems to veer from one to the next in a way I am sure I never saw before. I will find out which is true. Born into Darkness as a title sounds scary, but I've always loved scary books. This, however, turns out not to be a scary story at all. Instead, it's sad, gut-wrenching, and every other emotion you can think of. Maybe it's because I have met him in person. I don't think I took my hand away from my mouth for the four hours it took me to finish it.

The book details his life from five years old until recently, filled with more abuse and hardship than I had ever heard from any of my patients. After every chapter, my urge to wrap my arms around him and give him a great big hug, surges. I slide the laptop to my side but can't get myself to close it yet. I'm processing what I have just read, wondering how the hell Matt can even act as adjusted as he seems. His life started with abuse, then his uncontrollable anger got a hold of him, settling into depression for over a decade. How does someone climb out from that to live a normal life?

There is a specific instance in the book that I must look into. Matt was young, incredibly young, when he got into an altercation with his uncle, Bo. After it was said and done, Matt thought he had killed him. He showed no emotion or remorse for just having killed another human being, then again, his uncle was abusing him, so I had no remorse at reading that he was dead either. It turned out that his uncle survived the beating and lost any recollection of it happening. It made me a little angry that he lived and went on to hurt many more people after that.

At the end of the book, Matt doesn't know what happened to Bo, but he heard that he had died a few years earlier. Out of curiosity, I want to see what the evil piece of shit looks like. I put the laptop back on my thighs and type the name Bo Ellis with no results. It makes sense that Matt would have a different last name since he would have taken his father's. A quick Google search for Matthias Ellis leads me to an obituary about the McCarty family. 'Dana McCarty died in her sleep and is survived by her son Matthias Ellis.' I check the date; he penned it only a few years ago. Most likely around the time Matt reports seeing a therapist for depression. I'm reminded of a section in his book. He wrote about how much he hated her but after she died, it caused grief and turmoil within him. My chest tightens when I imagine the pain he must have gone through.

I open a new browser page and type Bo McCarty in the search bar. Immediately, news articles flood the page, all repeating the same information, virtually verbatim. The police found Bo McCarty dead in the smoldering remains of his home. There are no details of his death, except that it is an open murder investigation and that it's clear he was tortured prior to the killing. What's the date of this article?

"Oh my—"

I slap my hand over my mouth when I realize...Bo was murdered three days ago, on Friday night. A thin layer of sweat builds on my forehead and my heart rate spikes. His murder isn't what's bothering me. One of the last lines from Matt's book is. He wrote that he heard Bo had died years ago. Why would he even bother to put that in his book if not to...

"Holy shit. He did it. Matt killed him."

I have sat pleasantly in a room with a killer, which should bother me greatly, but when I think about it, he killed a terrible, bad man. Who am I to judge him? I have killed before too and in some strange way, this makes me feel closer to him. I close the laptop and release a long lung-filled sigh. I can't wait to meet him again.

When Wednesday comes, I'm a little nervous. Not scared. More like, excited. I look over the counter at him in the waiting area with his face buried in his phone. Carol taps me on the arm. When I redirect my sight to her, she raises her brow and smirks at me. I smile and then step to the door.

"Matt?"

"Yep, coming. How ya doing, Cristy?"

"It's been a long day. How about you?"

"I just woke up. Haha."

"Oh yeah, you work nights. I remember."

"That's a pretty nasty scar on your hand."

I bring my hand up and stare at the scar for a few seconds, trying to decide if I want to tell him how it happened. I don't. Instead, I take a seat at the desk without acknowledging his statement and wait for him to sit.

"So…?"

"So what?"

"Did you try what I asked? Envisioning a happy place?"

"Yeah, it worked."

"Really?"

His short response is an indication that he's lying. He wants to get the answer out as quickly and short as possible to move on to the next question. He knows if he says no, that he didn't bother trying my solution, it would lead to a deeper discussion about his anger. I won't let it end so easily.

"How's your anger?"

"I'm still angry."

"Do you think about hurting others?"

"Same as before. I wish I could slap the hell out of some people for being assholes, but other than that, not really."

There it is again. "Not really." Why does he say that when it should be a simple yes or no answer? I'm sitting across from and staring in the face of an angry man, a killer, who can't help himself. He reminds me of Jeremy in that he has anger issues, but still, there's so much good in him. Am I deluding myself? Perhaps so. But I want to help him. And I will want to help Matt until he shows me that my willingness to assist is misguided.

"You know…So, I have a patient. You remind me of him a little in that he is always very angry too, but he is unable to control himself. He was recently court-ordered to see me after he beat his wife so bad that she was hospitalized, about three years ago."

"Oh wow, that's terrible."

"Yeah, it was. What's worse is that he was only in prison for a few years. After two months with me, the authorities will allow him to go back to his normal life. I saw him walking through Walmart a few weeks ago with his wife and two kids."

"Did she look okay?"

"No… it was obvious he was still beating her. She looked terrible. Well, I assume he was still beating her. She had that look."

He stares at me awkwardly, as if trying to figure out what I want him to say.

"So, he lives around here then?"

"Yes. Green Valley. The point is, that you and I need to work through your emotions to make sure that you don't escalate into harming someone else. You and anger are the worst of enemies and eventually, one gives up the battle and lets the other simply continue."

"I think I get what you're saying, but there's no one in my life to release anger on, so—"
"That's what I'm getting at, Matt. Can you imagine what that guy would be doing if he didn't have his wife to take his anger out on?"

"Yeah, that crazy bastard would be out killing people, I bet."

"Exactly! I wish I could help him. Help his wife. The poor woman. But I can't. I want to help you, Matt. I want to help you, partly because I can't help her."

His eyes gloss over and stare off into the distance. I watch as his eyes flutter side to side for almost a minute.

"You okay, Matt?"

He appears to be pulling out of a trance of some sort.

"Yeah, I just feel so bad for the poor woman. I think the guy should be strung up by his heels. He doesn't deserve to be alive. No abuser does. Been there, done that."

He looks disgusted, almost as if it makes him physically sick.

"Well, that's pretty extreme, but I don't disagree. Do you think you could really do that—or anything like that? String someone up by their heels?"

"Seriously? No, I don't know how anyone could do something like that."

"Good."

"Are you comfortable talking about your childhood? I promise I won't write any notes concerning anything you disclose."

"Not much to talk about. My family beat me a lot as a kid. Never enough to go to hospital. I suppose I'm grateful for that although sometimes, I think if someone at the hospital had seen it, the authorities would have put me somewhere safer. Never mind. It is what it is."

"Do the memories of those instances trouble you now?"

"No. I never think about it really. I worked through all that stuff when I was seeing the therapist before, so… nope. Not really."

Not really. I could scream at hearing these words. Does Matt use 'not really' as a 'get out of jail free' card when the answer is—or should be—yes? Does 'not really' confirm my suspicions? Or maybe it's just a bad habit of his, a phrase he tends to tack onto every negative. That's possible. People do that. Some add 'I suppose' or 'know what I mean?'

"The people physically abusing you, who were they, Matt? Can you tell me?"

"Oh, just my grandmother. We lived alone. I really don't think that has anything to do with my current problem though. As I said, I worked through all that years ago. I didn't come here to go through all the old stuff again. What's done is done, you know?"

"Okay, fair enough. Well, do you have anything you would like to discuss before we end today's session?"

"I can't think of anything, offhand."

"All right then. I'm hoping we can meet again. How does Monday sound?"

"Work's been incredibly busy lately. Can I just call and make another appointment when I'm free? I never manage to stick to schedules if I book too far ahead. My job won't let me—"

I've seen this before. An open promise to continue treatment with no set date. He's not coming back. This 'my work won't allow me' is a frequent get-out clause, an excuse. I have a sight sinking feeling. Is coming to me that bad? Does he not believe I can assist him with his struggles at all? Evidently not. But we have barely begun yet. I think Matt is just one of those who thinks he doesn't like questions. He comes for therapy but expects me to do all the talking, and he sees anything I ask as prying.

"Of course. Just let the front desk know that you're my patient. I can usually get you in by the next day."

"Great! Thank you, Cristy. Have a good rest of your day."

"You too."

I purse my lips somewhat when he walks out the door, knowing I may never see him again. There is just something about him, something intriguing and risky that makes me want to know more. Not in a sexual way, at least I don't think. I don't really know because I haven't been sexually attracted to someone in a very long time. Maybe this is some form of long-forgotten lust. Regardless, he's gone. There is nothing I can do about it now.

The next day flies by, leaving no imprint of what we discussed during any of my appointments. I feel as if I've been running on autopilot since Matt left the clinic. Now Friday, I'm driving to work, trying to remember one single conversation I had with a patient yesterday, but the only thing I can remember is lunch. There's solace in knowing I only have one appointment this morning, then my weekend starts. One of the perks of being a contractor. When I walk through the door, Carol waves me over. She's on the phone and doesn't skip a beat in the conversation, handing me a note:

Madison Brewer will not be able to make today's appointment and wishes to reschedule for Monday at nine-thirty.

I'm relieved after reading it. I only had one session today, but I had completely forgotten that it was with Madison. Actually, for the last two days, I had forgotten about her completely. I give Carol a thumbs up, accepting the reschedule, then walk right back out the door. How can I have gotten so preoccupied that I stopped thinking about the Maddy issue altogether? At least I have a few more days to think about it before I have to see her again.

"Is that…?"

Passing by a diner, I notice a car exactly like Matt's and quickly turn into the lot to investigate. Still, in my car, I easily spot him through the window.

"Oh, Matt. Always with your face in that phone."

I park the car, check that my hair and makeup are presentable, then casually walk into the diner. I expected that the sound of the bell over the door would have made him look up, but he doesn't acknowledge the jingle, so I walk over and stand next to him.

"Hey, you! Strange seeing you here."

He looks up at me confused as if trying to figure out if I'm really here.

"Uh, no. It's strange seeing *you* here. I eat here almost every day."

"Really? I bet you eat the same thing too."

"How'd you know that?"

"Matt, I'm a psychiatrist. My job is to know things. Comprehend people's emotions and thoughts into something tangible."

Why did I say that? Why can't I ever just turn it off?

"Are we in a session? Why are you talking that way?"

"Haha, no. Sorry, I always talk this way. I don't mean anything by it. Mind if I sit with you?"

There he goes. I can tell he's lost in thought again. It looks so strange, how his eyes shake rapidly and stop blinking. Nystagmus, that's called—an involuntary, nervous-looking eye flicker. It's always hard to pin down why that happens. Should I interrupt him? Yeah.

"Matt?"

"Oh, yeah. Sorry. Um…sure. Have a seat."

I sit across from him and place my arms crossed on the table, then lean in slightly.

"Do you come here often?"

"Not really. The first time I visited was just last week. The food was good, so I decided to try it again. Well, you know what the food is like; you eat here almost every day. Why here?"

"The food's always the same—I mean, it's good—and they leave me alone."

"They? The servers?"

"Yeah, I don't like talking to people. They know what I like and just bring it to me."

"Wow, that's interesting. You know it's strange that I became a therapist because I actually don't like talking to people either. That's why I don't date or go out. Just work and home."

I realize what I said makes no sense at all. Did I honestly claim that I became a therapist because I hate talking to people? In what world does that statement begin to add up? This job means I have to talk to people every single day. And often, I have to listen to and talk about things that don't even interest me in the slightest. Thankfully, Matt doesn't point out the huge discrepancy in what I've just told him. He seems to let most things pass.

"Can I get you something to drink, ma'am?"

The waitress slides a plate in front of Matt. I look at the plate, then at the waitress.

"Oh, he already has his food, so I'll probably just pop back outside. I'm not really hungry."

"You're not going to eat?"

"Nah, I don't want to impose on your peaceful breakfast. Oh, hey. Before I go, would you like my personal number? I know you're probably not going to see me at the clinic again, but I would love to keep in touch."

"Yeah, sure. You can just put it in my phone. Here."

"Great, feel free to call or text whenever. It doesn't need to be about therapy or anything. I just think you are an interesting guy."

"Thank you. I think you are an interesting woman too. I'll be in touch."

On my walk to the door, I stop momentarily, then turn and smile at him. I want him to call me. Maybe if he thinks that I like him, he will contact me. I really hope it didn't come across as me trying to carry on with the therapy that he's decided not to do. We'll see. He seems awkwardly charming, which is promising. My phone rings on the way home, but I don't know how to set it up on Bluetooth, so I let it go to voicemail. When I pull into the driveway, I check the message. It's Carol.

"Hey Cristy, you know that crazy-ass guy you see every week, Jeremy Biggs? He's all over the news, been missing since last night and they're saying it looks like a possible homicide. That guy pissed someone off and got himself dead. Shit's crazy. Anyway, call me back."

Wow. Jeremy is missing…presumed dead? The constant residual stress from knowing I will have to see him again disappears, replaced by churning in my stomach. It can't be a coincidence that this happened right after I told Matt about him. But how? I never told him Jeremy's name, only some random information. There's no way he could have found him with so few details. Could he?

A crazy idea snaps into my head. I can't tell if it came from my conscious or subconscious, but it's solidly in the forefront of my mind now. The hairs on my arms stand up and my hands begin to tremble at the thought. The answer that I've been looking for. The solution to Maddy's problem. Finally, a way to save that little girl.

"I can get Matt to kill Doug."

Best Laid

Work files strewn all over my coffee table and floor manage to consume the whole Saturday. Using what little I know about Matt, I'm trying to formulate a plan. He seems to only kill truly bad people. I hate to admit it, but that only fascinates and attracts me even more. I write down a list of requirements.

- Make sure it can't link back to me or Madison.
- Develop trust with him.
- He must think it's his idea, reached on his own.
- Use multiple murders to dilute suspicion of Maddy.
- Create a personal connection to Maddy so Matt will feel driven to kill her ex.

I put the pen down, walk to my closet, then pull a box down from the top shelf. After rummaging my hand through it, I pull out a small plastic block and hold it in my open palm. This is the wireless tracking device that was found attached to my car a year after James's death. I have no clue how long he was monitoring me, but I wouldn't have ever known about it if I hadn't taken my car in for a tire change. When the mechanic handed it to me, I had no clue what it was. When he explained it, it gave me a creepy feeling like James was spying on me from hell.

"Dudes be usin' these things to track women. Sometimes, we find em on girls' cars even when they're single and ain't got no man. Those ones are even scarier, man. This thing be tellin' somebody out there everywhere ya been goin'."

I always knew James was abusive and irrational but when I found out he had been spying on me, I was terrified of what he would have been capable of if I'd let him live. That's one of the reasons I've been telling myself I will never date again. You think you love a person, only to find out they're an abusive psychopath. If I, a trained psychiatrist, couldn't see it, who could? The heart makes you blind to the truth no matter how obvious it is.

"I always knew there was a reason I held onto this. Time to put you to some good use."

I walk back to the living room, take a seat on the couch, then add one more thing to my list.

- Monitor Matt's movements.

Confident that I have everything figured out, I feed Rani, then remove a leftover chicken breast and some romaine lettuce to make a salad, but before I can start the preparation, I receive a text. *Lunch in about thirty minutes?*

I can't believe it. Matt actually contacted me. Not just contact, but he's even asked me out. I gleefully reply. *Sure. I'm free. Where would you like to meet?* My guess is that he didn't expect me to accept because it's taking him way too long to answer. Feeling on the cusp of rejection, I hear the notification. *Mexican restaurant by Taco Bell?* I'm already typing while I'm reading it. *Sure, see you in 30.* The tracker is already charged as I never use it but keep it plugged in just in case; no point in paying a tracking subscription if I'll never have it to hand when I want it. The main purpose was originally to put onto Jeremy's car so I could see if he was stalking me, but I never had the nerve to go through with it.

I'm kind of glad to have a reason to use the thing after paying so much to keep it online and live. I plug it into my phone and log into my tracker panel with the service provider. It all looks good, and it gives me a pinpoint accurate image of where I am now. Movement, coordinates, pictures of the road and nearby properties—everything. It's amazing how easy it is to set this thing up. 'Do you accept this and this?' Sure, and done.

When I arrive, I park around the side to see if Matt is waiting for me. I spot him out front of the restaurant waving his arms and talking to someone, but I can see no one else. I sneak around the outside of the lot, careful to stay below his line of sight. Just my luck. I find his car on the opposite side of where I parked. A family of four walks by as I crouch and lean against his Charger. I press my index finger to my lips.

"Shh. My son's trying to find me. I'm just playing a prank."

They lightly giggle and walk by without a second thought. I pull the tracker from my purse and then reach underneath the back of his car. I feel around endlessly, waiting for it to find some sort of a magnetic surface. These days, with modern cars, there are so few magnetic parts. I feel every second tick by, each one feeling like many minutes. Still nothing magnetic shows up for me. I have to get my knees and hands down on the gravel, then lie on my side, reaching under as far as I can. The gravel cuts into my skin and already, I am filthy with motor oil, also blackened from fumbling around the underside of the car and its greasy, dirty tires, plus all that detritus from the gravel.

Finally, holding my hand in a really awkward position and reaching as far up into the vehicle as I can, the tracker shoots from my hand and then projects a loud thud. I exhale, then awkwardly stand with pain in every joint, looking about myself. The magnetic force was stronger than I anticipated and when this thing found its spot, it was as though it had a mind of its own. I dust myself off, frantically trying to wipe the oil from my hands too, then trot over to meet Matt. The second I turn the corner, I realize I should have come from the other direction since that's where I parked, but it's too late. I just hope he doesn't notice that I'm going the wrong way when I leave.

"Hey, I was worried you wouldn't keep in touch. Were you just talking to yourself?"

"What? No, I was singing a song I just heard in my car."

That's not what it looked like. Maybe he really is crazy. Still, right now, crazy is what I need.

"Ah. I hate it when you can't get a song out of your head. It just keeps nagging and nagging in your mind until you finally just give up and have to sing it."

"Yeah…That's exactly how it was. Anyway, what's happened to your hands?" he asks. "You look like you've been fighting with a coal delivery man."

I laugh aloud. "Oh, God. I know! I need to find the bathroom. I thought I had a tire going flat so stopped to look. My tire was filthy but it's fine. I felt all around and there's no damage."

When we walk in, the restaurant is around half-filled, and he seems a little out of place. I mean he looks ill at ease as if he'd rather not be here. He looks more at home in the café.

"Have you ever been here?"

"Yeah, a few times. They have great fajitas."

"What were you doing when I texted you?"

I can't tell you. If you knew, you would think that I was the crazy one.

"Just case notes and stuff. Boring crap you don't want to hear about. More interestingly, what were *you* doing? I was surprised to hear from you."

"I was at Anamax Park, just walking around."

Now that's crazy. I was just there a few days ago, feeding pigeons while trying to figure out how to save a girl's daughter from her ex-husband.

"Really? That sounds like a nice relaxing time."

"It was until I saw a woman beating her kid. Not spanking. Really beating. It was brutal and yes, it made me angry before you ask me that."

It's a perfect opportunity to support his need to release anger and develop a little trust.

"I wasn't going to ask you that. I was going to say that it was terrible and that I hate people like that. You have every right to be angry about what she was doing."
You have every right? What the fuck? Now, I'm giving him permission to feel what he feels?

I grin at him playfully to show I'm not in therapist mode even if I sound as if I am.

"So, what happened to the woman at the park?"

"Nothing. I looked away for a moment and when I looked back, she was gone."

Another opportunity to bond and show that I know what he's going through.

"It's so sad the poor child has to go through that. I hear about those things all the time and it makes me angry that they can get away with it. Even in your case. I don't want to bring up bad memories or anything, but it's amazing that you made it out of that house with everything your grandmother and uncle did to you."

Oh, my God. Did I just say that? What the hell am I thinking? Maybe he didn't notice.

"How did you know about my uncle?"

Shit. No going back now. Just admit it and apologize. If he digs too deep, then revert to unmitigated regret.

"Oh, sorry. I read your book. I just wanted to know more about what you went through so I could help you. I'm sorry if that makes you mad, but I figured since you told me about the book, it was okay for me to read it."

"I'm not mad. I just wish you would have asked me."

Wow, he isn't acting out angrily as I thought he would.

"Look. You're not my patient anymore and I'm not here as your therapist. When I read your book, it was when I assumed you would still be coming to see me. I'm sorry."

"It's fine, really. That was the past. I told you I'm over it. Anyway, what's with all these people getting away with doing that sort of shit to a child?"

What awkward timing. The server is standing inches away from us, looking unsure whether she even wants to take our order after hearing Matt talk about child abuse. But I'm probably imagining it, my mind in overdrive. Matt points at me with his right hand, his face half buried in his left.

"You go first."

"I'll take the steak fajitas, well done, and a side of guacamole."

"I'll have the same."

I think I could have ordered dog crap on flax bread, and he would have ordered the same. He almost said 'I'll have the same' before I even finished.

"All right, I will have that right out."

The Arizona air dries my skin really bad. I apply lotion twice a day to prevent my hands from cracking. I reach into my purse and apply a generous amount to my palm before rubbing it in.

"What were we saying? Oh yeah, I think these people get away with it because the kids are too scared to say anything. These predators have a way of intimidating the kids into silence."

"I know what you mean. I felt that way as a child."

My first breakthrough.

"Matthias, are you sharing?"

"Haha. No, just trying to be polite. I'm just saying, I know how the kids in those situations can feel pressured into staying quiet."

Now is my chance to plant the first seed and hope that he figures it out, but how much information should I give him? As far as I have seen, he's a very brilliant problem solver. He found Jeremy with little more than a description of his actions. What kind of a person can do that? How obsessive do they have to be? I'm confident that he will find him before I even open my mouth. To be certain he is paying attention, I ensure the seriousness in my gaze is unmistakable and lasting.

"A guy in Twin Peaks was molesting his kids a few years ago, and that bastard is already out of jail. Gerald Watson or Wallace or something. Either way, he only did about two years for that. The system is so fucked up."

Gerald's file used to be one of the dozens on the floor of my home, having been assigned to his case during his trial, to assess whether he would be prone to recidivism. But since the defense were the ones to hire me, they let me go. I warned them that he showed every sign of a repeat offender. They didn't like my assessment. He's one of the few that made the cut for my plan.

"I think the judges in those cases should do time for being too lenient."

"Right? Oh, here comes our food."

We make casual small talk while we eat, but all I can think about is whether I should bring up Gerald's name again, so he will remember it. I use two last names to make it slightly more obscure that I'm leading him. Oh, God. What if there really is a Gerald Wallace around here? I don't know if I could handle an innocent man's death because of my actions, but it's too late to go back now. Once we're done and outside, I regain my composure and focus on the plan again.

"Well, it was really fun. Maybe we can do it again sometime?"

"Definitely. I had a really great time too. I'll text you when I'm free."

I press my body to his and wrap my arms around him, then whisper in his ear.

"I hope you do. Have a good night."

When I walk to my car, I feel his eyes watching me as I purposefully rock my hips, hoping it's enough to distract him from the fact that I'm going the opposite way from where he saw me come from. I get in my car and purposefully drive by him on my way out to see his reaction. Still standing in the same spot I had left him, he casually waves as I pass by.

The moment I get home, I bring up the locator app on my phone and instantly become nauseous. Is it because I'm nervous or disgusted about what I am doing? Either way, I don't feel good about it. Watching his blue dot move around the map, I envision James doing the same thing to me all those years ago. I place the phone down on the table.

"What the hell am I doing? This is wrong."

Of course, spying on Matt is wrong, but so is killing people. I need to be able to know exactly where he is at all times if I want to guarantee my plan's success. I promise myself that I will remove the device and stop as soon as it's over, but it doesn't make me feel any less sickened, reminding myself that this is all for the safety of a little girl. I peek at the phone one more time and notice that he's stopped in a housing edition. Using two fingers, I zoom in and my eyes go wide; I know exactly where he is. I lived in the house at the end of that street with James, not eighty yards from where Matt's parked his car right now. I short-sold the home and moved out a month after the incident.

***

Sunday, I spend cleaning around the house and thinking about any loose ends I may have forgotten about. I know Matt works tonight, so he won't be up till around three or four in the afternoon. I'm thinking about asking him to meet for lunch before work, but it may be too soon. It might make me seem too desperate. Instead, I sit down with the chicken salad I was preparing yesterday before Matt invited me to lunch, flipping to the news. Has any more information been released on Jeremy's death? I'm aware that I should feel disturbed right now. At a minimum, a little nervous but I'm not.

They are talking about a man they presume has been murdered, and I sit here almost positive that I know who did it. Yet I continue to stuff my mouth with chicken salad, unfazed that I have been meeting with the likely killer regularly. I take another bite. Hell, I might just try to catch him tomorrow for breakfast and see if he needs some more incentive to find Gerald. I've been working so hard to plot this whole thing out that I have grown numb to the reality of what it means. There are people dying because of me, but does it make me a bad person? After all, they are just monsters plaguing the lives of innocents. They deserve this…right?

I picture Matt's face the first time I saw him in the clinic. I had no clue that when he said he was angry, he was already capable of hurting someone, much less killing them. Yes, he's awkward and obviously holds hatred inside for the people who raised him, but there is something in him that I don't see in any of my other patients dealing with vindictive anger. Morality.

"Blood was found at the scene. So much so, that officials doubt he would have survived his injuries unless he sought medical treatment immediately. They stated that a note found—"

I jump from my seat. A note? What note? Why the hell would he leave a note? *You're going to get yourself caught before we can save Madison's daughter, Matt. You fucking idiot.* I clutch at my chest to prevent my heart from smashing through.

"Evil, Tom. That's it. Just the single word 'Evil' written on the road in paint." *Oh. I thought they meant an actual note, like the Zodiac Killer used to send to the media.* I don't see much harm in a single word spray-painted on the pavement unless he used some strange, rare paint. I walk to the kitchen to put away my bowl, then laugh at how stupid I was to think Matt would be that careless.

Out of curiosity, I wonder if he left a note like it at the scene of his uncle's murder, so I amble back to my laptop and type, 'Bo McCarty murder'. 'Suspect Identified' screams the article's headline. *Oh, my God. They have someone in custody for Bo's murder already.* Maybe I've been wrong about Matt. How could I have gone so far with this assumption? The first line states that there is a correction to the story and that they have released the suspect without charge, redacting his name from the report. All other information is accurate as of the date of publication.

I'm relieved that Matt is back to being my number one suspect, but concern quickly returns. The crime entailed extreme torture. Broken fingers, lacerations, blunt force trauma, and many others too disturbing to put into print. I thought Matt was just killing these people, but no. He really is an incredibly angry person, taking out his anger on these people before killing them. While it makes sense that he would put so much energy into his vengeance, I wonder if it makes him feel better and for how long. I also wonder if Jeremy endured that level of wrath from Matt. Not that I feel bad for Jeremy, but I don't know if I feel comfortable with torture. Although I'm more comfortable with it than I am with domestic and sexual abuse.

You know what? Maybe I am comfortable with it. Fuck those guys. Tomorrow is Memorial Day and I usually take it off, but I didn't think about it before accepting the appointment with Madison. It's fine though because she's my only patient which will give me plenty of time to explain my plan. Peeking down at my watch, it's almost ten o'clock, so I get up, rub my eyes, then release a shallow yawn while walking to the bedroom.

"Come on, Rani. Time for bed. Momma's gotta get up early tomorrow. She has another date."

Pulling the Strings

I jump out of bed before the alarm finishes its first cycle and turn it off, then immediately turn on the locator app. Matt's car is standing still over out at the airfield, so I have time to get ready, but not much. I rush a twenty-minute shower into ten, then start drying my hair. It's still moderately damp when I hear a bicycle bell ring on my phone; Matt is on the move.

"Shit. Shit. Shit."

I open the phone, watching him get closer to his house as I pass a blow-dryer over my hair. If I text him now and he accepts, he'll beat me to the diner, and I need to get there first so I can order our food. But if I wait till he gets home and comfortable, he'll most likely decline the offer. My hair is dry enough for now. It'll frizz up some as it finishes, but who cares? The hairdresser always says, 'make sure you get it bone dry'. But they never had to deliver an urgent plan like mine, did they?

I throw on some jeans and a tee-shirt, then rush out the door, all the while watching Matt's dot. He's pulling up to his house at almost the exact moment I am pulling into the diner. I text him while walking in. *Hey, haven't heard from you. Are you off work yet?* He doesn't respond. I take a seat at our booth and wait almost ten minutes.

"What the hell, Matt? I know you're home."

Having the tracker on his car makes this so much more awkward and nerve-wracking. It feels as if he's ignoring me on purpose now, whereas previously, I just told myself he was caught up at work and had no ability to check his messages or respond. *Come on. Don't be ignorant.*

Apparently, it's my turn to say something at an awkward time because the server has walked up from behind and is standing right next to me, almost staring down at my screen.

"Can I start you off with something to drink?"

"Uh, yeah. Hold on one second."

I text Matt two more times. *Wanted to see if you were free for breakfast. I know you usually eat later, but it might be good to eat before you go to bed.* Still nothing.

"Can I just get iced tea and let you know when I'm ready to order? I'm hoping a friend might come and join me."

"Sure."

After five minutes, he finally replies. *You're not working today?* I am, but he doesn't need to know that. *Haha! It's Memorial Day. We regular people get it off.* It doesn't take him long to reply this time. *Sure. I'll meet you at the diner in 30.* Finally! I thought I had woken up early for nothing. *AWESOME!!! See ya then!* I wave the server over.

"Okay, do you know the guy that always sits here? Cute, with brown hair and hazel eyes?"

"Do you mean Matt?"

"Oh. Well, yeah. I didn't think anyone knew his name."

"Everyone here knows Matt. We always fight to get his table since he tips so much!"

"Oh! Does he?"

"Sure does! A couple of years back, he came in, walked straight to the counter, and said his name was Matt and he has a problem talking with people. Said if we just gave him the same order and left him alone, we'd get a huge tip, even better if we can give him his regular table over there. He's been doing it for years now. You're the first person we've seen him talk with."

"Okay well, he's going to be here in about twenty-five minutes. Here's fifty bucks. Can I get two of what he usually orders started right after he gets here?"

"Sure thing, hun."

A little while later, Matt walks through the door. I effortlessly read the pleasant surprise on his face. It's more obvious watching him sauntering toward me.

"So, how was your night?"

"It was work. Boring, except for my coworker who was annoying as usual. The dude will not stop talking."

"Try being a therapist. Everyone I meet won't shut up."

When he laughs at my joke, it's hard to imagine that he could ever become angry enough to hurt anyone. He looks so sweet when he smiles, almost childlike in his innocence.

"How about you? Do anything fun last night?"

"You know me, always working. I've been seeing a girl for a few days now who's had a rough life. She was addicted to drugs and became a prostitute. Anyway, she's been clean for a while now and wants to get custody of her daughter, but I have to clear her first. I spent most of the night going through a foot-high stack of files on her."

"Good Lord, that's a lot. Do you think you'll clear her?"

"I don't think she will ever be well enough to be cleared. When they took her daughter away, she was only five years old, and they found her locked in a closet covered in her feces and crying. Any person who could do that to their child will never be normal. You know what I mean?"

I have obviously struck a nerve. Matt's eyes are doing that thing again. I watch him a little before interrupting him.

"Hey, you know what I mean?"

"Yes, sorry. I was just thinking about something."

"Where do you go when you trail off like that?"

"What do you mean?"

"Sometimes, you get a blank stare on your face and don't say anything for a while. It's like you're stuck in limbo."

"Void."

Void...as in empty? What did he mean by that?

"What? Did you say void?"

"Void? No, I said boy as in, 'oh boy where is this going?'"

That was the weakest redirect he has ever tried with me. I'd love to explore deeper what he meant by it, but I'm pretty sure it would irritate him. Maybe I can ask in a way that doesn't seem like I'm prying.

"Seriously though, I'm interested. What's going on in that fascinating head of yours?"

"I don't know. I just think a lot. Sometimes when I hear something, it makes me think. There's nothing particular that I think about. It's always different. For instance, that time I was thinking about how you said she'd never be normal, and it reminded me of how I always wanted to be normal and will never be."

The server is coming from behind him now, carrying our plates. The timing couldn't be more perfect for this.

"Normal is subjective, Matt. You are who you are, regardless of what other people perceive as normal."

I keep my eyes locked onto Matt's as the server slides both of our plates in front of us.

"If you like your food delivered to you without talking to anyone and the people are okay with that, then it's now normal. Do you see what I mean?"

His face lights up as if he has just met the perfect woman. The first person to ever understand who he is and accept him for it. My goal here is to get him to trust me but oddly, it feels more like I'm trying to get myself to trust him. As much as I hate to admit it, I like him.

As we're walking to the door, I'm debating on whether I should kiss him or not. I don't want this to progress too fast, to the point he's falling in love with me, but I do want him to want more. Maybe I'll kiss him on the cheek. Make it flirtatious. Maybe that's what I did…

***

When I get in my car, I open the tracker app to see where he goes. Damn this. His dot is still in the lot. After a few minutes, I get out and begin walking back to the front of the diner when I hear Matt yelling. Glancing around the corner, I see him there, standing right next to a car with a man in it. They aren't talking, just sitting there staring at each other. Eventually, Matt turns around and murmurs something. From his voice earlier, I thought he was angry, but the look on his face right now is sadness. He's like a lost puppy walking to his car.

I watch as he drives off, but the other man stays parked. *I wonder what all that was about. That guy looks terrified.* I don't have time to sit around and ponder though, because I need to rush home and change before my appointment with Maddy. I have so much to tell her. I just hope she's as excited about the plan as I am. After I'm done changing into something a little more professional, I walk over and through mounds of paper strewn all around to make it to the front door. Looking through to the back of the house, I stare at the back door, missing how simple my life was just a few weeks earlier.

My mornings of coffee and birds are gone; I have replaced them with stress and conspiracy to commit murder. I keep telling myself that this is to save Maddy and her daughter, but it still feels wrong. The only comfort I have is that the choice will be Matt's alone. I have not implicated myself, merely providing information and never suggesting he does anything with it. When I get to work, Maddy is already waiting in the chair by the doorway.

"Oh hey, Maddy. Come on back. What room do I have today, Carol?"

"Um, four is empty."

"Great, thank you."

Madison follows closely behind me. Her manner is more energetic than before but still sluggish. Once she enters the consulting room, I close the door behind her as I have done hundreds of times before for all my other patients, but this time feels different. This time, it isn't only for patient privacy; it's to plan a murder.

Madison has her hair in a bun today, so I think it would be nice to compliment her on how great she looks with her hair up. It's a more self-confident look than I saw her with last week. Most of our conversation was through her long bangs, beneath which she would peer at me.

"I like your hair like that. You look beautiful. You should own those cheekbones, girl. I'd kill for them instead of these flat uninteresting ones I have."

She smiles shyly while running her fingers across her cheeks and releases a soft half giggle.

"Thank you. I've been trying to be more confident since I saw you last, like you keep saying. Doug had me doubting myself for so long that I thought I was ugly."

"Doug? Is that your ex?"

Her fingers begin drumming on her legs as if she has told me too much, and her eyes move away from me to the floor. I put my hands over hers, that rest on her knees.

"Hey, it's okay. He can't hurt you now. I have a plan. Do you wanna hear it?"

She nods without raising her head like she knows whatever I'm about to say will be disappointing. I place two fingers under her chin and gently elevate her eyes to mine.

"We are going to kill him."

At first, I interpret her saucer eyes as disbelief, but the accompanying smile reassures me that she is pleased with the idea. I tell her about my interactions with Matt, what I believe he has done, and methodically explain the plan. Every step of the plot, she becomes more upright and invested.

"Also, I need him to show some kind of connection to you."

"What do you mean?"

"I think he only kills if he has some personal vendetta against the person."

"Oh, ok. So, what do I need to do?"

"Nothing. I want you as far away from this as possible. I'm going to tell him that you are a patient of mine—"

"But I am."

"Yes, I know but, in this case, you've come to me because you were a drug-addicted prostitute who has cleaned up. You want to save your child."

She rolls her eyes around, confused.

"Listen. His mother abandoned him. She was a drug addict and a prostitute. When she died, it tore him apart emotionally because he knew she'd never have a chance to get her shit together and be a mother to him. You'll remind him of his mother, Maddy. Except you'll be the version that he wished he had; one who actually tried for her child. You see? See what I'm saying?"

"How do you know so much about this guy?"

"Long story. But he wrote a book about it."

"Sounds like a real psycho."

"Aww, he's actually quite nice."

She glares at me suspiciously.

"Okay, I know that look. At least he only kills bad people…as far as I know. Speaking of, I already gave him a second name, a really bad guy. If he turns up dead, we'll know for certain that he's the one doing it, and then we can steer him toward Doug. That will be three. If he gets caught, there's no way to link you or me; he's been doing this a while now."

She continuously nods her head in understanding, then suddenly stops, lowering her brow.

"What about your friend? When he's done with Doug, what are you going to do about him?"

Huh. I haven't really thought that far ahead. All my focus has been on saving Maddy's daughter. I guess in the back of my mind, I thought once Matt was done with Doug, it would all just be…over. Now that I have time to think about it, I'm a little sad. I won't be able to see him again because the more time I spend with him, the more likely the police can link us. I like Matt, but he is technically a psychotic murderer, so… I don't want to spend the rest of my life in prison, and I certainly don't want that for Madison. This is all Matt's doing. If the police get on to me, if they ask me about the fact Matt tells them where he got the information, then I'll just come clean. I made a mistake and gave away details I shouldn't have. But then I'll play gutted that he's misused the information, betrayed my trust, and killed. I push down a huge lump in my throat.

"After he's done with your ex-husband, I'll stop all contact with him and destroy any records I have pertaining to you."

Her face still carries the weight of concern but not for herself.

"D'you think you can really do it? The way you were talking earlier, you seemed into him."

Yes. Into him I am. Hell. I can't make eye contact with her. There is certainly an attraction between Matt and me, but deep inside, I have always known that we can never be together. What would that even look like? 'Welcome home, honey. Did you kill anyone today?' I feel dumb for even entertaining any emotion for him.

"Yes, he's a psychotic killer, Maddy. Once he's done, I will be done with him too, and Doug will have gone. You will be back with your daughter."

She reaches into her purse and grabs a hold of something but doesn't remove it. Instead, she pauses, looks at me with concern, then leans in toward me.

"Do you have anything for protection? A gun, mace, anything?"

I shake my head while goose bumps trail down my neck. She is scaring me a little, the way she's looking at me. I'm afraid she is about to pull a gun from her purse, and I don't know how I will react to seeing it because I am terrified of guns. She slowly pulls out a blocky yellow device sort of resembling the shape of a gun.

"This is a taser. Got it from a friend of mine for protection. It's really easy to use. Just—"

This is unbelievable! What does she think I am? Imagine the police taking me for questioning and I'm walking about with this thing in my tote!

"Maddy, I can't use that thing. I don't even think I'll need it. Matt wouldn't hurt me."

I'm fifty years old, staring at this girl half my age, who's looking at me as if I'm the most naïve person that she has ever met.

"Are you serious right now, Cristy? You're spending time with a guy who's been killing people, who you are hoping will kill even more people, and you don't think you need some sort of protection from him? I mean, even I know that's real stupid.

"And I'll never, ever even be a tenth as clever as you are. But even *I* know…"

When she puts it that way, I see how ignorant I'm being right now but, in my heart, I know he wouldn't hurt me. I've seen into his soul. Oh God, what am I thinking? The heart makes you blind to the truth.

"Okay, give it to me. How does it work?"

"It's really easy. You see this trigger? Put your finger in there, aim this part at the person, then pull. Keep holding it, and it will keep shocking them. Just hold it down until they give up."

She speaks as if she's used one of these before, probably the most confidence I've seen her show. She reaches out and passes it over to me. It feels heavier than it looks but comfortable in my hands. It doesn't look as scary as a gun because it's bright yellow for one thing. I'm not even anxious holding it.

"It's not so bad, right?"

"Actually, no. Not at all. It's kinda cute."

"Well, that cute thing will drop a four-hundred-pound man like a lead weight."

I raise my brows at her. She is way too excited about the idea of shooting someone with this thing. Since this was my only meeting today, I didn't bring my tote. I gently slide it into the side pocket of my lab coat.

"Promise me that if shit gets bad, you won't hesitate to use it on him."

I'm never going to use this thing, but I also know that she'll never let the matter go, so I reluctantly agree.

"I promise. If he tries to hurt me, I'll shoot him with it."

"And keep it with you at all times?"

I stand up as a signal that it's time to go and she quickly understands.

“Yes and keep it with me at all times.”

“Okay, good. You can have it for a while. I’ve got a few.”

“Haha. Why thank you. Stop worrying about me, Maddy. Just focus on what’s coming. You are about to be reunited with your daughter. Plus, I have to say, I’m kind of worried about you also carrying these weapons around like this.”

“It’s not a weapon,” she says, slightly irritable. “It’s for defense.”

“So is a Glock, Maddy.”

She just shrugs, and her smile could light the whole room as she walks out the door. She mouths a silent thank you before turning away and walking down the hall. I close the door, sit back down at the desk, then pull the taser out from my pocket.

“When the hell am I ever going to use this thing? I don’t care what Matt’s done; I know that he would never hurt me unless…I do something to hurt him.”

Behind the Mystery

Cristy's Story

The park is virtually empty right now, but I'm not here to be a part of a crowd anyway. I'm here to think. For the last few hours, Matt has been weighing heavy on my mind. I keep trying to tell myself that he is a bad guy, a monster, someone I shouldn't allow myself to have feelings for. But I can't help my emotions. Maybe I'm broken and can only be attracted to emotionally damaged men. Even if that were the case, Matt is on a whole new plateau of damage, on a level decidedly outside the strata of accepted norms. I know I could never change or fix him, so what is it that I hope to accomplish? I don't care. When this is over, I want to be with him.

I bring my wrist up to turn the alarm off as it chimes, setting it to alert me when Matt's going to be getting ready for work. Walking back to my car, I check the locator. He hasn't left yet. At the diner, I grab the attention of a passing server.

"I wonder, could I briefly borrow a pen? Oh, and a scrap of paper if you have one?"

The waitress tears a sheet of paper from the order pad and pops the pen on the table corner, promising to come back and retrieve it shortly. While I am writing, I get the bicycle bell tone, alerting me. Matt is on the move.

"Ma'am? Can you make an order for Matt and place it on top of this note for him? I'll put it on his table."

"Yeah, sure. When would you like to start it?"

"Now. He's on his way. Here's the tab."

I walk over to the table, gently laying the note down. As I'm walking out, three ladies behind the counter are smiling broadly at me as though I'm some sort of ditzy little schoolgirl with a simple schoolyard crush. They couldn't begin to comprehend how complicated this relationship actually is. No one could. But then again, perhaps I do feel like a ditzy little schoolgirl with a crush! God knows, it's how I have been behaving around Matt ever since we met.

When I get to my car, I wait patiently for him to arrive. He appears, immediately doing the cutest thing. He approaches the window from the side to see if I'm at his booth, then puts his hands on his hips as if I have broken a promise, even though we didn't have plans to meet today. He walks through the door, taking his usual turn toward his booth but stops, then looks around, confused. He's looking for me. I wish I could watch him read the note. See if it evokes a softer side of him. I can't though. Carol is on vacation, and I promised her that I'd take care of her dogs for her before dark. I get to Carol's house, then locate the spare key she left for me in the flowerpot.

Her dogs are going crazy inside, listening to me walk around on the porch. Opening up, her two large German Shepherds bombard me as though they never saw a person in their lives before. Even though Carol has only been gone since this morning, they act as though they have been stranded alone for ages.

"It's okay, boys. We are going to go for a walk. Do you want to go for a walk? Huh? Wanna go outside?"

They are going wild with excitement. So much so, that it's difficult to get their leashes fastened. When I finally get the second leash secured, I get an alert that Matt is on the move. Sure enough, I check my phone to see his dot moving toward his worksite.

"I hope you had a good breakfast, Matt. I'll see you tomorrow."

Once outside, it's like trying to avoid two trains pulling me in two directions. If I had to guess, I would say that each of these enormous beasts must way at least a hundred and fifty pounds, their combined weight almost three times my own. Now I know how Carol has such muscular legs. After thirty minutes of hanging on for dear life, I'm worn out and begin leading them back toward the house. Before we make it, I get another alert that Matt is on the move, but I can't check it and hold onto the dogs at the same time, so I wait until I get them back into the house. Then I plop onto the couch, drenched in sweat.

"Where are you going, hun?"

His blue tracker dot is leaving Walmart in Green Valley and now he looks to be heading to his house. *It's strange that he isn't at work, but there could be many reasons for it.* Maybe he became ill or just decided to take the night off. I don't need to read too far into it. I give the pups a little more loving attention then lock the front door behind me, making sure to put the key back into the flowerpot.

When I get home, I'm so exhausted that I don't feel like eating. I pour a glass of red wine, sit on the couch, then turn on the television. Why do I even pay for cable? It's rarely something I watch. Most stations are flooded with so-called reality tv shows. Anyone with half a brain cell can tell that they're all scripted and staged. No one's life could contain so much naturally occurring drama to fill multiple seasons of entertainment. I put the television on mute and place the remote on the couch next to me, then pick up my phone. Did Matt make it home yet? No. He is not only not at his house, but also, he is traveling north toward Tucson. Where is he going? I watch intently as he exits west from interstate ten, then my stomach begins to knot.

"Oh, my God. He's going to Gerald's."

Until now, I have doubted that Matt really is a killer. Everything slotted in, but as crime shows always demonstrate, even the police and the best detectives often think they have arrested a killer, only to find it's someone else—as in the case of Bo's murder and the false arrest. Subconsciously, I have been hoping that I was wrong about my assumptions, afraid of what that means for us.

Watching the blue dot hurl closer to where Gerald was last residing, I still keep telling myself that I am being paranoid. *But I need to know for sure.*

I hurriedly grab my keys and jog to my car, terrified of what I'm doing and what I may see, but I'm driven by the need for the truth. On the highway, I frequently check the app to see if Matt's car has moved from the spot at which it stopped earlier. It hasn't. I can't imagine what he's doing right now. I do not wish to imagine it either. He's been sitting there for so long, I wonder if he's staking out Gerald's home. It would make sense that a seasoned killer would take his time and meticulously plan their murders, but Matt strikes me as more of an emotional, in-the-moment type of person, driven by his anger and immediate need to get revenge, impulsive and rash.

When I get to the area, I park at the end of the street. Where is Matt's car in relation to mine on the map? He's around three hundred yards down the same road, while Gerald's house sits about midway between us, close enough for me to see his porch lights from where I am. I watch down the dimly lit road for over an hour before catching a flash of something. It went by so fast that I couldn't tell what it was, but it was big. Too big to be a cat or a dog.

Watching and listening quietly for a few minutes, my mind tries to make out any faint movements or sounds, but nothing stands out. When I first arrived, I was so nervous that I could easily have vomited, but now I'm growing bored and impatient, eager to see what's taking so long. I reach into the pocket of my lab coat lying on the passenger seat, removing the taser. My hand trembles holding the grip, creating a rattling sound.

"Get your shit together, Cristy. Just go over there and see what's going on. You don't have to do anything else."

I step out with the taser in hand, creeping toward the home. My legs grow stringy and weak the closer I get. By the time I reach the front curb, I feel as though I've been dragging bags of sand strapped to my ankles. Other than the porch light, the only light in the house is from the living room.

Matt's voice flows through the air, softly talking to someone, followed by muffled whimpering. I inch closer to the window taking slow, careful steps, stopping a foot away. Through the glass and partially open blinds, I see Matt's back. He's on top of someone, the person fighting to get up. Suddenly, my heart begins sprinting and my mouth dries out, my tongue sticking to my teeth. It's happening right now. Right in front of me.

That tiny doubt about Matt being a killer is dashed away, my mind inundated with a flurry of thoughts and emotions, almost all explicable except one. Arousal. As I stand out here, wide-eyed, watching Matt extinguish a life, the warmth of arousal is spreading through me. It feels wrong, but I can't stop it, can't take my eyes off it either. The man in there being murdered is finally getting what he deserves. As gruesome as this is, it is serving justice to a lifelong abuser. For a moment, I wish that were me in there, handing out the sentence.

The commotion abruptly halts so I lean into the window to investigate. Matt's clutching at his throat, and on the back of his neck, he clasps his fingers together. Oh, my God. Somehow, Gerald has gotten loose; he's choking Matt! *Oh God, no! Oh God, oh my God!* I rush to the front door and jerk the knob, finding it locked, quickly making my way to the back. Here, an enormous sliding glass door stands wide open. Soon, I'm by the living room.

"You fucking psycho. You've really fucked up now. Trying to kill me in my own home? Seriously? Wake up and look at me, you crazy fuck."

I pass the threshold. Gerald is kneeling over Matt's body, a knife in his hand. I fear that Matt may already be dead, but Gerald is talking to him as if he can hear. My eyes well with tears at the thought that I have just delivered Matt to his death. Raising the taser with both hands, they start to shake. The rattling of plastic startles Gerald; his eyes dart straight to mine.

"What the holy shit are you doing here? Oh, of course! Who else would it be? I should have guessed *you'd* be behind this. I knew you were a whack job bleeding heart back when I met you in jail."

His face is mangled, covered in so much blood that I can't tell where his face ends and his neck starts, so horrific that I can't get my mouth open to speak. Instead, I am just standing there, the taser rattling at him.

"You just going to stand there and act like all this is normal? You couldn't wait to open up your fucking mouth and run it to everyone who would listen and now you won't say a damn word? You know what? All that matters is that you are in my house and tried to kill me, so I have every right to shove this fucking blade into your goddamn neck!"

He stands up and casually walks toward me.

"Do—don't. Not one more fucking step,"

He stops, lightly running the back of the knife across his throat while smiling, then turning toward the door.

"Stop. I'll shoot you. I will,"

He laughs and continues to the door. I know that every step he takes is one closer to me being in prison, so I grip the taser tightly, squeezing my eyes closed. The moment he opens the door, I pull the trigger and hold it.

I hear a short shriek, followed by a small thud. When I open my eyes, he's thrashing wildly on the floor. I still have my finger on the trigger, but don't let go, instead continuing to shock him for a few more seconds. When I let go, his body rests motionless in the doorway. I put the taser down, grab his feet, then pull him far enough in to close the door. There is no pulse that I can find. At first, I think being tased may have killed him, but looking around the room, it's more than clear he's lost an enormous amount of blood from the huge gash on his face. Even though I believe he's dead, I can't take the risk.

Pulling the taser prongs out, I roll them up, then put it in my pocket. With all my strength, I roll him onto his back and pick up the knife from the floor, then squat next to him. My mouth begins salivating heavily as I fight from releasing all of the contents in my stomach. I lift the knife over my head and then look down at the wicked man before me.

"Someone should have done this to you years ago."

I thrust the knife straight down, burying it deep within his chest. The snapping sound it makes as it passes through his ribs causes vomit to climb to the top of my throat. I swallow incessantly to force it back down. Once I have it under control, I rush over to check on Matt. His breathing sounds wheezy, so I tilt his head back to open his airway.

"God, what have I done to you, Matt? I'm so sorry I got you into this."

I rub the back of his head lightly, gazing through never-ending sheets of tears. Entangling my fingers with his, I bend over and kiss the back of his hand. Frightened, I jump back as he suddenly jerks his hand from mine. His moans and gasps are comforting signs that he is going to be okay, but I want to ensure that he makes it out all right, so I don't leave. Instead, I go to the bedroom and wait. For five minutes, I listen as his moans become louder and more frequent, and then he says his first words.

"Did I leave that open?"

His voice is battered and hoarse. I can't see him but do know every time he moves because he lets out a pain-filled groan. The sound of his shuffling feet passing by the room causes me to hold my breath and place my hand over my mouth. Although I am glad he's okay, I have no clue how he will react to seeing me here. Anyone in his path right now may well suffer the same fate as Gerald. After a few minutes of pacing through the home, Matt finally steps outside and closes the door, but doesn't leave.

Peeking through a tiny slit in the blinds, I wait for him to walk away, but he's doing something on the porch out of my view. Maybe he's leaving another note or trying to figure out what happened. I don't care what it is. I just wish he would leave already so I can get out of this house. I exhale a heavy sigh, seeing him run across the yard toward his car. When I'm certain he is gone, I grab a rag from Gerald's bathroom and wipe down any evidence from the back door handle, then wipe both front doorknobs.

Taking in the scene one last time, I imagine his kids finding him like this. I don't know if they ever visit, but I can't handle the idea of psychological ruin for them at the sight of their butchered father on the floor. So, I leave the door partially open in hope that someone will find him tomorrow.

In my car, I bury my face into my palms, sobbing uncontrollably. This was never supposed to happen. I wasn't supposed to become this involved. How did things get so out of hand? Pulling my hands away, I rub at blood-encrusted fingertips. When Matt kills the people to whom

I lead him, there is also metaphorical blood on my hands, but the glaring truth is I literally have blood on them right now. I envision Gerald's body on the floor, expecting the thought to feed my anxiety, but instead, it's calming. It's over. He's dead and I'm the one to have taken his last breath from him. There is nothing I can do about it now. I start the car, put it in drive, then wipe the tears from my face.

"Good riddance. The world will not miss you."

The Aftermath

Cristy's Story

My head is an anvil being worked by a hammer when I walk through the door. I toss my car keys randomly onto the floor, then drop to the couch like a freshly felled tree. My right eye barely glances over the cushion, locked onto the files on the coffee table. I don't want the ability or temptation to read through them again. I've held onto some of them for years, never really knowing why. It wasn't until I came up with this convoluted, ridiculous plan, that I had a use for them. Perhaps I thought one day that I would be able to do something. I don't know. Not this, of course—no one on earth hopes for this—but *something*.

Rolling off the couch and onto my knees, I scoop up the manila folders into a pile, then crawl over to the fireplace. I haven't used this thing since the week I moved in, so it takes me a while to remember how to turn it on. I push and hold the off and flame buttons at the same time, then hear three electrical pops followed by a whoosh. The fire lights up. One by one, I toss in the files, ensuring the fire completely destroys them before hurling in another. Only a pile of crumbling ash remaining, I kill the flame, then trudge to my bedroom.

In the shower, my grimy, blood-splattered clothes drop one by one to the floor. In the corner of my eye, my reflection is moving with me but I'm afraid to look at her, too terrified of what she has become. I climb into the shower without making eye contact, then rest my head under the jets of steaming hot water. I alternate staring blankly at the shower wall and sobbing uncontrollably for an hour until there is no longer any hot water left, then I turn it off. I haven't cleaned myself in all that time, but don't care, wanting just to go to bed and to wake up realizing this was all a bad dream.

Exhausted from the day's events, my body aches for sleep. The moment my head hits the pillow, my consciousness melts away into it. I make no effort to prevent its gravitational pull from dragging me deeper. In quick succession, it grows dimmer and darker, then fades to black.

***

I'm seated on a park bench. The sky is dark and angry, the wind hitting in powerful, quick bursts. The air is cold, my limbs shivering from the bite of the breeze. I cross my arms at my chest and raise my sight to the field across from me, filled with people strewn all around, resting motionless in various poses. I rise to my feet, then aimlessly wander through the carnage. Left and right, I look over each person that I pass, recognizing them as people I have treated for various abusive tendencies throughout my career.

Deeper into the killing field, someone's voice calls in the distance, not calling for or speaking to me, but summoning me. I march over the bodies in my path to the voice, careful not to trample them. Stumbling upon a person kneeling over another, the voice becomes clear.

"Love and hate are two sides of the same coin, Cristy. Your passions for both are… equal in their ferocity, yet so far out of reach."

I step to the side of them, crouching down. The person on the ground is Matt, and the one kneeling next to him…is me. Matt lies motionless, a knife protruding from his chest, vivid blood trickling from his partially gaping mouth. He reaches his hand out to the other me, cupping her cheek, slowly opening his eyes. Even though he is touching her, his soft palm on my face generates a small electrical charge across my skin.

"None of this is your fault, Cristy. It was my choice to allow my anger to consume me."

***

The wretched phone alarm stirs me awake, the alarm that I set to wake me when Matt was scheduled to leave work. I forgot to turn it off last night before bed, knowing he had left work early. I'm groggy, but don't feel as if I could fall back asleep, so I roll out of bed to brush my teeth. There is no mistaking the reflection in the mirror this morning, I had a very rough night of sleep. My hair is matted and wiry, and the makeup not removed before bed is caked around my eyes.

After I finish brushing my teeth, I pick up my phone and text Matt. I know he's probably asleep and if he isn't, he won't feel like meeting me, but I need to make sure that he's okay. Before and after work is the only logical time I would be contacting him. *Hey, you wanna have breakfast?* When he replies, a huge weight lifts from my chest. *Sorry Cristy, but I'm not feeling well at all. Throat hurts. Maybe this afternoon after I get some rest.*

The poor thing. I can only imagine how bad his throat is hurting right now after Gerald choked him inches from death. *Aww, okay. Well, feel better. Let me know.* I clean up and then dress for work as usual, but my hands won't stop shaking. I need to find a way to calm myself before meeting my first patient at nine, so I drape a shawl over my shoulders, make a cup of coffee, then sit on my back porch. I've sat back here hundreds of times before but for some reason, this seems foreign to me. I feel like a stranger in my backyard.

For the last few weeks, I have been inching toward transformation, becoming someone else. The events of last night may not have been part of the plan, but they happened and now I have to live with what that makes me. Someone who can no longer see the beauty in any sunrise. Taking down the last bit of coffee, I feel a little better but still maintain a nervous tremble in my hands. Rubbing them together, the anxiety transfers to my gut like ripples of electricity causing my stomach to vibrate. I press my fingertips to my abdomen, seeking to massage away the angst, but it remains unchanged. I fill my chest with air, then slowly release it.

"Just three patients. That's all you have to get through today, Cristy."

In my usual fashion, I spend the next twenty minutes searching for my keys. Walking to check the least likely place, on the key rack by the door, I'm instantly reminded of where I put them. *Ouch. They're under my goddamn foot.* I pick them up. Why the hell do I keep doing this to myself? I walk out the door in a huff.

On route to the clinic, my inner voice tells me over and over, *it's all okay, Cristy. You got this. It's all gonna be just fine*. Just three appointments. The problem is, I have no clue why any of today's patients are seeing me. Another—even greater—problem is that I couldn't care less. When I walk through the door, the typical geriatric aroma of menthol medicated rub greets me. There are four elderly men and a middle-aged woman in the waiting area. None falls into the usual patient demographic. Very odd!

"Hey, Debra. Which room do I have today?"

"You can take three or four. Dr. Stevens is out today, so both rooms will be empty."

"Great. Thank you. How's Carol liking it up north?"

"You know Carol. She could take a trip to a thrift store, and she'd say it was amazing."

"Haha. That's so true. Can you send back my first patient when she arrives, please?"

"Sure thing, Cristy."

I walk into room three and take a seat at the desk, then log on to review my first patient's report. This is her introductory meeting with me, so I don't have a formal file yet. The only information provided is that she is thirty-four, prior Air Force, and has been depressed recently. This should be simple enough. I'll just let her talk about her feelings, get them out into the open and off her chest, then make another appointment with her next week. Fifteen minutes later, Debra knocks on the door and then slowly opens it.

"Hey, Cristy, Angela Gamez is here. Are you ready for me to bring her back?"

"Yes, send her back. Thank you, Debra."

A few seconds later, Debra escorts a dark-haired Hispanic woman into the room.

"You can have a seat over there. This is Dr. Ruiz, but everyone calls her Cristy."

I stand and reach out to shake her hand. She looks at my hand and then proceeds to take a seat. When I look at Debra, she gives me a grin as if to say that I have my work cut out for me with this one. I close the door and then return to the desk facing Angela.

"Okay then. What brings you in today, Angela?"

She fiddles with her hands, digging at her fingertips with her nails. I've seen this behavior before. It's not hard to figure out. Her lips are pale and slightly chapped and she's wearing a thin long sleeve shirt even though it's already over ninety degrees outside. I would bet my car that underneath her sleeves is an array of needle tracks. I try to withhold my judgments and give her the benefit of the doubt. The doubt doesn't last long.

"I've been in pretty severe pain. It's been going on for so long that I've got depressed. My old doctor in New Mexico used to prescribe me Vicodin, but since I moved, he won't refill it."

"You know that I'm not that kind of doctor right, Angela?"

She stops and glares at the wall.

"But you can prescribe medications, right? They don't have any available appointments to see a physician for another three weeks."

Her willingness to attempt so freely to manipulate me is infuriating. The only reason she is sitting in front of me right now is that she can't wait three weeks to trick a physician into writing her a prescription.

"Can I ask you something? Have you ever lost a child?"

Her confusion is palpable. The question is so far outside her realm of preparation that she doesn't know how to respond.

"Real pain is losing a child. That would be a great reason to drown yourself in medication. How about death? Have you ever caused the death of another human being, watching the last sparkle of life fade from their eyes?"

Her confusion slowly morphs into fear as her eyes grow wider. I can tell she's considering running out the door. The only reason she hasn't is that she has to go by me to get to it.

"Your pain is self-induced, Angela. There are people out there with real physical and emotional pain who choose to cope without the help of drugs. Some join therapy groups, and some find constructive hobbies. Others take knives and plunge them into the root of their pain."

As I lean in toward her, she rocks her body away.

"Do you feel like you need drugs to help you through the pain, Angela?"

She shakes her head in silence, never taking her eyes from mine. I rise to my feet and open the door.

"If I see you in here again, I will show you how I deal with things that cause me pain."

She rushes by me and straight out the front door without looking back. Debra glances over the counter at me, surprised that I was able to get Angela out so quickly.

"Debra, can you do me a favor? My last two appointments aren't until one-thirty. I'm not feeling well at all. Can you please move them to next week? Thursday and Friday are open."

"Sure, I'll call them right now. Go home and get some rest."

Driving home, I can't stop worrying about Matt, envisioning him lying on the floor unconscious, soaked in Gerald's blood. I feel responsible for his current condition. No, I don't just *feel* responsible; I *am* responsible. He needs to get better before I can forgive myself for what I have done to him.

When I pass by an Italian deli, I instantly U-turn back to it and purchase a large bowl of meatball soup, then drive to his house and place it on his porch with a get-well note inside. A few hours later, I'm sitting on my back porch, struggling to reconcile the hole into which I have dug myself when Matt texts me. *Thank you so much for the soup, but how did you know where I lived?*

***

The sun slowly creeping below the tree line is the first soothing sensation I've had all day. My nerves have been constantly on edge, trying to figure out what to do about Matt. I take a sip from my wine glass while lightly rocking in my chair. Only two options keep rattling around in my otherwise empty mind. I can follow through with this absurd plan or come clean to Matt and hope he understands. There is minor comfort in knowing I have a little time to decide. I can't imagine that he's feeling physically up to much right now, so I decide it's best to sleep on it and figure it out in the morning.

***

Jolting awake from a deep slumber, Matt's words repeat in my head from the same dream I experienced last night. He once again told me that it was his choice, that it wasn't my fault. His reassuring words wrap me in a warm blanket, and I know what I must do. I will continue with the plan and lead him to Madison's ex-husband. I let Matt sleep in for a bit before putting the final stage into motion.

At exactly eleven o'clock, I text him. *Breakfast?* It's been a few days since his altercation with Gerald, so he should be feeling a little better by now. *It's Friday, don't you have work?* I rarely schedule patients on Fridays. *No more patients today. Come on. I'll meet you in 30. I'll buy!* He accepts, and my heart thumps, partly because I want to see him and partly because this whole thing is one step closer to being over. *Okay fine. I'm on my way.* I quickly dress and drive straight to the diner. A few minutes later, Matt arrives, and I'm instantly reminded of the night he almost died. I need to maintain my composure and act ignorant of his condition.

"Oh my God. What happened to you?"

"I got into a fight last night."

"A fight? Weren't you at work?"

What am I doing? I already know the truth. I should keep my mouth shut.

"Uh, yeah. It happened at work. Some guy I work with attacked me. It's fine now."

"That's crazy. What was it about?"

Oh my God. Stop probing. Just take what he says and roll with it.

"I'd rather not talk about it. Let's talk about you. How was your day?"

Now is the time to roll out the red carpet. I lay out all the details I had prepared but Matt appears half-vested in the conversation as I explain to him how abusive her ex-husband was to her, to their child, and even to his parents. When I mention his family name though, Matt's attention seems to perk up.

"Is there any way you can influence the judge to reconsider?"

"I wish, but the Brewers are pretty well off, and according to the judge, they are a stable family for the baby."

"Did you say Brewers? The father of the little girl isn't Doug Brewer, is he?"

What? How in the hell does he know that? How does he know Doug?

"How did you know that?"

He sits more upright in his chair and in a confused, low tone, explains how he knows Doug.

"Uh, I work with the guy. He's a weird dude."

"Yeah, I know. You don't need to tell me."

I'm thrown off by how coincidental this whole thing is. What are the odds that he would work with the guy that I am trying to have him kill? Oh well. It doesn't change the fact that he is a very bad man and needs to be eliminated for the sake of his daughter.

"Hey, aren't we going to eat?"

"Eat? No, I already ate. I thought you were sick, so I have soup in the car for you to take home."

"But we've been sitting here for so long."

"They know it's our table."

"Oh my God I love—"

What did he almost say? I can feel my heart skipping every other beat.

"Did you just say—"

"No, let's go."

We both slide out of the booth, and I drop a fifty-dollar bill onto the table then he walks me to my car where I give him a hug. I have hugged him before but this time, emotion threatens to overwhelm me from hearing him almost say that he loves me. I equally desire and hate the thought of it because I want his love, but it makes me feel horrible for using him. I pull away slightly and stare into his eyes, expecting him to kiss me. But he just sits there, clueless.

"Oh, good Lord!"

I grab his face with both hands, pushing my lips to his. When I pull away, his body tries to follow, but I put my arm out to stop him.

"Whoa boy. Let's not get ahead of ourselves. One step at a time."

I give him one last peck on the lips before climbing into my car and driving out, waving as I pass by.

"I love you too."

Unveiling the Truth

I don't want to think or worry about anything today, just wanting to lie down in the grass with my shoes off and read a good book. It's early enough in the morning that people haven't swarmed into the park yet, and the sun hasn't reached high enough in the sky to warrant shade. A few kids are playing on the jungle gym and occasionally, a bicyclist or jogger streams by but otherwise, it's peaceful out here. I finish the last paragraph of a chapter, place a bookmark between the pages, and then rise to leave.

The moment I stand, I notice a familiar face sitting on the bench fifty meters away. It's Madison sitting next to a man with her hand on his leg. I didn't know that she had a boyfriend, but I guess there wasn't really a reason for her to tell me about him. There's no harm in saying hello before I leave. As I approach them, Madison looks up at me with dread.

"Hey, Maddy. How have you been? Is this your new boyfriend?"

She grips his hand tighter and brings it over onto her lap. He releases a superficial laugh while reaching out to shake my hand.

"New? No. Boyfriend? Also, no. I'm her husband Anton."

"I'm confused. You guys are married?"

Madison sits quietly staring down at her feet. Her right leg hopping up and down nervously.

"Yeah, we've been married for, what, almost three years now, hun? Who are you again?"

I reach out to grab his hand that he's been extending out to me since I walked up.

"Oh, I'm sorry. Where are my manners? My name is Cristy. I'm Madison's, um…doctor."

"Ah, she did say that she's been having some back issues lately. Are you the chiropractor?"

What the hell is going on right now? Maybe she's too embarrassed to tell him that she has been seeing a psychiatrist. Still, something seems really strange about all of this.

"Yes, I have been treating her back problems."

Madison's head is still down but she lifts her eyes up to me. She seems afraid but of what? Before I walked over here, she was laughing and showing affection to her husband. The only other variable is me but why would she be afraid of me? I am the one trying to help her get her daughter back.

"Look. Look. I found a ladybug, Maddy!"

I look down to find a cute little blonde girl with a ladybug cupped in her hand. She looks to be around five years old. The same age as Madison's daughter. Madison brings her head up for the first time since I arrived.

"Oh, nice. Now go put it back in the grass so it can grow big and strong."

"Yes, let's go get big and strong, ladybug."

Madison can see the confusion on my face, yet she doesn't address it. I have so many questions but I'm unsure of which ones would be appropriate to ask in front of her husband, so I ask the least accusatory.

"Is that your daughter?"

Anton laughs again as if the question was more ridiculous than my previous one.

"Maddy can't have kids. That's her niece. We take care of her when Maddy's brother is at work because he works late at night. Hell, we have her more often than he does. I like Doug, but he needs to get a job with better hours. You have to make the tough decisions when you're raising a child."

Doug? I'm feeling lightheaded; so close to fainting that my legs are weak and stringy. Madison has been using me, but why? What does she stand to gain from Matt killing her brother?

"Hey Mommy Maddy, can we get ice cream from the truck over there?"

"Absolutely. Can you take her to get an ice cream, honey?"

"Sure, let's go, Dania. It was nice meeting you, Cristy!"

My mouth mimes 'you too' silently as I watch him walk away with the little girl. I take a few steps past Madison, then casually sit next to her. I expect her to still be facing the ground in shame but when I look at her, she is fixed on me. Her eyes could burn a hole straight through me. They are so full of rage; I worry that she is about to attack me.

"What's going on, Maddy?"

She responds to my inquiry by penetrating her sight deeper into me, then slides closer. Our legs touch.

"Dania is my daughter. Do you hear me? I have raised her since her mother died two years ago. All my brother does is work and play video games. He doesn't give a shit about her."

"What about all that custody and abuse stuff? His family trying to take her away. All a lie?"

"Yes, I made it all up. I came to you hoping that you would contact the authorities and he would be investigated more seriously. I had been filing anonymous reports with them for months with no results but if a doctor called them, they would take it more seriously. It wouldn't matter that none of it was true. I'm already her legal guardian, so it would have been one step closer to winning custody once I filed. When you came up with the whole murder thing though, I thought, even better. Quicker and less paperwork."

"But he's your brother."

"Do you think I give a fuck about Doug? Seriously? I was willing to let you have him killed for Christ's sake. Well, not *was*. I mean to say that I *am* willing."

"You really think I'm going to let Matt go through with this now?"

She pushes her shoulder into me, then presses her cheek to mine.

"You are going to let everything go as planned or I will tell the cops what he's done and how you helped him."

It feels like every neuropathway in my brain is firing continuously. I can't believe how easily Madison has played me and how far I was willing to go to help her. Risking my job, my freedom, and my life, all so she could get custody of her brother's child. How fucking stupid am I to fall for this?

"You are going to keep doing what you've been doing until Doug is dead. After that, I don't care what you do. Understand?"

I nod my head in defeat. I'm trapped, with no choice but to do as she says.

"Mommy Maddie! I got a princess pop. Look how pretty it is. I'm gonna bite it!"

"Aww, that is a pretty princess, just like you. I'm gonna bite you!"

I rise from the bench as she begins chasing Dania around, making chomping sounds. My feet drag behind me like lead weights scraping the concrete.

"Don't forget what I said, Cristy!"

In my car, I can't get myself to drive away. Every muscle in my body is shivering uncontrollably and I feel as if I'm going to vomit. I haven't felt this way since returning home from the hospital after my miscarriage. I remember the terror consuming me to the point of losing control of my body. Back then, I gave up, letting James do whatever he wanted to me. Now, I am forced to do the same and carry out Madison's bidding. I slam my forehead into the steering wheel and begin sobbing loudly in self-pity.

I've spent years avoiding friendship and love, only to put myself in this situation the first time I open up to both. I'm starting to think there's a reason I became a psychiatrist. I'm so fucked up that I need to surround myself with fucked up people to feel normal. The whole reason I started this was because Madison reminded me of myself. The fact that I have taken it so far shows my perception wasn't far off. I wipe the tears from my face and look into the rearview mirror.

"Accept who you are, take responsibility for what you have done, and finish this."

I check the locator app. Matt's still at home. I text him, *Hungry?* He replies almost immediately. *Can't right now. A little busy.* I'm in the middle of writing a long response, begging him to meet with me when he changes his mind. *Actually yes, I am hungry. Meet at the Vietnamese restaurant in Green Valley?* Relieved, I erase my text and then type a short reply. *Sure, see ya in 30.*

I head to the restaurant, planning to make Matt hate Doug so much that he won't be able to think about anything else, but when he steps out of his car, all I can think about is, if I do, this could be the last time I will ever get to see him? It can wait until tomorrow. I want this to feel like our first real date. When he approaches, I playfully tease him and give him a kiss, but I can tell something is weighing heavily on his mind.

"Hey, are you okay? What's wrong?"

He begins sobbing heavily. This is the first time I have ever seen this side of him, and it tears at my heart. I wipe his tears away and then lightly kiss him on the cheek.

"Hey–hey, tell me what's going on."

He's too flustered to answer, so I wrap my hands behind his head and pull him into my chest.

"Shh–Shh–Shh. It's okay. Whatever it is…It will be okay. You don't have to tell me if you don't want to."

He slips through my arms and backs away.

"I'm sorry. I never wanted you to see me like this. It's just been so much craziness lately."

"No, please don't be sorry. I always knew you were hurting inside. I don't want to pry, but I'm here if you wanna talk about it. Hey, let's go in and get something to eat. You'll feel better after a bowl of pho."

His smile is reassuring when I cup his cheek in my hand. Then I open the door and wave him through. It feels as if we are a real couple as we sit and talk. I haven't felt this comfortable around another person in years. It's strange to think that the man in front of me is capable of so much destruction; how can he be? He is so charming and compassionate. *I can't do this. I can't lie to him anymore.*

Once we get outside, I have every intention of telling him the truth, but I can't, too overwhelmed with emotion and beginning to weep.

"Okay, now what's going on with you?"

I want to tell him so badly, but don't want him to be mad at me. Maybe I can get Madison to change her mind if I tell her that she will be implicated if she goes to the cops. I need to make sure Matt doesn't do anything crazy while I figure this out.

"I need to talk to you, but not right now. I want you to promise me something."

"Sure, anything."

"I promise I will tell you everything if you promise me that you will get some rest and calm down emotionally. I saw how torn up you were earlier, and it scares me."

"You're scared of me?"

"What? No. I'm scared *for* you, not of you."

I grab him by both cheeks and then kiss him more passionately than I had ever before. My heart flutters in my chest from the touch of his warm lips against mine. When I pull away, I can tell that I have left him light-headed when he speaks with his eyes still closed.

"I'll see you tomorrow."

"You better. You made a promise."

I run my fingers along his neck, cast a warm grin, and then get into my car. Barreling down the road, I need Madison's contact information from her file on my kitchen table. I just hope she takes my threat of incriminating her seriously, ending the plot to murder her brother. Sitting at a stoplight, the bicycle chime on my phone alerts me that Matt is on his way home. I briefly glance at it and to my surprise, he is going in the opposite direction. He's headed toward the Whiskey River bar.

"Oh my God. He's doing it right now."

I cut across into the turn lane and U-turn back the way I came, barely dodging oncoming traffic. The adrenaline coursing through me causes my heart to beat heavy and hard against my ribs and my vision begins to blur. Everything around me is flying by so fast that I get the sensation of teleporting. My hands tremble in fear but I don't care. I have to stop him. I will never forgive myself if I cause an innocent person's death.

Matt's car is parked along the curb in front of a home. I pull into the driveway. Why would he park so close to where he is about to commit murder? I can only pray that this is the right house. I slam the car door behind me loud enough that he can hear it if he's inside, then walk to the front door. I stare at it for a moment, take a deep breath, then lightly tap on it with my knuckles. No acknowledgment comes from within the home, so I turn the handle and slowly push the door open. My eyes instantly lock with Matt's. He's standing in the hallway, peeking around the corner with a pistol in his hand.

"What—What the hell are you doing here?"

"I promise to tell you everything, but we need to get out before you make a huge mistake."

"I don't understand. What the fuck are you doing here? Did you follow me?"

"Please, just trust me. I'll explain what's going on, but we have to leave right now."

He tucks the pistol into his waist band and conceals it with his shirt, then walks past me through the doorway. At my car, he stops, opens the door, then motions for me to get inside.

"I'd invite you to my house but I'm afraid of what I'd do to you if we were alone right now."

An enormous lump builds in my throat that I can't seem to swallow and my head fills with pressure. I move to enter my vehicle as instructed, trying to hold back my tears but tiny drops escape and congeal into pools over my eyes. He lightly pushes my head to clear the doorway as I bend down to get into the car, and then scowls at me heatedly.

"Diner. Right now, and be ready to talk."

Two Dark in the Void

Matthias' Story

It's a quiet night in the middle of the woods of Madera Canyon. The quaint, rustic décor of the cabin is the perfect setting for this, the howling winds rattling the loose panes on the windows which are exposed, allowing moonlight to sprinkle in through the surrounding pine trees. The only other source of light is a small battery powered lantern dimly casting on an unconscious woman in a wooden chair. Her arms and legs have been constrained with rope and her torso is secured to the back of the chair with duct tape.

I lift her limp head from her chest and brush her bangs from her face, then pull her right eyelid open. She stirs awake in a panic and lets out a high-pitched wail, but it's cut short when I tightly wrap my hands around her throat. Her eyes enlarge in terror confronted with the apathy on my face. I slowly release my grip but keep my fingers loosely on her skin.

"Do you know who I am?"

She shakes her head while keeping her eyes locked with mine.

"My name is Matthias Ellis."

Her neck begins to tremble between my fingers as she sobs quietly. I pull my hands away from her, watching as she processes the situation.

"So, you do know me, Madison. That will make this go by so much smoother. You are aware what I am capable of?"

She nods tearfully.

"Great, then I should expect that you will answer my questions truthfully. Otherwise, you will get to see first-hand what I can do. Why did you do this to me?"

Her face shoots up at me in disagreement.

"It wasn't me. It was Cristy. She started this whole thing."

"Don't worry about Cristy. We have come to an, let's just say, *understanding.*"

She buries her face into her shoulder.
"Please no. I swear. I—"

"You will not get another chance to be truthful, Madison. Your lies will only be a burden carried by your own flesh and I will have no problem relieving you of that burden."

Her mind churns, sifting through all of the lies to find the small specks of truth entangled within them. When her head slumps to the side, I know that she is ready to release herself. Now, she can be freed from deceit, able to be honest with herself for once.

"It wasn't my intention to have you kill my brother at first. My original plan was to have Cristy file a few reports and make him look like a shitty father so I could use it in court and get custody of Dania. I didn't mean for it to go this far. I'm not that kind of person."

"Oh Madison, a sprinkle of truth garnished with more lies. You aren't that kind of person?"

She shakes her head, confused.

"Let me give you some background about me. I'm what some might call a psychopath. Most psychopaths are intelligent and goal driven; the goal usually being to kill someone. I'm a bit different than your usual psychopath though. You see, I only have the urge to kill people who have done very bad things."

"I don't understand. I haven't done bad things to you or anyone else."

I grasp her shoulder firmly and dig my fingertips into her skin. She squeals and then trails off into a whimper.

"Don't interrupt me. Where was I? Oh, right. So, very bad things. The fact that you were a part of playing me into your sick game to get your brother's daughter wouldn't be enough to warrant capital punishment from me. Even the not-so-inconsequential detail that you would have let me kill an innocent person, still wouldn't warrant it. There is one thing though that does. Do you know what that is?"

Her forehead creases and her eyebrows lower as she considers every mistake she has made in her lifetime.

"You don't have to think that far back, Madison. I'll narrow it down for you. Two years ago, on April fifteenth."

I can feel her confused fear filling the room like a thick lakeside morning fog. She closes her eyes and then shakes her head back and forth in small quick bursts.

"How did you? No, it was an accident."

"Oh Madison. You aren't here with me tonight because of an accident and you aren't here because of your brother or your niece. You are here with me, in this cabin, in the middle of the woods…because you killed your brother's wife."

"No, I swear—"

"To whom? To God? It'd better be to God. He's the only one who won't slice your fucking face open for lying. Look me in the face and swear to me right now that you didn't do it?"

She begins crying so forcefully that her breathing becomes labored and sporadic. I let her wallow in the muddy puddle of her self-pity while pacing the room in front of her. When she finally calms down, I stop pacing and stand over her, staring at the top of her head and listening to her annoying mucus-filled sniffles.

"I really didn't mean for it to happen."

I slam my fist into the side of her neck. Her head snaps quickly to the side as she projects an earsplitting wail that immediately trails off into multiple feral groans. She gutturally wheezes, a long thin strand of saliva oozing from her mouth.

"I warned you. Try again, Madison. Think really hard about what you want to say this time."

Once again, I give her time to recover her bearings before continuing but this time, it's taking her longer to calm down. I can tell that she has finally given up the idea of limiting her culpability when she takes in a deep breath and slowly releases it. One of the signs of a defeated person ready to accept responsibility.

"So?"

She raises her head to face me, her eyes bloodshot and puffy. After a few blinks, she drops her chin back down toward the floor.

"Yes."

"Yes, what?"

"I did it. I killed her."

"You wouldn't be saying that just because you know that's what I want to hear, would you? How did you do it?"

She wipes the snot from her nose onto her shirt sleeve, then forcefully sniffs.

"We were taking pictures and I told her that it would be cool to take one of her on the handrail overlooking the canyon. Once she sat on top of it, I walked over, grabbed her legs, and then pushed her over."

"Why?"

"Why? Why did I do it?"

"Yes."

"Because I knew once she was gone, Doug couldn't take care of Dania on his own. He would need me to help with her and eventually, I could adopt her."

"Wow, and people think that *I* am evil. That's some cold-blooded shit, right there. At least I only kill bad people. Well, I try to."

I back away from her slightly, inspecting her reaction to finally letting the truth out. She seems almost proud of it. In her crazy ass mind, she probably thinks this is a bonding experience from one killer to another, but we are nothing alike. She sits silently staring as I consider how to proceed with crossed arms. Ultimately, I decide that this is no longer my project; I have gotten what I needed from her.

"I want to thank you for finally being honest with me. Hell, honest with yourself, for that matter. Sadly, my part here is done now. Not that I wouldn't love to show you what I can do, but your fate is not mine to deliver. It's hers."

Cristy slowly walks from the doorway and stands in front of Madison with an eight-inch knife grasped in her hand.

"Oh, what the fuck? Please, Cristy, I'm sorry. I promise I'll forget any of this ever happened."

"See, hun. I told you they always beg and make promises they don't intend to keep. If they were really sorry, they wouldn't have done the things that put them in the chair to begin with."

I recognize the fire in Cristy's eyes, the same look that I had when I came to realize who I was, accepting my urges and the reality that I must feed. I place my hand on her shoulder and she turns her head to face me.

"Remember what I taught you? The floor is yours, hun."

She creeps closer to Madison, pressing the back of the blade against her cheek. Madison clenches her eyes shut and sobs through tightly pursed lips.

"Okay, Madison. Here's what's going to happen."